THE COMPUTER

was giving its answer at last.

Jason already had explained his and his companions' situation, surrounded by the hostile inhabitants of Felicity. He had outlined in detail his daring plan to conquer and bring peace to the most violent planet in the universe.

Now, to Jason's growing horror, the computer was telling him that his calculations had been incorrect, his decisions wrong.

Now there was but one question left to ask: Was there any way to escape their swiftly approaching doom?

HARRY HARRISON

DEATHWORLD 3

A DELL BOOK

Published by
DELL PUBLISHING CO., INC.
750 Third Avenue
New York, New York 10017

Dell ® TM 681510, Dell Publishing Co., Inc.

Printed in U.S.A.

First printing—May 1968

for
Kingsley and *Jane*

—gratefully

1

GUARD LIEUTENANT TALENC lowered the electronic binoculars and twisted a knob on their controls, turning up the intensity to compensate for the failing light. The glaring white sun dropped behind a thick stratum of clouds, and evening was close, yet the image intensifier in the binoculars presented a harshly clear black-and-white image of the undulating plain. Talenc cursed under his breath and swept the heavy instrument back and forth. Grass, a sea of wind-stirred, frost-coated grass. Nothing.

"I'm sorry, but I didn't see it, sir," the sentry said reluctantly. "It's always just the same out there."

"Well I saw it—and that's good enough. Something moved and I'm going to find out what it is." He lowered the binoculars and glanced at his watch. "An hour and a half until it gets dark, plenty of time. Tell the officer of the day where I've gone."

The sentry opened his mouth to say something, then thought better of it. One did not give advice to Guard Lieutenant Talenc. When the gate in the charged wire fence opened, Talenc swung up his laser rifle, settled the grenade case firmly on his belt, and strode forth—a man secure in his own strength, a one time unarmed-combat champion and veteran of uncounted brawls. Positive that there was nothing in this vacant expanse of plain that he could not take care of.

He had seen a movement, he was sure of that, a flicker of motion that had drawn his eye. It could have been an animal; it could have been anything. His decision to investigate was prompted as much by the boredom of the guard routine as by curiosity. Or duty. He stamped solidly through the crackling grass and turned only once to look back at the wire-girt camp. A handful of low buildings and tents, with the skeleton of the drill tower rising above them, while the clifflike bulk of the spaceship shadowed it all. Talenc was not a sensitive man, yet even he was aware of the minuteness of this lonely encampment, set into the horizon-reaching plains of emptiness. He snorted and turned away. If there was something out here, he was going to kill it.

A hundred meters from the fence there was a slight dip, followed by a rising billow, an irregularity in the ground that could not be seen from the camp. Talenc trudged to the top of the hillock and gaped down at the group of mounted men who were concealed behind it.

He sprang back instantly, but not fast enough. The nearest rider thrust his long lance through Talenc's calf, twisted the barbed point in the wound and dragged him over the edge of the embankment. Talenc pulled up his gun as he fell, but another lance drove it from his hand and pierced his palm, pinning it to the ground. It was all over very quickly, one second, two seconds, and the shock of pain was just striking him when he tried to reach for his radio. A third lance through his wrist pinioned that arm.

Spread-eagled, wounded, and dazed by shock, Guard Lieutenant Talenc opened his mouth to cry aloud, but even this was denied him. The nearest rider leaned over casually and thrust a short saber between Talenc's teeth, deep into the roof of his mouth, and his voice was stilled forever. His leg jerked as he died, rustling a clump of grass, and that was the only sound that marked his passing. The riders gazed down upon him silently, then turned away with complete lack of interest. Their mounts, though they stirred uneasily, were just as silent.

"What is all this about?" the officer of the guard asked, buttoning on his weapon belt.

"It's Lieutenant Talenc, sir. He went out there. Said he saw something, and then went over a rise. I haven't seen him since, maybe ten, fifteen minutes now, and I can't raise him on the radio."

"I don't see how he can get into any trouble out there," the officer said, looking out at the darkening plain. "Still— we had better bring him in. Sergeant." The man stepped forward and saluted. "Take a squad out and find Lieutenant Talenc."

They were professionals, signed on for thirty years with

John Company, and they expected only trouble from a newly opened planet. They spread out as skirmishers and moved warily away across the plain.

"Anything wrong?" the metallurgist asked, coming out of the drill hut with an ore sample on a tray.

"I don't know . . ." the officer said, just as the riders swept out of the concealed gully and around both sides of the knoll.

It was shocking. The guardsmen, trained, deadly and well-armed, were overrun and destroyed. Some shots were fired, but the riders swung low on their long-necked mounts, keeping the animals' thick bodies between themselves and the guns. There was the twang of suddenly released bow-strings and the lances dipped and killed. The riders rolled over the guardsmen and rode on, leaving nine twisted bodies behind them.

"They're coming this way!" the metallurgist shouted, dropping the tray and turning to run. The alarm siren began to shriek and the guards poured out of their tents.

The attackers hit the encampment with the sudden shock of an earthquake. There was no time to prepare for it, and the men near the fence died without lifting their weapons. The attackers' mounts clawed at the ground with pillar-like legs and hurled themselves forward; one moment a distant threat, the next an overwhelming presence. The leader hit the fence, its weight tearing it down even as electricity arced brightly and killed it, its long thick neck crashing to the ground just before the guard officer. He stared at it, horrified, for just an instant before the creature's rider planted an arrow in his eye socket and he died.

Murder, whistling death. They hit once and were gone, sweeping close to the fence, leaping the body of the dead beast, arrows pouring in a dark stream from their short, laminated bows. Even in the half darkness, from the backs of their thundering, heaving mounts, their aim was excellent. Men died, or dropped, wounded. One arrow even tore into the gaping mouth of the siren so that it rattled and moaned down into silence.

As quickly as they had struck they vanished, out of sight in the ravine behind the shadowed rise, and, in the stunned silence that followed, the moans of the wounded were shockingly loud.

The light was almost gone from the sky now and the dark-

9

ness added to the confusion. When the glow tubes sprang on, the camp became a pool of bloody murder set in the surrounding night. Order was restored only slightly when Bardovy, the expedition's commander, began bellowing instructions over the bullhorn. While the medics separated the dying from the dead, mortars were rushed out and set up. One of the sentries shouted a warning and the big battlelamp was turned on—and revealed the dark mass of riders gathering again on the ridge.

"Mortars, fire!" the commander shouted with wild anger. "Hit them hard!"

His voice was drowned out as the first shells hit, round after round poured in until the dust and smoke boiled high and the explosions rolled like thunder.

They did not yet realize that the first charge had been only a feint and that the main attack was hitting them from the opposite side of the camp. Only when the beasts were in among them and they began to die did they know what had happened. Then it was too late.

"Close the ports!" the duty pilot shouted from the safety of the spacer's control room high above, banging the airlock switches as he spoke. He could see the waves of attackers sweeping by, and he knew how lethargic was the low-geared motion of the ponderous outer doors. He kept pushing at the already closed switches.

In a wave of shrieking brute flesh, the attackers rolled over the charged fence. The leading ones died and were trampled down by the beasts behind, who climbed their bodies, thick claws biting deep to take hold. Some of the riders died as well, and they appeared to be as dispensable as their mounts, for the others kept on coming in endless waves. They overwhelmed the encampment, filled it, destroyed it.

"This is Second Officer Weiks," the pilot said, activating all the speakers in the ship. "Is there any officer aboard who ranks me?" He listened to the growing silence and, when he spoke again, his voice was choked and unclear.

"Sound off in rotation, officers and men, from the Engine Room north. Sparks, take it down."

Hesitantly, one by one, the voices checked in, while Weiks activated the hull scanners and looked at the milling fury below.

"Seventeen—that's all," the radio operator said with

shocked unbelief, his hand over the microphone. He passed the list to the Second Officer, who looked at it bleakly, then slowly reached for the microphone.

"This is the bridge," he said. "I am taking command. Run the engines up to ready."

"Aren't we going to help them?" a voice broke in. "We can't just leave them out there."

"There is no one out there to leave," Weiks said slowly. "I've checked on all the screens and there is nothing visible down there except these—attackers and their beasts. Even if there were, I doubt if there is anything we could do to help. It would be suicide to leave the ship. And we have only a bare skeleton flight crew aboard as it is."

The frame of the ship shivered as if to add punctuation to his words.

"One of the screens is out—there goes another—they hit it with something. And they're fixing lines to the landing legs. I don't know if they can pull us over—and I don't want to find out. Secure to blast in sixty-five seconds."

"They'll burn in our jets, everything, everyone down there," the radio operator said, snapping his harness tight.

"Our people won't feel it," the pilot said grimly, "and—let's see how many of the others we can get."

When the spacer rose, spouting fire, it left a smoking, humped circle of death below it. But, as soon as the ground was cool enough, the waiting riders pressed in and trampled through the ash. More and more of them, appearing out of the darkness. There seemed no end to their teeming numbers.

2

"PRETTY STUPID to get hit by a sawbird," Brucco said, helping Jason dinAlt to pull the ripped metalcloth jacket off over his head.

"Pretty stupid to try and eat a peaceful meal on this planet!" Jason snapped back, his words muffled by the heavy cloth. He pulled the jacket free and winced as sharp pain cut into his side. "I was just trying to enjoy some soup, and the bowl got in the way when I had to fire."

"Only a superficial wound," Brucco said, looking at the red gash on Jason's side. "The saw bounced off the ribs without breaking them. Very lucky."

"You mean lucky I didn't get killed. Whoever heard of a sawbird in the mess hall?"

"Always expect the unexpected on Pyrrus. Even the children know that." Brucco sloshed on antiseptic and Jason ground his teeth together tightly. The phone pinged and Meta's worried face appeared on the screen.

"Jason—I heard you were hurt," she said.

"Dying," he told her.

Brucco sniffed loudly. "Nonsense. Superficial wound, fourteen centimeters in length, no toxins."

"Is that all?" Meta said, and the screen went dark.

"Yes, that's all," Jason said bitterly. "A liter of blood and a kilo of flesh, nothing more bothersome than a hangnail. What do I have to do to get some sympathy around here—lose a leg?"

"If you lost a leg in combat, there might be sympathy," Brucco said coldly, pressing an adhesive bandage into place. "But if you lost a limb to a sawbird in the mess hall, you would expect only contempt."

"Enough!" Jason said sharply, pulling his jacket back on. "Don't take me so literally and, yes, I know all about the sweet consideration I can expect from you friendly Pyrrans. I don't think I'll ever miss this planet, not for five minutes."

"You're leaving?" Brucco asked, brightening up. "Is that what the meeting is about?"

"Don't sound so wildly depressed at the thought. Try to control your impatience until 1500 hours, when the others will be here. I play no favorites. Except myself, that is," he added, walking out stiffly, trying to move his side as little as possible.

It was time for a change, he thought, looking out of a high window across the perimeter wall to the deadly jungle beyond. Some light-sensitive cells must have caught the motion because a tree branch whipped forward and a sudden flurry of thorndarts rattled against the transparent metal of the window. His reflexes were so well trained by now that he did not move a muscle.

Past time for a change. Every day on Pyrrus was another spin of the wheel. Winning was just staying even, and when your number came up, it was certain death. How many people had died since he first came here? He was beginning to lose track, to become as indifferent to death as any Pyrran.

If there were going to be any changes made, he was the one who would have to make them. He had thought once that he had solved this planet's deadly problems, when he had proved to them that the relentless, endless war was their own doing. Yet it still went on. Knowledge of the truth does not always mean acceptance of it. The Pyrrans who were capable of accepting the reality of existence here had left the city and had gone far enough away to escape the pressure of physical and mental hatred that still engulfed it. Although the remaining Pyrrans might give lip-service to the concept that their own emotions were keeping the war going, they did not really believe that this was true. And each time they looked out at the world that they hated, the enemy gained fresh strength and pressed the attack anew. When Jason thought of the only possible end for the city, he grew depressed. There were so many of the people left who would not accept the change—or help of any kind. They were as much a part of this war and as adapted to the war as the hyperspecialized life forms outside, molded in the same way by the same generations of mixed hatred and fear.

There was one more change coming. He wondered how many of them would accept it.

It was 1520 hours before Jason made his appearance in Kerk's office: he had been delayed by a last-minute exchange of messages on the jump-space communicator. Everyone in the room shared the same expression, cold anger. Pyrrans had very little patience and even less tolerance for a puzzle or a mystery. They were so alike—yet so different.

Kerk, gray-haired and stolid, able to control his expression better than the others. Practice, undoubtedly, from dealing so much with off-worlders. This was the man whom it was most important to convince because, if the slapdash, militaristic Pyrran society had any leader at all, he was the one.

Brucco, hawk-faced and lean, his features set in a perpetual expression of suspicion. The expression was justified. As physician, researcher and ecologist, he was the single authority on Pyrran life forms. He had to be suspicious. Though at least there was one thing in his favor: he was scientist enough to be convinced by reasoned fact.

And Rhes, leader of the outsiders, the people who had adapted successfully to this deadly planet. He was not possessed by the reflex hatred that filled the others, and Jason counted upon him for help.

Meta, sweet and lovely, stronger than most men, whose graceful arms could clasp with passion—or break bones. Does your coldly practical mind—hidden in that beautiful female body—know what love is? Or is it just pride of possession you feel toward the off-worlder Jason dinAlt? Tell him sometime; he would like to know. But not right now. You look just as impatient and dangerous as the others.

Jason closed the door behind him and smiled insincerely. "Hello there, everybody," he said. "I hope you didn't mind my keeping you waiting?" He went on quickly, ignoring the angry growls from all sides.

"I'm sure that you will all be pleased to hear that I am broke, financially wiped out, and sunk."

Their expressions cleared as they considered the statement. One thought at a time—that was the Pyrran way.

"You have millions in the bank," Kerk said, "and no way of gambling and losing them."

"When I gamble, I win," Jason informed him with calm dignity. "I am broke because I have spent every last credit. I have purchased a spaceship, and it is on its way here now."

"Why?" Meta asked, speaking the question that was foremost in all their minds.

"Because I am leaving this planet and I'm taking you—and as many others as possible—with me."

Jason could read their mixed feelings easily. For better or for worse—and it was certainly worse than any other planet in the known galaxy—this was their home. Deadly and dangerous, but still theirs. He had to make his idea attractive, to gain their enthusiasm and make them forget any second thoughts that they might have. The appeal to their intelligence would come later; first he must appeal to their emotions. He knew well this single chink in their armor.

"I've discovered a planet that is far more deadly than Pyrrus."

Brucco laughed with cold disbelief, and they all nodded in agreement with him.

"Is that supposed to be attractive?" Rhes asked, the only Pyrran present who had been born outside the city and was therefore immune to their love of violence. Jason gave him a long, slow wink to ponder over while he went on to convince the others.

"I mean deadly because it contains the most dangerous life form ever discovered. Faster than a stingwing, more vicious than a horndevil, more tenacious than a clawhawk—there's no end to the list. I have found the planet where these creatures abide."

"You are talking about men, aren't you?" Kerk said, quicker to understand than the others, as usual.

"I am. Men who are more deadly than the ones here, because Pyrrans have been bred by natural selection to defend themselves against any dangers. *Defend.* What would you think of a world where men have been bred for some thousands of years to attack, to kill and destroy, without any thought of the consequences? What do you think the survivors of this genocidal conflict would be like?"

They considered it and, from their expressions, they did not think very much of the idea. They had taken sides, united against a common enemy in their thoughts, and Jason hurried on while he had them in agreement.

"I'm talking about a planet named 'Felicity,' apparently called this to sucker in the settlers, or for the same reason that big men are called 'Tiny.' I read about it some months back in a newsfax, just a small item about an entire mining settlement being wiped out. This is a hard thing to do. Mining-operation teams are tough and ready for trouble—and the John & John Minerals Company's are the toughest. Also—and equally important—John Company does not play for small stakes. So I got in touch with some friends and sent them some money to spread around, and they managed to contact one of the survivors. It cost me a good

15

deal more to get accurate information from him, but it was well worth it. Here it is." He paused for dramatic effect and held up a sheet of paper.

"Well, read it. Don't just wave it at us," Brucco said, tapping the table irritably.

"Have patience," Jason told him. "This is an engineer's report, and it is very enthusiastic in a restrained engineering way. Apparently Felicity has a wealth of heavy elements, near the surface and confined to a relatively restricted area. Opencut mining should be possible and, from the way this engineer talks, the uranium ore sounds like it is rich enough to run a reactor without any refining."

"That's impossible," Meta broke in. "Uranium ore in a free state could not be so radioactive that—"

"Please," Jason said, holding both hands in the air. "I was just making a small exaggeration to emphasize a point. The ore is rich, let it go at that. The important thing now is that, in spite of the quality of the ore, John Company is not returning to Felicity. They had their fingers burned once, badly, and there are plenty of other planets they can mine with a lot less effort. Without having to face dragon-riding barbarians who appear suddenly out of the ground and attack in endless waves, destroying everything they come near."

"What is all that last bit supposed to mean?" Kerk asked.

"Your guess is as good as mine. This is the way the survivors described the massacre. The only thing we can be sure about it is that they were attacked by mounted men, and that they were licked."

"And this is the planet you wish us to go to," Kerk said. "It does not sound attractive. We can stay here and work our own mines."

"You've been working your mines for centuries, until some of the shafts are five kilometers deep and producing only second-rate ore—but that's not the point. I'm thinking about the people here and what is going to happen to them. Life on this planet has been irreversibly changed. The Pyrrans who were capable of making an adjustment to the new conditions have done so. Now—what about the others?"

Their only answer was a protracted silence.

"It's a good question, isn't it? And a pertinent one. I'll tell you what's going to happen to the people left in this

16

city. And when I tell you, try not to shoot me. I think you have all outgrown that kind of instant reflex to a difference of opinion. At least I hope that everyone in this room has. I wouldn't tell this to the people out there in the city. They would probably kill me rather than hear the truth. They don't want to find out that they are all condemned to certain death by this planet."

There was the thin whine of an electric motor as Meta's gun sprang halfway out of its power holster, then slipped back. Jason smiled at her and waggled his finger; she turned away coldly. The others controlled their trigger reflexes better.

"That is not true," Kerk said. "People are still leaving the city—"

"And returning in about the same numbers. Argument invalid. The ones who were able to leave have done so; only the hard core is left."

"There are other possible solutions," Brucco said. "Another city could be constructed—"

The rumble of an earthquake interrupted him. They had been feeling tremors for some time, so commonplace on Pyrrus that they were scarcely aware of them, but this one was much stronger. The building moved under them and a jagged crack appeared in the wall, showering cement dust. The crack intersected the window frame and, although the single pane was made of armorglass, it fractured under the strain and crashed out in jagged fragments. As though on cue, a stingwing dived at the opening, ripping through the protective netting inside. It dissolved in a burst of flame as their guns surged from their power holsters and four shots fired as one.

"I'll watch the window," Kerk said, shifting his chair so he could face the opening. "Go on."

The interruption, the reminder of what life in this city was really like, had thrown Brucco off his pace. He hesitated a moment, then continued.

"Yes . . . well, what I was saying—other solutions are possible. A second city, quite distant from here, could be constructed, perhaps at one of the mine sites. Only around this city are the life forms so deadly. This city could be abandoned and—"

"And the new city would recapitulate all the sins of the old. The hatred of the remaining Pyrrans would recreate the

17

same situation. You know them better than I do, Brucco, isn't that what would happen?"

Jason waited until Brucco had nodded a reluctant yes.

"We've been over this ground before and there is only one possible solution. Get those people off Pyrrus and to a world where they can survive without a constant, decimating war. *Any* place would be an improvement over Pyrrus. You people are so close to it that you seem to have forgotten what a hell this planet really is. I know that it's all that you have and that you're adjusted to it, but it is really not very much. I've proved to you that all of the life forms here are telepathic to a degree and that your hatred of them keeps them warring upon you. Mutating and changing and constantly getting more vicious and deadly. You have admitted that. But it doesn't change the situation. There are still enough of you Pyrrans hating away to keep the war going. Sanity save me but you are a pigheaded people! If I had any brains, I would be well away from here and leave you to your deadly destiny. But I'm involved, like it or not. I've kept you alive and you've kept me alive and our futures run on the same track. Besides that, I like your girls."

Meta's sniff was loud in the listening silence.

"So—jokes and arguments aside, we have a problem. If your people stay here, they eventually die. All of them. To save them, you are going to have to get them away from here, to a more friendly world. Habitable planets with good natural resources are not always easy to find, but I've found one. There may be some differences of opinion with the natives, the original settlers, but I think that should make the idea more interesting to Pyrrans rather than the other way around. Transportation and equipment are on the way. Now who is in with me? Kerk? They look to you for leadership. Now—lead!"

Kerk squinted his eyes dangerously at Jason and tightened his lips with distaste. "You always seem to be talking me into doing things I do not really want to do."

"A measure of maturity," Jason said blandly. "The ego rising triumphant over the id. Does that mean that you will help?"

"It does. I do not want to go to another planet and I do not enjoy the thought. Yet I can see no other way to save the people in the city from certain extinction."

"Good. And you, Brucco? We'll need a surgeon."

18

"Find another one. My assistant, Teca, will do. My studies of the Pyrran life forms are far from complete. I am staying in the city as long as it is here."

"It could mean your life."

"It probably will. However, my records and observations are indestructible."

No one doubted that he meant it—or attempted to argue with him. Jason turned to Meta.

"We'll need you to pilot the ship after the ferry crew has been returned."

"I'm needed here to operate our Pyrran ship."

"There are other pilots. You've trained them yourself. And if you stay here, I'll have to get myself another woman."

"I'll kill her if you do. I'll pilot the ship."

Jason smiled and blew her a kiss that she pretended to ignore. "That does it then," he said. "Brucco will stay here, and I guess Rhes will also stay to supervise the settling of the city Pyrrans with his people."

"You have guessed wrong," Rhes told him. "The settlements are now handled by a committee and going as smoothly as can be expected. I have no desire to remain—what is the word?—a backwoods rube for the rest of my life. This new planet sounds very interesting and I am looking forward to the experience."

"That is the best news I have heard today. Now let's get down to facts. The ship will be here in about two weeks, so if we organize things now, we should be able to get the supplies and people aboard and lift soon after she arrives. I'll write up an announcement that loads the dice as much as possible in favor of this operation, and we can spring it on the populace. Get volunteers. There are about 20,000 people left in the city, but we can't get more than about 2,000 into the ship—it's a demothballed armored troop carrier called the *Pugnacious,* left over from one of the Rim Wars—so we can pick and choose the best. Establish the settlement and come back for the others. We're on our way."

Jason was stunned, but no one else seemed surprised.

"One hundred and sixty-eight volunteers—including Grif, a nine-year-old boy—out of how many thousand? It just isn't possible."

"It is possible on Pyrrus," Kerk said.

"Yes, it's possible on Pyrrus, but only on Pyrrus." Jason paced the room, with a frustrating, dragging step in the doubled gravity, smacking his fist into his open palm. "When it comes to unthinking reflex and sheer bullheadedness, this planet really wins the plutonium-plated prize. 'Me born here. Me stay here. Me die here. Ugh.' Ugh is right!" He spun about to stab his finger at Kerk—then grabbed at his calf to rub away the cramp brought on by overexertion in the heightened gravity.

"Well, we're not going to worry about them," he said. "We'll save them in spite of themselves. We'll take the one hundred and sixty-eight volunteers and we'll go to Felicity, and we'll lick the planet and open the mine—and come back for the others. That's what we're going to do!"

He slumped in the chair, massaging his leg, as Kerk went out.

"I hope . . ." he mumbled under his breath.

3

MUFFLED CLANKING sounded in the airlock as the transfer-station mechanics fastened the flexible tubeway to the spacer's hull. The intercom buzzed as someone plugged into the hull jack outside.

"Transfer Station 70 Ophiuchi to *Pugnacious*. You are sealed to tubeway, which is now pressurized to ship standard. You may open your outer port."

"Stand by for opening," Jason said, and turned the key in the override switch that permitted the outer port to be open at the same time as the inner one.

"Good to be back on dry land," one of the ferry crewmen said as they came into the lock, and the others laughed uproariously, as though he had said something exceedingly funny. All of them, that is, except the pilot, who scowled at the opening port, his broken arm sticking out stiffly before him in its cast. None of them mentioned the arm or looked in his direction, but he knew why they were laughing.

Jason did not feel sorry for the pilot. Meta always gave fair warning to the men who made passes at her. Perhaps, in the romantically dim light of the bridge, he had not believed her. So she had broken his arm. Tough. Jason kept his face impassive as the man passed by him and out into the tubeway. This was constructed of transparent plastic, an undulating umbilical cord that connected the spacer to the transfer station, the massive, light-sprinkled bulk that loomed above them. Two other tubeways were visible, like theirs, connecting ships to this way station in space, balanced in a null-*g* orbit between the suns that made up the two star system. The smaller companion, 70 Ophiuchi B, was just rising behind the station, a tiny disk over a billion miles distant.

"We've got a parcel here for the *Pugnacious*," a clerk said, floating out of the mouth of the tubeway. "A transhipment waiting your arrival." He extended a receipt book. "Want to sign for it?"

Jason scrawled his name, then moved aside as two freight handlers maneuvered the bulky case down the tube and through the lock. He was trying to work a pinch bar under the metal sealing straps when Meta came up.

"What is that?" she asked, twisting the bar from his hands with an easy motion and jamming it deep under the strap. She heaved once and there was the sharp twang of fractured metal.

"You'll make some man a fine husband," Jason told her, dusting off his fingers. "I bet you can't do the other two that easily." She bent to the task. "This is a tool, something that we are going to need very much if we are going into the planet-busting business. I wish I had had one when I first came to Pyrrus, it might have saved a good number of lives."

Meta threw back the cover and looked at the wheeled ovoid form. "What is it—a bomb?" she asked.

"Not on your life. This is something much more important." He tilted up the crate so that the object rolled out onto the floor.

It was an almost featureless, shiny metal egg that stood a good meter high with its small end up. Six rubber-tired wheels, three to a side, held it clear of the floor, and the top was crowned by a transparent-lidded control panel. Jason reached down and flipped up the lid, then punched a button marked *on* and the panel lights glowed.

"What are you?" he said.

"This is a library," a hollow, metallic voice answered.

"Of what possible use is that?" Meta said, turning to leave.

"I'll tell you," Jason said, putting out his hand to stop her, ready to move back quickly if she tried any arm-busting tricks. "This device is our intelligence, in the military sense, not the IQ. Have you forgotten what we had to go through to find out anything at all about your planet's history? We needed facts to work from and we had none at all. Well, we have some now." He patted the library's sleek side.

"What could this little toy possibly know that could help us?"

"This little toy, as you so quaintly put it, costs over 982 thousand credits, plus shipping charges."

She was shocked. "Why—you could outfit an army for that much. Weapons, ammunition . . ."

"I thought that would impress you. And will you please get it through your exceedingly lovely blond head that armies aren't the solution to every problem. We are going to bang up against a new culture soon, on a new planet, and we want to open a mine in the right place. Your army will tell us nothing about mineralogy or anthropology or ecology or exobiology—"

"You are making those words up."

"Don't you just wish I were! I don't think you quite realize how much of a library is stuffed into this creature's metal carcass. Library," he said, pointing to it dramatically, "tell us about yourself."

"This is a model 427-1587, Mark IX, improved, with photodigital laser-based recorder memory and integrated circuit technology—"

"Stop!" Jason ordered. "Library, you will have to do better than that. Can't you describe yourself in simple newsfax language?"

"Well, hello there," the library chortled. "I'll bet you never saw a Mark IX before, the ultimate in library luxury—"

22

"We've hit the *sales talk* button, but at least we can understand it."

"—and the very newest example of what the guys who built this machine like to call 'integrated circuit technology.' Well, friends, you don't need a galactic degree to understand that the Mark IX is something new in the universe. That 'integrated so-and-so' double-talk just means that this is a thinking machine that can't be beat. But everyone needs something to think about as well as to think with, and just like the memory in your head, the Mark IX has a memory all its own. A memory that contains the *entire library* at the University of Haribay, holding more books than you could count in a lifetime. These books have been broken down into words and the words have been broken down into bits, and the bits have been recorded on little chips of silicon inside the Mark IX's brain. That memory part of the brain is no bigger than a man's clenched fist—a *small* man's fist—because there are over 545 million bits to every ten square millimeters. You don't even have to know what a bit is to know that that is impressive. All of history, science and philosophy are in this brain. Linguistics, too. If you want to know the word for 'cheese' in the basic galactic languages, in the order of the number of speakers, it is this—"

As the high-speed roar of syllables poured out Jason turned to Meta—and found she was gone.

"It can do other things besides translate 'cheese,' " he said, pressing the *off* button. "Just wait and see."

The Pyrrans were happy enough to vegetate, to doze and yawn, like tigers with full stomachs, during the trip to Felicity. Only Jason felt the urge to use the time efficiently. He searched all the cross-references in the library for information about the planet and the solar system it belonged to, and was drawn from his studies only by Meta's passionate, yet implacable, grasp. She felt that there were far more interesting ways to pass the long hours, and Jason, once he had been severed from his labors, enthusiastically agreed with her.

One ship-day before they were scheduled to drop from jump-space into the Felicity system, Jason called a general meeting in the dining room.

"This is where we are going," he said, tapping a large

diagram hung on the wall. There was absolute silence and 100 percent attention, for a military-style briefing was meat and drink to the Pyrrans.

"The planet is called 'Felicity,' the fifth planet of a nameless class-F1 star. This is a white star with about twice the luminosity of Pyrrus's own G2 sun and it puts out a lot more ultraviolet. You can look forward to getting nice suntans. The planet has nine-tenths of its surface covered by water, with a few chains of volcanic islands and only one land mass big enough to be called a continent. This one. As you can see, it looks like a flattened-out dagger, point downward, divided roughly in the middle by the guard. The line here, represented by the guard, is an immense geological fault that cuts across the continent from one side to the other, an unbroken cliff that is three to ten kilometers high across the entire land mass. This cliff and the range of mountains behind it have had a drastic effect on the continental weather. The planet is far hotter than most other habitable ones—the temperature at the equator is close to the boiling point of water—and only this continent's location right up near the northern pole makes life bearable. Moist, warm air sweeps north and hits the escarpment and the mountains, where it condenses as rain on the southern slopes. A number of large rivers run south from the mountains and signs of agriculture and settlements were seen here—but were of no interest to the John Company men. The magnetometers and gravitometers didn't twitch a needle. But up here"—he tapped the northern half of the continent, the "handle" of the dagger—"up here the detectors went wild. The mountain building that pushed the northern half up so high, causing this continent-splitting range in the middle, stirred up the heavy metal deposits. Here is where the mines will have to be, in the middle of the most desolate piece of landscape I have ever heard about. There is little or no water, the mountain range stops most of it, and what does get past the mountains usually falls as snow on this giant plateau. It is frigid, high, dry, and deadly—and it never changes. Felicity has almost no axial tilt to speak of, so the seasonal changes are so slight they can scarcely be noticed. The weather in any spot remains the same all of the time. To finish off this highly attractive picture of the ideal settlement site, there are men who live up here who are as deadly—or deadlier—than

24

any life forms you ever faced on Pyrrus. Our job will be to sit right down in the middle of them, build a settlement and open a mine. Do I hear any suggestions as to how this can be done?"

"I know," Clon said, standing slowly. He was a hulking, burly man with a thick and protruding brow ridge. The weight of this bony ledge must have been balanced by even thicker bone in the skull behind, leaving room for only the most minuscule of brain cavities. His reflexes were excellent, undoubtedly short-circuited in his spinal column like some contemporary dinosaur, but any thoughts that had to penetrate his ossified cranium emerged only with the most immense difficulty. He was the last person Jason expected to answer.

"I know," Clon repeated. "We kill them all. Then they don't bother us."

"Thanks for the suggestion," Jason said calmly. "Your chair's right behind you, that's it. Your suggestion is a sound Pyrran one, Pyrran also in the fact that you want to apply it to a second planet even though it failed on the first one. Attractive as it may look, we shall not indulge in genocide. We shall use our intelligence to solve this problem, not our teeth. We are trying to open this world up, not close it forever. What I propose is an open camp, the opposite of the armed *laager* the John Company men built. If we are careful, and watch the surrounding countryside carefully, we should not be taken by surprise. My hope is that we will be able to contact the locals and find out what they have against miners or off-worlders, and then try to change their minds. If anyone has a better suggestion for a plan of action, let me know now. Otherwise, we land as close to the original site as we can and wait for contact. Our eyes are open, we know what happened to the first expedition, so we will be very careful that it doesn't happen to us."

Finding the original mine site was very easy. A year's slow growth of the sparse vegetation had not been enough to obscure the burned scar on the landscape. The abandoned heavy equipment showed clearly on the magnetometer, and the *Pugnacious* sank to the ground close by. From above, the rolling steppe had appeared to be empty of life, and it looked even more so once they were down. Jason stood in the open airlock and shivered as the first blast of dry, frigid air hit him, the grass rustling to its passing, while grains of sand hissed against the metal of the hull. He had planned to be first out, but Rhes happened to knock against him as Kerk came up so that the gray-haired Pyrran slipped by and leaped to the ground.

"A lightweight planet," he said as he turned slowly, his eyes never still. "Can't be over 1G. Like floating, after Pyrrus."

"It's closer to 1.5G," Jason said, following him out just as warily. "But anything is better than 2G."

The first landing party, ten men in all, emerged from the ship and carefully surveyed the area. They stayed close enough to be able to call to one another, yet not so close that they blocked each other's vision or field of fire. Their guns stayed in their power holsters and they walked slowly, apparently indifferent to the frigid wind and blown sand that reddened Jason's skin and made his eyes water. In their own, strictly Pyrran way, they were enjoying themselves after the forced relaxation of the voyage.

"Something moving 200 meters to the southeast," Meta's voice spoke in their earphones. She was one of the observers at the viewports in the ship above.

They spun and crouched, ready for anything. The undulating plain still appeared to be empty, but there was a sudden hissing as an arrow arced toward Kerk's chest. His gun sprang into his hand and he shot it from the air as calmly and efficiently as he would have dispatched an attacking stingwing. Another arrow flashed toward them and Rhes stepped aside so that it missed him. They all waited, alert, to see what would happen next.

An attack, Jason thought, or is it just a diversion? It can't be possible—so soon after our arrival—that any kind of concerted attack could be launched. Yet, why not?

His gun jumped into his hand and he started to wheel about—just as hard pain slammed into his head. He had no awareness of falling, just a sudden and complete blackness.

4

JASON DID NOT enjoy being unconscious. A red, cloying pain engulfed him and, barely rational, he had the feeling that, if he could only wake up all the way, he could take care of everything. For some reason he could not understand, his head was rocking back and forth, adding immeasurably to the agony, and he kept wishing it would stop, but it did not.

After what must have been a very long time, he realized that, when he was feeling the pain, he must be conscious, or very close to it, and he should use these periods most advantageously. His arms were secured in some manner—he could feel that even if he could not see them—but they still had some degree of movement. The bulk of the power holster was there, pressed between his arm and his side, but the gun would not leap into his hand. His groping fingers eventually found out why when they contacted the ragged end of the cable that connected the gun with the holster.

His shattered thoughts groped for understanding with the same disconnected numbness as had his fingers. Something had happened to him; someone, not something, had hit him. Taken his gun away. What else? Why couldn't he see anything? Anything other than a diffuse redness when he tried to open his eyes. What else was gone? His equipment belt, surely. His fingers fumbled back and forth at his waist but could not find it.

They touched something. In its separate holder the medikit still remained on the back of his hip. Careful not to hit the *release* button—if it slipped out of his hand, it was gone—he pressed the heel of his hand up against the device until his flesh contacted the actuating probe. The analyzer buzzed distantly and he never felt the stab of the hypodermic needles through the all-pervading agony in his head. Then the drug took effect and the pain began to seep away.

Without the overriding presence of the pain, he could concentrate that small remaining part of his consciousness on the problem of his eyes. They could not be opened: something was sealing them shut. Something that might or might not be blood. Something that probably was blood considering the condition of his head, and he smiled at his success in completing this complicated line of thought.

Concentrate on one eye. Concentrate on right eye. Squeeze tight shut until it hurt, pull with lids to open. Squeeze shut again. It worked, the pulling, squeezing, tears-dissolving, and he felt the lids start to part stickily.

The white-burning sun shone directly into his eye and he had to blink and look away. He was moving backward across the plains, a jarring and uneven ride, and there was something like a grid not too far from his face. The sun touched the horizon. That was important, he kept telling himself, to remember that the sun touched the horizon directly behind him, or perhaps a little bit to the right.

Right. Setting. A little to the right. The medikit's drugs and the traumatic shock were pushing him under again. But not yet. Setting. Behind. To the right.

When the last white glimmer dropped behind the horizon, he closed the tortured eye and this time welcomed unconsciousness.

"_____!" a voice roared, an incomprehensible gout of sound. The sharp pain in his side made a far stronger impression and Jason rolled away from it, trying to scramble to his feet at the same time. Something hard and unyielding bruised his back and he dropped onto all fours. It was time to open his eyes, he decided, and he brushed at his sealed eyelids and managed to unglue them. One look convinced him that he had been far happier with them shut, but it was too late for that now.

The voice belonged to a big, burly man who clutched a two-meter-long lance, with which he had been prodding Jason's ribs. When he saw that Jason was sitting up with his eyes open, he pulled back the lance and leaned on it, examining his captive. Jason understood their relative positions when he realized that he was in a bell-shaped cage of iron bars, the top of which just cleared his head when he was sitting down. He leaned against the bars and studied his captor.

He was a warrior, that was clear, arrogant and self-assured, from the fanged animal skull that decorated the top of his padded helm to the needle-sharp prickspurs on the heels of his knee-high boots. A molded breastplate, apparently made of the same kind of material as his helm, covered the upper half of his body and was painted in garish designs around the central figure of an unidentifiable animal. In addition to the lance, the man had an efficient-looking short sword slung, without scabbard, through a thong on his belt. His skin was tanned and wind-burned, glistening with some oily substance and, standing upwind of Jason, he exuded a rich and unwashed animal odor.

"— — — — — — — — — — —!" the warrior shouted, shaking the lance in Jason's direction.

"That's a pretty poor excuse for a language!" Jason shouted back.

"— — — — — — — — — —!" the man answered, in a shriller voice this time, accompanied with shark clicking sounds.

"And that one is not much better."

The man cleared his throat and spat in Jason's general direction. *"Bowab* you," he said, "you can speak the in-between tongue?"

"Now that's more like it. A broken-down and corrupt form of standard English. Probably used as some sort of second language. I suppose that we'll never know who originally settled this planet, but one thing is certain—they spoke English. During the Breakdown, when communication was cut off between all the planets, this fine world slipped down into dog-eat-dog barbarism and must have generated a lot of local dialects. But at least they kept the memory of English, debased though it is, as a common language among the tribes. It's just a matter of speaking it badly enough to be understood."

"What you say?" the warrior growled, shaking his head over Jason's incomprehensible burble of words.

Jason tapped his chest and said, "Sure, me speak in-between tongue just as good as you speak in-between tongue."

This apparently satisfied the warrior because he turned and pushed his way through the throng. For the first time,

29

Jason had a chance to examine the passing men who had just been a blur in the background before. All males, and all warriors, dressed in numerous variations on a single theme. High boots, swords, half armor and helms, spears and short bows decorated in weird and colorful patterns. Beyond them and on all sides were rounded structures colored the same yellowish gray as the sparse grass that covered the plains. Something moved through the crowd, and the men gave way to a swaying beast and rider. Jason recognized the creature from the description given by the survivors of the massacre, of the mounts that had been ridden during the attack.

It was horselike in many ways, yet twice as big as any horse, and covered with shaggy fur. The creature's head had an equine appearance, but it was disproportionately tiny and set at the end of a moderately long neck. It had long limbs, especially the forelegs, which were decidedly longer than the hind legs, so that its back sloped downward from the withers to the rump, terminating in a tiny, flicking tail. The strong, thick toes on each foot had sharp claws that dug into the ground as the beast paced by, guided by the rider who sat just behind the forelimbs at the highest point on the humped back.

A harsh blast on a metallic horn drew Jason's attention and he turned to see a compact group of men striding toward his cage. Three soldiers with lowered lances led the way, followed by another with a dangling standard of some kind on a pole. Warriors with drawn swords walked alertly, surrounding the two central figures. One of them was the lance-jabber who had prodded Jason to life. The other, a head taller than his companions, had a golden helm and breastplate inset with jewels, while curling horns sprouted from both sides of his helm.

He had more than that, Jason saw when he approached the cage. The look of the hawk, or a great jungle cat secure in his rule. This man was the leader and he knew it, accepted it automatically. He, a warrior, leader of warriors. His right hand rested on the pommel of his bejeweled but efficient-looking sword while he stroked the sweep of his great red mustachios with the scarred knuckles of his left hand. He stopped close to the bars and stared imperiously at Jason, who tried, but failed, to return the other's gaze with the same intensity. His cramped position inside the cage and his battered, scruffy appearance did not help his morale.

"Grovel before Temuchin," one of the soldiers ordered, and buried the butt end of his lance in the pit of Jason's stomach.

It might have been easier to grovel, but Jason, bent double with the pain, kept his head up and his eyes fixed on the other.

"Where are you from?" Temuchin asked, his voice so used to command that Jason found himself answering at once.

"From far away, a place you do not know."

"Another world?"

"Yes. Do you know about other worlds?"

"Only from the songs of the jongleurs. Until the first ship came down, I did not think they were true. They are." He snapped his fingers and one of the men handed him a blackened and twisted recoilless rifle. "Can you make this spout fire again?" he asked.

"No." It must have been one of the weapons of the first expedition.

"What about this?" Temuchin held up Jason's own gun, its cable dangling where it had been torn from his power holster.

"I don't know." Jason was just as calm as the other. Let him just get his hands on the gun. "I will have to look at it closely."

"Burn this one, too," Temuchin said, throwing the gun aside. "Their weapons must be destroyed by fire. Now tell me at once, other-world man, why do you come here?"

He'd make a good poker player, Jason thought. I can't read his cards and he knows all of mine. Then what should I tell him? Why not the truth?

"My people want to take metal from the ground," he said aloud. "We harm no one, we will even pay—"

"No." There was a flat finality to the sound. Temuchin turned away.

"Wait, you haven't heard everything."

"It is enough," he said, halting for a moment and speaking over his shoulder. "You will dig and there will be buildings. Buildings make a city and there will be fences. The plains are always open." And then he added in the same flat voice,

"Kill him."

As the band of men turned to follow Temuchin, the standard-bearer passed in front of the cage. His pole was topped with a human skull and Jason saw that the banner itself was made up of string after string of human thumbs, mummified and dry, knotted together on thongs.

"Wait!" Jason shouted at their retreating backs. "Let me explain. You can't just do this—"

But, of course, he could. A squad of soldiers surrounded the cage and one of them bent underneath it and there was the rattling of chains. Jason cowered back as the entire cage swung up on creaking hinges, and he clutched at the bars as the soldiers reached for him.

He sprang over them, kicking one in the face as he went by and crashed into the soldiers beyond. The results were a foregone conclusion, but he made the most of the occasion. One soldier lay sprawled on the ground and another sat up holding his head when the rest carried Jason away. He cursed them, in six different languages, even though his words had as much effect on the stolid, expressionless men as had his blows.

"How far did you travel to reach this planet?" someone asked.

"*Ekmortu!*" Jason mumbled, spitting out blood and the chipped corner of a tooth.

"What is your home world like? Much as this one? Hotter or colder?"

Jason, being carried face down, twisted his head around to look at his questioner, a gray-haired man in ragged leather garments that had once been dyed yellow and green. A tall, sleepy-eyed youth stumbled after him dressed in the some motley, though his were not so completely obscured by grime.

"You know so many things," the old man pleaded, "so you must tell me something."

The soldiers pushed the two men away before Jason could oblige by telling him some of the really pithy things that came to mind. With so many men holding him, he was completely helpless when they backed him against a thick iron pole set firmly in the ground and tore at his clothing. The metalcloth and fasteners resisted their fingers until one of them produced a dagger and sawed through

32

the material, ignoring the fact that he was slicing Jason's skin at the same time. When his clothing had been pulled open to his waist, Jason was bleeding from a dozen cuts and was groggy from the mauling he had taken. He was pushed to the ground and a leather rope lashed around his wrists. Then the soldiers went away.

Although it was early afternoon, the temperature must have been just above the freezing point. With his insulated clothing stripped away, the shock of the cold air on his body brought him instantly to full, shivering consciousness.

What the next step would be was obvious. The strap that secured his wrists was a good three meters long and the other end was fastened to the top of the pole. He was alone in the center of a cleared area, and there was a bustle on all sides as the hump-backed riding beasts were saddled and mounted. The first man ready uttered a piercing, warbling cry and charged at Jason with his lance leveled. The beast ran with frightful speed, claws digging into the soil, hurtling forward like an unleashed thunderbolt.

Jason did the only thing possible, jumping to the other side of the pole and keeping it between himself and the attacking rider. The man jabbed with his lance but had to pull it back swiftly as he went by the pole.

Only fighting intuition saved Jason then, for the sound of the second beast's charge was lost in the thunder of the first. He grabbed the pole and spun around it. The lance clanged against the metal as the second attacker went by.

The first man was already turning his mount and Jason saw that a third had saddled up and was ready to attack. There could be only one possible outcome to this game of deadly target practice: he could dodge just so often.

"Time to change the odds," he said, bending and groping in the top of his right boot. His combat knife was still there.

As the third man started his charge, Jason flipped the knife into the air and caught the hilt between his teeth, then sawed his leather bindings against its razor edge. They fell away and he crouched behind the slim pole to avoid the stabbing lance. The charge went by and Jason attacked.

He sprang, the knife in his left hand, reaching out with his right to grab the rider's leg in an attempt to unseat him.

But the creature was moving too fast and he slammed into its flank behind the saddle, his fingers clutching at the beast's matted fur.

After that everything happened very fast. As the rider twisted about, trying to stab down and back at his attacker, Jason sank his dagger right up to its hilt in the animal's rump.

The needlelike spikes of the prickspurs that the warriors used in place of rowels on their spurs indicated that the creatures they rode must not have very sensitive nervous systems. This was true of the thick hide and pelt over the ribs, but the spot that Jason's dagger hit, not too far below the animal's tail, appeared to be of a different nature altogether. A rippling shudder passed through the creature's flesh and it exploded forward as though a giant spring had been released in its guts.

Already off balance, the rider was tipped from his saddle and disappeared. Jason, clutching at the fur and worrying the knife deeper with his other hand, managed to hold on through one bound, then a second. There was the blurred vision of men and animals streaming by while Jason fought to keep his grip. This proved impossible and, on the third ground-shaking leap, he was tossed free.

Sailing headlong through the air, Jason saw he was aiming toward the space between two of the dome-shaped structures. This was certainly better than hitting one of them, so he relaxed and tucked his chin under as he struck the ground and did a shoulder roll, then another. Landing on his feet, he ran, his speed scarcely diminished.

The domed structures, dwellings of some kind, were scattered about with lanes between them. He was in a wide, straight lane and thoughts of spearheads between the shoulder blades sent him darting off at right angles at the next opening. Outraged cries from behind him indicated that his pursuers did not think highly of his escape. So far, he was ahead of the pack and he wondered how long he could keep it that way.

A leather flap was thrown back on one of the domes ahead and a gray-haired man looked out—the same one who who had been trying to question Jason earlier. He appeared to take in the situation in a glance and, opening the flap wider, he motioned Jason toward it.

It was a time for quick decisions. Still running headlong, Jason glanced around and saw that, for the moment, no one else was in sight. Any port in a storm. He dived through the opening dragging the old man after him. For the first time he was aware that the combat knife was still in his hand, so he pressed it up through the other's beard until the point touched his throat.

"Give me away and you're dead," he hissed.

"Why should I betray you?" the man cackled. "I brought you here. I risk all for knowledge. Now back, while I close the opening." Ignoring the knife, he began to lace the flap shut.

Looking quickly about the dark interior, Jason saw that the sleepy-eyed youth was dozing by a small fire, over which hung an iron pot. A withered crone was stirring something in the pot, completely ignoring the commotion at the entrance.

"In back, down," the man said, pushing at Jason. "They'll be here soon. They mustn't find you, oh no."

The shouting was coming closer outside and Jason could see no reason to find fault with the plan. "But the knife is still ready," he warned, as he sat against the back wall and allowed a collection of musty skins to be draped over his shoulders.

Heavy feet thundered by, shaking the earth, and voices could be heard from all sides now. Graybeard hung a leather shawl over Jason's head so that it obscured his face, then scrabbled in a pouch at his belt for a reeking clay pipe that he poked into Jason's mouth. Neither the old woman nor the youth paid any attention to all of this.

They still did not look up when a helmeted warrior tore open the entrance and poked his head inside.

Jason sat, motionless, looking out from under the leather hood, the hidden knife in his hand, ready to dive across the floor and sink it into the intruder's throat.

Looking quickly about the dark interior, the intruder shouted what could only have been a question. Graybeard answered with a negative grunt—and that was all there was to it. The man vanished as quickly as he had come and the old woman tottered over to lace the entrance tightly shut again.

In his years of wandering around the galaxy, Jason had

encountered very little unselfish charity and was justifiably suspicious. The knife was still ready. "Why did you take the risk of helping me?" he asked.

"A jongleur will risk anything to learn new things," the man answered, settling himself cross-legged by the fire. "I am above the petty squabbles of the tribes. My name is Oraiel, and you will begin by telling me your name."

"Riverboat Sam," Jason said, putting the knife down long enough to pull up the top of his metalcloth suit and push his arms into it. He lied by reflex, like playing his cards close to his chest. There were no threatening moves. The old woman mumbled over the fire while the youth squatted behind Oraiel, sinking into the same position.

"What world are you from?"

"Heaven."

"Are there many worlds where men live?"

"At least 30,000, though no one can be completely sure of the exact number."

"What is your world like?"

Jason looked around, and, for the first time since he had opened his eyes in the cage, he had a moment to stop and think. Luck had been with him so far, but he was still a long way from getting out of this mess alive.

"What is your world like?" Oraiel repeated.

"What's your world like, old man? I'll trade you fact for fact."

Oraiel was silent for a moment and a spark of malice glinted in his half-closed eyes. Then he nodded. "It is agreed. I will answer your questions if you will answer mine."

"Fine. You'll answer mine first as I have more to lose if we're interrupted. But before we do this twenty-questions business, I have to take an inventory. Things have been too busy for this up until now."

Though his gun was gone, the power holster was still strapped into place. It was worthless now, but the batteries might come in useful. His equipment belt was gone and his pockets had been rifled. Only the fact that the medikit was slung to the rear had saved it from detection. He must have been lying on it when they searched him. His extra ammunition was gone as well as the case of grenades.

The radio was still there! In the darkness they must not have noticed it in the flat pocket almost under his arm.

It only had line-of-sight operation, but that might be enough to get a fix on the ship or even call for help.

He pulled it out and looked gloomily at the crushed case and the fractured components that were leaking from a crack in the side. Some time during the busy events of the last day, it had been struck by something heavy. He switched it on and got exactly the result he expected. Nothing.

The fact that the chronometer concealed behind his belt buckle was still keeping perfect time did little to cheer him. It was 10 in the morning. Wonderful. The watch had been adjusted for the 20-hour day when they had landed on Felicity, with noon set for the sun at the zenith at the spot where they had landed.

"That's enough of that," he said, making himself as comfortable as was possible on the hard ground and pulling the furs around him. "Let's talk, Oraiel. Who is the boss here, the one who ordered my execution?"

"He is Temuchin the Warrior, The Fearless One, He of the Arm of Steel, The Destroyer—"

"Fine. He's on top. I can tell that without the footnotes. What has he got against strangers—and buildings?"

" 'The Song of the Freemen,' " Oraiel said, digging his elbow into the ribs of his assistant. The youth grunted and rooted about in the tangled furs until he produced a lutelike instrument with a long neck and two strings. Plucking the strings for accompaniment he began to sing in a high-pitched voice.

> Free as the wind,
> Free as the plain on which we wander,
> Knowing no home,
> Other than our tents. Our friends
> The Moropes,
> Who take us to battle,
> Destroying the buildings,
> Of those who would trap us . . .

There was more like this and it went on for an unconscionably long time, until Jason found himself beginning to nod. He interrupted, broke off the song, and asked some pertinent questions.

A picture of the realities of life on the plains of Felicity began to emerge.

From the oceans on the east and west, and from the Great Cliff in the south, to the mountains in the north there stood not one permanent building or settlement of man. Free and wild, the tribes roved over the grass sea, warring on themselves and each other in endless feuds and conflicts.

There had been cities here, some of them were even mentioned by name in the Songs, but now, only their memory remained, and an uncompromising hatred. There must have been a long and bitter war between two different ways of life, if the memory, generations later, could still arouse such strong emotions. With the limited natural resources of these arid plains, the agrarians and the nomads could not possibly have lived side by side in peace. The farmers would have built settlements around the scant water sources and fenced out the nomads and their flocks. In self-defense, the nomads would have had to band together in an attempt to destroy the settlements. They had succeeded so well in this genocidal warfare that the only trace of their former enemies that remained was a hated memory.

Crude, unlettered, violent, the barbarian conquerors roamed the high steppe in tribes and clans, constantly on the move as their stunted cattle and goats consumed the scant grass that covered the plains. Writing was unknown; the jongleurs—the only men who could pass freely from tribe to tribe—were the historians, entertainers and bearers of news. No trees grew in this hostile climate so wooden utensils and artifacts were unknown. Iron ore and coal were apparently plentiful in the northern mountains, so iron and mild steel were the most common materials used. These, along with animal hides, horns and bones, were almost the only raw materials available. An outstanding exception were the helms and breastplates. While some were made of iron, the best ones came from a tribe in the distant hills who worked a mine of asbestos-like rock. They shredded this to fibers and mixed it with the gum of a broad-leaved plant to produce what amounted to an epoxy-fiber-glass material. It was light as aluminum, strong as steel, and even more elastic than the best spring steel. This technique, undoubtedly inherited from the first, pre-breakdown settlers on the planet, was the only thing that physically distinguished the nomads from any other race of

38

iron-age barbarians. Animal droppings were used for cooking fuel; animal fat, for lamps. Life tended to be nasty, brutish and short.

Every clan or tribe had its traditional pasture ground over which it roamed, though the delimitations were vague and controversial, so that wars and feuds were a constant menace. The domed tents, *camachs,* were made of joined hides over iron poles. They were erected and struck in a few minutes, and when the tribe moved on, they were carried, with the household goods, on wheeled frames called *escungs,* like a travois with wheels, which were pulled by the *moropes.*

Unlike the cattle and goats, which were descendants of terrestrial animals, the *moropes* were natives of the high steppes of Felicity. These claw-toed herbivores had been domesticated and bred for centuries, while most of their wild herds had been exterminated. Their thick pelts protected them from the eternal cold, and they could go as long as 20 days without water. As beasts of burden—and chargers of war—they made existence possible in this barren land.

There was little more to tell. The tribes roved and fought, each speaking its own language or dialect and using the neutral in-between tongue when they had to talk to outsiders. They formed alliances and treacherously broke them. Their occupation and love was war and they practiced it most efficiently.

Jason digested this information while he attempted, less successfully, to digest the unchewable lumps from the stew that he had forced himself to swallow. For drink there had been fermented *morope* milk, which tasted almost as bad as it smelled. The only course he had missed was the one reserved for warriors, a mixture of milk and still-warm blood, and for this he was grateful.

Once Jason's curiosity had been satisfied, Oraiel's turn had come and he had asked questions endlessly. Even while Jason ate, he had had to mumble answers, which the jongleur and his apprentice filed away in their capacious memories. They had not been disturbed, so he considered himself safe—for the time being. It was already late in the afternoon and he had to think of a way to escape and return to the ship. He waited until Oraiel ran out of breath then asked some pointed questions of his own.

"How many men are there in this camp?"

The jongleur had been sipping steadily at the *achadh*, the fermented milk, and was beginning to rock back and forth. He mumbled and spread his arms wide. "They are the sons of the vulture," he intoned. "Their numbers blacken the plain and the fearful sight of them strikes terror—"

"I didn't ask for a tribal history, just a nice round figure."

"Only the gods know. There may be a hundred, there may be a million."

"How much is 20 and 20?" Jason interrupted.

"I do not bother my thoughts with such stupid figurations."

"I didn't think you could do higher mathematics—like counting to one hundred and other exotic computations."

Jason went over and peered out of the opening between the laces. A blast of frigid air made his eyes water. High, icy clouds drifted across the pale blueness of the sky, while the shadows were growing long.

"Drink," Oraiel said, waving the leathern bottle of *achadh*. "You are my guest and you must drink."

The silence was broken only by the rasp of sand as the old woman scrubbed out the cooking pot. The apprentice's chin was on his chest and he appeared to be asleep.

"I never refuse a drink," Jason said, and walked over and took the bottle.

As he raised it to his lips, he saw the old woman glance up quickly, then bend low again over her work. There was a slight stirring behind him.

Jason hurled himself sideways, the drinking skin went flying and the club skinned his ear and crashed into his shoulder.

Still rolling, without looking, Jason kicked backward and his foot caught the apprentice in the pit of the stomach. He folded nicely and the spiked iron bar rolled free of his limp hands.

Oraiel, no longer drunk, pulled a long, two-handed sword from under the furs beside him and swung on Jason. Though the spikes had missed, the bar itself had numbed Jason's right shoulder and his arm, which hung limply at his side. There was nothing wrong with his left arm, however, so he flung himself inside the arc of the sword before it could descend and locked his hand around the jongleur's

40

throat, thumb and index finger on the major blood vessels. The man kicked spasmodically, then slumped unconscious.

Always aware of his flanks, Jason had been trying to keep one eye on the old woman, who now produced a gleaming, saw-edged knife—the *camach* was an armory of concealed weapons—and hopped to the attack. Jason dropped the jongleur and chopped her wrist so the knife fell at his feet.

The entire action had taken about ten seconds. Oraiel and his apprentice were draped over each other in an unconscious huddle, while the crone sobbed by the fire, cradling her wrist.

"Thanks for the hospitality," Jason said, trying to rub some life back into his numbed arm. When he could move his fingers again, he tied and gagged the woman, then the others, arranging them in a neat row on the floor. Oraiel's eyes were open, radiating bloodshot waves of hatred.

"As ye sow, so shall ye reap," Jason said, picking over the furs. "That's another one you can memorize. I suppose you can't be blamed for trying to get your information, and the reward money as well. But you were being a little too greedy. I know that you're sorry now and want me to have enough of these moth-eaten furs to disguise myself with, as well as that greasy fur hat which has seen better days, and perhaps a weapon or two."

Oraiel growled and frothed a little around his gag.

"Such language," Jason said. He pulled the hat low over his eyes and picked up the spiked club, which he had wrapped in a length of leather. "Neither you nor the old girl have enough teeth for the job, but your assistant has a fine set of choppers. He can chew through the leather gag, then chew the thongs on your wrists. By which time I shall be far from here. Be thankful I'm not one of your own kind, or you would be dead right now." He picked up the skin of *achadh* and slung it from his shoulder. "I'll take this for the road."

There was no one in sight when he poked his head out of the *camach*, so he stopped long enough to lace the flap tightly behind him. He squinted up at the sky once, then turned away among the domed rows.

Head down, he shuffled away through the barbarian camp.

5

No ONE PAID HIM the slightest attention.

Bundled as they were against the perpetual cold, most of the people looked as ragged and nondescript as he did, male and female, young and old. Only the warriors had any distinction of dress, and they could be easily avoided by scuttling off between the *camachs* whenever he saw one approaching. The rest of the citizenry avoided them as well, so no notice was taken of his actions.

There appeared to be no organized planning of the encampment that he could see. The *camachs* staggered in uneven rows, thrown up apparently wherever the owners had stopped. They thinned out after a while and Jason found himself skirting a herd of small, shaggy and evil-looking cows. Armed guards, holding tethered *moropes,* were scattered about, so he made his way by as quickly as was prudent. He heard—and smelled—a flock of goats nearby, and avoided them as well. Then, suddenly, he was at the last *camach,* and the featureless plain was ahead, stretching out to the horizon. The sun was almost down and he squinted at it happily.

"Setting right behind me, or just a little to the right. I remember that much about the ride here. Now if I reverse the direction and march into the sunset I should come to the ship."

Sure, he thought, if I can make as good time as the thugs did who brought me here. And if I am going in the right direction, and they made no turns. And if none of these bloodthirsty types find me. If—

Enough ifs. He shook his head and braced his shoulders, then took a swig of the foul *achadh.* As he raised the skin to his mouth, he looked about him and saw that he was unobserved. Wiping his mouth on his sleeve, he strolled out into the empty steppe.

He did not go far. As soon as he found a gully that would shelter him from view of the encampment, he dropped down into it. It gave him some protection from the wind, and he pulled his knees up to his chest to conserve heat, then waited there until it was completely dark. It wasn't the most morale-building way to spend the time, chilled and getting colder as the wind rustled the grass above his head, but there was no other way. He put a rock on the far wall of the gully, ready to mark the exact spot where the sun set, then huddled back against the opposite wall. He brooded about the radio, and even opened it to see if anything could be done, but it was unarguably beyond repair. After that, he just sat and waited for the sun to reach the western horizon and for the stars to come out.

Jason wished that he had done some more stellar observation before the ship had landed, but it was a little late for that now. The constellations would be unfamiliar and he had no idea if there was a pole star or even a close circumpolar constellation that he could set his course by. One thing he did remember, from constant examination of the maps and charts as they prepared for the landing, was that they had set down almost exactly on the seventieth parallel, at 70 degrees of north latitude right on the head.

Now what did this mean? If there were a north polar star, it would be exactly 70 degrees above the northern horizon. Given a few nights and a protractor, it would be easy enough to find. But his present situation did not allow much time for casual observation. Or the temperature either; he stamped his feet to see if they still had any sensation remaining in them.

The north polar axis would be 70 degrees above the northern horizon, which meant that the sun at noon would be exactly 20 degrees above the southern horizon. It had to be this way every day of the year, because the axis of rotation of the planet was directly vertical to the plane of the ecliptic. No nonsense here about long days and short days— or even seasons for that matter. At any single spot on the planet's surface the sun always rose from the same place on the horizon. Day after day, year after year, it cut an identical arc across the sky, then set at the same spot on the western horizon as it had the night before. Day and night, all over the planet, were always of equal length. The angle of incidence of the sun's rays would always remain the same as well, which meant that the amount of radiation reaching any given area would remain constant the year round.

With days and nights of equal length, and the energy input always equal, the weather always remained the same and you were stuck with what you had. The tropics were always hot; the poles, locked in a frigid and eternal embrace.

The sun was now a dim yellow disk balanced on the sharp line of the horizon. At this high latitude, instead of dropping straight down out of sight, it slithered slantways along the horizon. When half the disk was obscured, Jason marked the spot on the far rim, then went over and stood the pointed stone up at that spot. Then he returned to the spot where he had been sitting and squinted along his bearing marker.

"Very fine," he said out loud. "Now I know where the sun sets—but how do I follow that direction after dark? Think, Jason, think, because right now your life depends upon it." He shivered, surely because of the cold.

"It would help if I knew just where on the horizon the sun set, how many degrees west of north. With no axial tilt, the problem should be a simple one." He scratched arcs and angles in the sand and mumbled to himself. "If the axis is vertical, every day must be an equinox, which means that day and night are equal every day, which means—ho-ho!" He tried to snap his fingers, but they were too cold to respond.

"That's the answer! If the length of the night is to equal the length of the day, then there is only one place for the sun to set and rise, at every latitude from the equator north and south. The sun will have to cut a 180-degree arc through the sky, so it must rise due east and set due west. Eureka!"

Jason put his right arm straight out from his shoulder and shuffled around until his finger was pointing exactly at his marker.

"This is simplicity itself. I am pointing west and facing due south. Now I craftily pull up my left arm and I am pointing due east. All that remains now is to stand in this uncomfortable position until the stars come out."

In the high, thin air, the first stars were already appearing in the east, though twilight still lingered on the opposite

44

horizon. Jason thought for a moment and decided that he could improve upon the accuracy of the finger-pointing technique. He put a stone on the eastern rim of the gully, just above the spot where he had been sitting. Then he climbed the opposite wall and sighted at it over the first marker stone. A bright blue star lay close to the horizon in the correct spot, and a clear Z-shaped constellation was beginning to be visible around it.

"My guiding star, I shall follow you from afar," Jason said, and snapped open his belt buckle to look down at the illuminated face of his watch. "Got you. With a 20-hour day, I can say ten hours of darkness and ten of light. So right now I walk directly away from my star. In five hours it will hit its zenith in the south, right on a line with my left shoulder as I walk. Then it swoops around and dives down to set directly in front of me about dawn. This is simplicity itself as long as I make adjustments for the new position every hour, or half hour, to allow for the changed position with the passage of time. Hah!"

Snorting this last, he made sure that the Z was directly behind his back, shouldered his club and tramped off in the correct direction. Everything seemed secure enough, but he wished, neither for the first nor the last time, that he had a gyrocompass.

The temperature dropped quickly as the night advanced, and in the clear, dry air the stars burned in distant, twinkling points. Overhead, the constellations wheeled silently high, while the little Z hurried in its low arc until it stood at its zenith at midnight. Jason checked his watch, then dropped onto a crackling hummock of grass. He had been walking for over five hours with only a single break. In spite of his training at 2G on Pyrrus, the going was hard. He swigged from the drinking skin and wondered what the temperature was. In spite of its mildly alcoholic content, the *achadh* was a half-frozen slush.

Felicity had no moons, but there was more than enough light to see by from the stars. The frigid grayness of the plain stretched away on all sides, silent and motionless except for the dark, moving mass coming up behind him.

Slowly, Jason sank to the ground and lay there, frozen, while the *moropes* and their riders came near, the ground shivering with the rumble of their feet. They passed, no more than 200 meters from where he lay, and he pressed flat and watched the dark, silent silhouettes until they vanished out of sight to the south.

"Looking for me?" he asked himself, standing and brushing at the furs. "Or are they heading for the ship?"

This latter seemed the most obvious answer. The compactness of the group and their hurried pace indicated some specific destination. And why not? He had been brought from the ship along this route, so it was perfectly understandable that others should follow it as well. He considered going over to attempt to follow their trail, but did not think too highly of the idea. There could be a good bit of traffic back and forth from the ship, and he did not feel like being caught on the barbarian highway by daylight.

When he stood up the wind had a chance to get at him, and a fit of shivering shook him with a giant hand. He was as rested as he was ever going to be, so he might as well press on before he froze to death. Slinging the drinking skin over his shoulder and picking up the club, he began walking again in the correct direction, paralleling the raiders' track.

Twice more during that seemingly endless night, groups of raiders hurried by in the same direction, while Jason concealed himself against chance observation. Each time it was harder to get up and go on, but the cold ground was a good persuader. By the time the sky began to lighten in the east, the 1.5 gravity had exacted its toll. It took Jason an effort of will to put one foot in front of the other. His guiding constellation was on the horizon, fading in the spreading grayness of dawn, and he went on until it was gone.

It was time to stop. Only by promising himself that he would not walk after sunrise had he managed to keep going at all. He could guide himself easily enough by the sun during the day, but it would be too dangerous. A moving figure could easily be seen at great distances on these plains. And, as the ship was not yet in sight, there was a good deal more walking to be done. He would have to get some rest if he were to go on, and this was possible only during the day.

He half fell, half crawled into the next gully. There was a small overhanging ledge, on the northern side where the sun would strike all day, just the burrow for him. The ledge would keep the wind off him and shield him from sight from above. Pulling his legs up to his chest, he tried to ignore the cold of the ground that struck through his furs and insulated clothing. While he was wondering if, chilled, uncomfortable, exhausted, stifling, he could possibly fall asleep, he fell asleep.

Some sound, some presence bothered him, and he opened one eye and peered out from under the edge of the hat. Two gray-furred animals, with skinny tails and long teeth, were surveying him with wide eyes from the other side of the gully. He said "Boo" and they vanished. The sun felt almost warm now and the ground had either warmed up or his side was too numb to feel anything. He went to sleep again.

The next time he awoke the sun had dropped behind the gully wall and he was in shadow. He knew just what a slab of meat in a frozen-food locker felt like. Moving took almost more effort than he cared to make, and he was afraid that, if he struck his hands or feet against anything, they would crack off. There was still some *achadh* left in the skin and he swilled it down, which brought on an extended coughing fit. When it was over he felt weaker, though a little bit more alive.

Once again he took his direction from the setting sun and, when the stars came out, started on his way. Walking was much worse than it had been the preceding night. Exertion, his wounds, the lack of food and the heightened gravity exacted their toll. Within an hour he was tottering like an octogenarian and knew that he could not go on like this. He dropped to the ground, panting with exhaustion, and pressed the release that dropped the medikit into his hand.

"I've been saving you for the last round. And, if I am not mistaken, I have just heard the final bell ringing."

Cackling feebly at this insipid witticism, he adjusted the control dial for *stimulants, normal strength*. He pressed the actuator to the inside of his wrist and felt the sharp bite of the needles striking home.

It worked. Within sixty seconds he became aware that his fatigue was beginning to slip away, masked behind a curtain of drugs. When he stood, he experienced a certain numbness in his limbs, but no tiredness at all.

"Onward!" he shouted, marking his guiding constellation as he slipped the medikit back into its holder.

The night was neither long nor short; it just passed in a pleasant haze. Under the stress of the drugs, his mind worked well and he tried not to think of the physical toll they were exacting. A number of war parties passed, all coming from the direction of the ship, and he hid each time even though most of them were far distant. He wondered if some battle had been fought and if they might have been beaten. Each time, he changed his course slightly to come closer to their line of march, so that there would be no chance of his getting lost.

Soon after three in the morning, Jason found himself stumbling and, at one point, actually trying to walk along on his knees. A full turn of the medikit control set it for *stimulants, emergency strength*. The injections worked and he went on again at the same regular pace.

It was almost dawn when he began to smell the first traces of some burned odor—which grew stronger with each pace forward. When the sky began to gray in the east, the smell was sharp in his nostrils, and he wondered what significance it might have. Unlike the previous morning, he did not stop but pressed on. This was the last day that he had and he must reach the ship before the stimulants wore off. It could not be too far ahead. He would just have to stay alert and chance walking during the day. He was much smaller than the *moropes* and their riders and, given any luck at all, he should be able to spot them first.

When he walked into the blackened area of grass, he would not believe it. A fire perhaps, accidentally ignited. It had burned in an exactly circular pattern.

Only when he recognized the rusted and destroyed forms of the mining machinery did he dare admit the truth.

"I'm here. Back at the same spot. This is where we landed."

He staggered crazily in a circle, looking at the massive emptiness stretching away on all sides.

"This is it!" he shouted. "This is where the ship was. We put the *Pugnacious* down right here next to the original landing site. Only the ship isn't here. They've left—gone without me. . . ."

Despair froze him and his arms dropped to his sides as he stood there, tottering, his strength gone. The ship, his friends, they were gone as well.

From close by came the rumble of heavy, running feet.

Over the hill rushed five *moropes,* their riders shouting with predatory glee as they lowered their lances for the kill.

6

WITH CONDITIONED REFLEX Jason swung up his arm, his hand crooked and ready for the gun—before he remembered that he had been disarmed.

"Then we'll do this the old-fashioned way!" he shouted, swinging the iron club in a whistling circle. The odds were well against him, but before he went down they would know that they had been in a fight.

They came in a tight knot, each man trying to be first to the kill, jostling one another and leaning far forward with outstretched lances. Jason stood ready, legs wide, waiting for the last possible instant before he moved. The shrieking riders were at the edge of the burnt area.

A muffled explosion was followed instantly by a great, roiling cloud of vapor that hid the attackers from sight. Jason lowered his club and stepped back as a tendril of the cloud twisted toward him. Only one *morope* made it through the gray vapor, carried along by its momentum, skidding and collapsing with a ground-shaking thud. Its rider catapulted toward Jason and even managed to crawl a short distance further, his jaw working with silent hatred, before he, too, collapsed.

When a wisp of the thinned-out gas reached Jason he sniffed, then moved quickly away. Narcogas. It worked instantly and thoroughly on any oxygen-breathing animal, producing paralysis and unconsciousness for about five hours, after which the victim recovered completely, with nothing worse than the nasty side effect of a skull-splitting headache.

What had happened? The ship had certainly gone, and

there was no one else in sight. Fatigue was winning out over the effects of the stimulants and his thinking was getting muzzy. He heard the growling rumble for some seconds before he recognized the source of the sound. It was the rocket launch from the *Pugnacious*. Blinking up into the clear brightness of the morning sky, he saw the high contrail stretching a white line across the sky toward him, growing larger with each passing second. The launch was first a black dot, then a growing shape, finally a flame-spouting cylinder that touched down less than a hundred meters away. The lock spun open and Meta dropped to the ground, even before the shock absorbers had damped the landing impact.

"Are you all right?" she called, running swiftly to him, the questing muzzle of her gun looking for enemies on all sides.

"Never felt better," he said, leaning on the club so he would not fall down. "What kept you? I thought you had all pulled out and forgotten about me."

"You know we wouldn't do that." She ran her hands over his arms, his back while she talked, as though looking for broken bones—or simply reassuring herself of his presence. "We could not stop them from taking you away, although we tried. Some of them died. An attack was launched on the ship at the same time."

Jason could well understand the shock of battle and dogged resistance behind her matter-of-fact words. It must have been brutal.

"Come to the launch," she said, putting his arm across her shoulders so she could bear part of his weight. He did not protest. "They must have been concealed on all sides and reinforcements kept arriving. They are very good fighters and do not ask for quarter, nor do they expect it. Kerk soon realized that there would be no end to the battle and that we could not help you by staying there. If you did succeed in escaping—which he was sure you would if you were still alive—it would have been impossible for you to reach the ship. Therefore, under cover of counter-attacks, we placed a number of spyeyes and microphones, as well as planting a good store of land mines and remote-controlled gas bombs. After that we left, and the ship has set up a base somewhere in the northern mountains. I dropped off at the foothills with the launch and have been waiting ever since. I came as soon as I could. Here, into the cabin."

"You timed it very well, thank you. I can do that myself."

He couldn't, but he wouldn't admit it, and made believe that he had climbed the ladder instead of being boosted in by a powerful push from her feminine right arm.

Jason staggered over and dropped into the copilot's acceleration couch while Meta sealed the lock. Once it was closed, the tension drained from her body as her gun whined back into its power holster. She hurried to his side, kneeling so she could look into his face.

"Take this filthy thing off," she said, hurling the fur cap to the floor. She ran her fingers through his hair and touched her fingertips lightly to the bruises and frostbite marks on his face. "I thought you were dead, Jason, really I did. I never thought I would see you again."

"Did that bother you so much?"

He was exhausted, his strength stretched well beyond the breaking point so that waves of blackness threatened to obscure his vision. He fought them away. He felt that, at this moment, he was closer to Meta than he had ever been before.

"It did, it bothered me. I don't know why." She kissed him suddenly, hard, forgetting the condition of his cracked and battered lips. He did not complain.

"Perhaps you are just used to having me around," he said, far more casually than he felt.

"No, it is not that. I have had men around before."

Oh, thanks, he thought.

"I have had two children. I am twenty-three years old. While piloting our ship, I have been to many planets. I used to think that I knew all there was to know, but now I do not believe so. You have taught me many new things. When that man, Mikah Samon, kidnapped you, I found out something I did not know about myself. I had to find you. These are very un-Pyrran things to feel, for we are taught to always think of the city first, never of other people. Now I am very mixed up. Am I wrong?"

"No," he said, fighting back the threat of overwhelming darkness. "Quite the opposite." He pressed his cracked and dirt-grimed fingers to the resilient warmth of her arm. "I think you are more right than any of the trigger-happy butchers in your tribe."

"You must tell me. Why do I feel this way?"

He tried to smile, but it hurt his face.

"Do you know what marriage is, Meta?"

"I have heard of it. A social custom on some planets. I do not know what it is."

An alarm buzzed angrily on the control board and she turned at once to it.

"You still don't know, and maybe it's better that way. Maybe I'll never tell you." He smiled, his chin touched his chest and he fell instantly asleep.

"There are more of them coming," Meta said, switching off the alarm and glancing into the viewscreen. There was no answer. When she saw what had happened, she quickly tightened the straps to secure him in the couch, then began the takeoff procedure. She neither noticed nor cared if any attackers were under the jets when she blasted skyward.

The pressure of deceleration woke Jason as they dropped down for the landing. "Thirsty," he said, smacking his dry lips together. "And hungry enough to eat one of those *moropes* raw."

"Teca is on the way," she told him, flipping off the switches as the launch grounded.

"If he is the same kind of sawbones his mentor, Brucco, is, he'll put me under for recovery therapy and keep me unconscious for a week. No can do." He turned his head, slowly, to look as the inner port opened. Teca, a brisk and authoritative young man, whose enthusiasm for medicine far exceeded his knowledge, climbed in.

"No can do," Jason repeated. "No recovery therapy. Glucose drip, vitamin injections, artificial kidney, whatever you wish as long as I'm conscious."

"That's what I like about Pyrrans," Jason said, as they carried him from the launch on a stretcher, the glucose-drip bottle swinging next to his head. "They let you go to hell in your own way."

Meta saw to it that it took a good while for the leaders of the expedition to gather. Jason, whose eyes had closed in the middle of a grumbled complaint, spent the time in a

52

deep, restorative sleep. He woke up when the hum of conversation began to fill the wardroom.

"Meeting will come to order," he said in what was intended to be a firm, commanding voice. It came out as a cracked whisper. He turned to Teca. "Before the meeting begins, I would like some syrup for my throat and a shot to wake me up. Can you take care of that?"

"Of course, I can," Teca said, opening his kit. "But I think it unwise due to the strain already imposed on your system." However, he did not let his thoughts interfere with the swift execution of his duties.

"That's better," Jason said as the drugs once more wiped away the barrier of fatigue. He would pay for this—but later. The work must be done now.

"I've found out the answers to some of our questions," he told them. "Not all, but enough for a beginning. I know now that, unless some profound changes are made, we are not going to be able to establish a mining settlement. And when I say 'profound,' I mean it. We are going to have to change the complete mores, taboos and cultural motivations of these people before we can get our mine into operation."

"Impossible," Kerk said.

"Perhaps. But it is better than the only other alternative— which is genocide. As things stand now, we would have to kill every one of those barbarians before we could be assured of establishing a settlement in peace."

A depressed silence followed this statement. The Pyrrans knew what this meant because they were themselves unwilling genocide victims of their home planet.

"We will not consider genocide," Kerk said, and the others unconsciously nodded their heads. "But your other alternative sounds too unreasonable."

"Does it? You might recall that we are all here now because the mores, taboos and cultural motivations of your people have recently been turned upside down. What's good enough for you is good enough for them. We bore from within, utilizing those two ancient techniques known as 'Divide and rule' and 'If you can't lick 'em, join 'em!' "

"It would help us," Rhes said, "if you explained what the mores exactly are that we are supposed to be disrupting."

"Didn't I tell you yet?" Jason searched his memory and realized that he hadn't. In spite of the drugs, he was not thinking so clearly as he should. "Then let me explain. I have recently had an involuntary indoctrination into how the locals live. 'Nastily' is one word for it. They are broken up into tribes and clans, all of whom seem to be perpetually at war with the others. Occasionally two or more of the tribes will join together to wipe out one of the others whom they all agree needs wiping out. This is always done under the leadership of a warlord, someone smart enough to make an alliance and strong enough to keep it working. Temuchin is the name of the chief who organized the tribes to destroy the John Company expedition. He is so good at his job that, instead of breaking up the alliance when the threat was over, he kept it going and has even added to it. The anti-city taboo appears to be one of the strongest they have, so it was easy to get recruits. He has kept his army busy ever since, consolidating more and more area under his control. When we arrived, it gave his recruiting an even bigger boost. Temuchin is our main problem. We can get nowhere so long as he is leading the tribes. The first thing we must do is to take away his reason for this holy war, and we can do that easily enough by leaving."

"Are you sure that you are not feverish?" Meta asked.

"Thank you for the consideration, but I am fine. I mean we must convince the tribes that we have left. Another landing must be made on the same site and some sort of digging in got under way. Trouble will arrive quickly enough and we'll have to fight them off to prove that we mean business. At the same time we will try to talk to them through loudspeakers, apparently to convince them of our peaceful intent. We'll tell them all about the nice things we will give them if they let us alone. This will only make them fight harder. Then we will threaten to leave forever if they don't stop. They won't stop. So we blast off, straight up, and drop back to a hiding place in the mountains on a ballistic orbit so we won't be seen. That is stage one."

"I assume there is a stage two," Kerk said with marked lack of enthusiasm, "for up to now it looks very much like a retreat."

"That's just the idea. In stage two we find an isolated spot in the mountains that simply cannot be reached on foot. We build a model village there to which we transplant, entirely against their will, one of the smaller tribes. They will have all the most modern sanitary conveniences, hot water, the only flush toilets on the entire planet, good

54

food and medical aid. They will hate us for it and do everything possible to kill us and to escape. We will release them—when this affair is over. But in the meanwhile we will utilize their *moropes* and *camachs* and the rest of their barbaric devices."

"What in the world for?" Meta asked.

"To form our own tribe, that's what for. The fighting Pyrrans. Tougher, nastier and more faithful to the taboos than any other tribe. We'll bore from within. We'll be so good at the barbarian game that our chief, Kerk the Great, will be able to squeeze Temuchin out of the top job. I know you will be able to get the operation rolling before I return."

"I did not know you were going," Kerk said, his baffled expression mirrored by the others. "What are you planning to do?"

Jason plucked an invisible string in midair. "I," he announced, "am going to become a jongleur. A wandering troubadour and spy, to sow dissent and prepare the way for your arrival."

7

"IF YOU LAUGH—or even smile—I'll break your arm," Meta said through tightly clenched teeth.

Jason had to use every iota of his gambler's facial control to maintain his bland, slightly bored expression. He knew she meant it about the broken arm. "I never laugh at a lady's new clothes," he said. "If I did, I would have split my sides many, many planets ago. I think you look fine for the job."

"You would," she hissed. "I think I look like some furry animal that has been run over by a ground car."

"Look, Grif is here," he said, pointing. She automatically turned toward the door. It was a timely entrance because, now that she had mentioned it, she did look like . . .

"Well, Grif, come in, my boy!" Making believe that the

wide grin and hearty laugh were for the grim-faced nine year old.

"I don't like this," Grif said, flushed and angry. "I don't like looking funny. No one wears clothes like this."

"All three of us do," Jason said, aiming his remarks at the boy but hoping they would register with Meta. "And where we are going, it is the usual dress. Meta here is in the height of fashion among the plains tribes." She was wrapped in stained leather and furs, her angry face scowling out from under a shapeless hood. He looked quickly away. "While you and I wear the indifferent motley of a jongleur and his apprentice. You'll soon see how well we fit in."

Time to change the subject from their ludicrous apparel. He looked closely at Grif's face and hands, then at Meta's.

"The ultraviolet and the tanning drugs have worked fine," he said as he took a small leather bag from the sack at his waist. "Your skins are about the same color as the tribesmen's, but there is one thing missing. As protection against the cold and wind, they grease their faces heavily. Wait, stop!" he said as both Pyrrans clenched their fists and death fluttered close. "I'm not asking you to smear on the rancid *morope* fat they use. This is clean, neutral, odorless silicone jelly that will be good protection. Take my word for it— you'll need it."

Jason quickly dug out a glob and rubbed it onto his cheeks. Reluctantly, the other two did the same. Before they were finished, the Pyrran scowls had deepened, which Jason had not thought possible. He wished they would relax—or this game would be over before it began. In the past week, once the others had approved, their plans had moved on teflon bearings. First the planned "retreat" from the planet, then the establishing of a base in this isolated valley. It was surrounded by vertical peaks on all sides and completely inaccessible except by air. Their resettlement camp was in the mountains nearby, a bit of plateau that was really only a large ledge set in a gigantic vertical cliff, a natural escape-proof prison. It was already occupied by a clean and embittered family of nomads, five males and six females, that had been caught away from their tribe and quieted by narcogas. Their artifacts and clothes, suitably cleaned and deloused, had been turned over to Jason—as had their *moropes*. Everything was ready now to penetrate

Temuchin's army, if Jason could only get these single-minded Pyrrans to cooperate.

"Let's go," Jason said. "It should be our turn by now."

With its capacious holds and cabins, the *Pugnacious* was still being used as a base, though some of the prefabs were almost erected. As they went down the corridor toward the lock, they met Teca coming from the opposite direction.

"Kerk sent me," he said. "They're almost ready for you."

Jason merely nodded and they started by him. Relieved of his message, Teca noticed for the first time their exotic garb and grease-covered faces. And the fierce scowls on the Pyrrans' faces. It was all very much out of place in the metal and plastic corridor. Teca looked from one to the other, then pointed at Meta.

"Do you know what you look like?" he said, and made the very great mistake of smiling.

Meta turned toward him, snarling, but Grif was closer, standing just next to the man. He sank his fist, with all of his weight, deep into Teca's midriff.

Grif was only nine—but he was a Pyrran nine-year-old. Teca had not expected the attack nor was he prepared for it. He said something like *whuf* as the air was driven from his chest, and sat down suddenly on the deck.

Jason waited for the mayhem to follow. Three Pyrrans fighting—and all of them angry! But Teca's mouth dropped open as he looked, wide-eyed, from one to another of the furry trio who surrounded him.

It was Meta who burst out laughing, and Grif followed an instant later. Jason joined in out of pure relief. Pyrrans rarely laugh, and when they do it is only at something broad and obvious, like a man's being knocked suddenly onto his backside. It broke the tension and they roared until their eyes streamed, laughing even harder when the red-faced Teca climbed to his feet and stalked angrily away.

"What was all that about?" Kerk asked when they emerged into the frigid night air.

"You would never believe me if I told you," Jason said. "Is that the last one?"

He pointed to the unconscious *morope* that was being rolled into a heavy cable sling. The launch, with vertijets screaming, was hovering above them and lowering a line with a stout hook at the end.

57

"Yes, the other two have already been delivered, along with the goats. You go out in the next trip."

They looked on in silence while the hook was slipped through the rings in the net and the launch was waved away. It rose quickly, the legs of its unconscious burden dangling limply, and vanished into the darkness.

"What about the equipment?" Jason said.

"It has all been moved out. We set up the *camach* for you and put everything inside it. You three look impressive in those outfits. For the first time, I think you may get away with this masquerade."

There were no hidden meanings in Kerk's words. Out here in the cold night, with a knifelike wind biting deep, their costumes were not out of place. They certainly were as effective as Kerk's insulated and electrically heated suit. Better perhaps. While his face was exposed, theirs were protected by the grease. Jason looked closely at Kerk's cheeks.

"You should go inside," he said, "or rub some of this grease on. It looks like you're getting frostbitten."

"Feels like it, too. If you don't need me here any more, I'll go and thaw out."

"Thanks for the help. We'll take it from here."

"Good luck then," Kerk said, shaking hands with them all, including the boy. "We'll keep a full-time radio watch so you can contact us."

They waited silently until the launch returned. They boarded quickly and the trip to the plains did not take very long, which was all for the best, as the interior of the cabin felt stuffy and tropical after the night air.

When the launch had set them down and gone, Jason pointed to the rounded form of the *camach*. "Get inside and make yourselves at home," he said. "I'm going to make sure that the *moropes* are staked down so they don't wander away when they come to. You'll find an atomic power pack there, as well as a light and a heater to plug in. We might as well enjoy the benefits of civilization one last evening."

By the time he had finished with the beasts, the *camach* had warmed up, and cheering light filtered through the lashings around the door flap. Jason laced it behind him and took off his heavy outer furs as the others had done. He rooted an iron pot from one of the hide boxes and filled it with water from a skin bag. This, and the other bags, had been lined with plastic which had not only leakproofed them, but made a marked difference in the quality of the water. He put it on the heater to boil. Meta and the boy sat silently, watching every move he made.

"This is *char*," he said, breaking a crumbly black lump off the larger brick. "It's made from one of the shrubs, the leaves are moistened and compressed into blocks. The taste is bearable and we had better get used to it." He dropped the fragments into the water, which instantly turned a repellent shade of purple.

"I don't like the way it looks," Grif said, eying it suspiciously. "I don't think I want any."

"You better try it in spite of that. We are going to have to live just like these nomads if we are to escape detection. Which brings up another very important point."

Jason pulled his sleeve up as he spoke and began to unstrap his power holster—while the other two looked on with shocked, widened eyes.

"What is wrong? What are you doing?" Meta asked when he took the gun off and stowed it in the metal trunk. A Pyrran wears his gun every hour of the day and night. Life is unimaginable without one.

"I'm taking off my gun," he patiently explained. "If I used it, or if a tribesman even saw it, our disguise would be penetrated. I'm going to ask you to put yours in here, too—"

Before the words were out of his mouth there was a sharp ripping sound as both of the other guns tore through the leather clothing and slapped into their owners' hands. Jason looked calmly at the unwavering muzzles.

"That is exactly what I mean. As soon as you people get excited, *zingo*, out come the guns. It's not that you can't be trusted; it's just that your reflexes are wrong. We're going to have to lock the guns away where we can get at them in an emergency, but where their presence can't betray us. We'll just have to handle the locals with their own weapons. Look here."

The guns zipped back into their power holsters as the Pyrrans' attention was captured by Jason's display. He unrolled a skin that clanked heavily. It was filled with a wicked assortment of knives, swords, clubs and maces.

"Nice, aren't they?" Jason asked, and they both nodded agreement. Babies and candy: Pyrrans and weapons. "With these we'll be just as well armed as anyone else—in fact better. For any one Pyrran is better than any three barbarians. I hope. But we're shading the odds with these. With the exception of one or two items, they are all copies of local artifacts, only made of much better steel, harder and with a more permanent edge. Now give me the guns."

Only Grif's gun appeared in his hand this time, and he had the intelligence to be a little chagrined as he let it slip back into the power holster. Fifteen solid minutes of wheedling and arguing reluctantly convinced Meta she should part with her weapon, and it took the two of them an hour more to disarm the boy. It was finally done and Jason poured out mugs of *char* for his unhappy partners—both of whom clutched swords to solace themselves.

"I know this stuff is terrible," he said, seeing the shocked expressions that appeared on their faces when they drank. "You don't have to learn to like it, but at least teach yourselves to drink it without looking as though you're being poisoned."

Except for occasional horrified looks at their bare right arms, the Pyrrans forgot the loss of guns while they readied the *camach* for the night. Jason unrolled the fur sleeping bags and turned off the heater while they packed the extra weapons away.

"Bedtime," he announced. "We have to get up at dawn to move to this spot on the chart. There is a small band of nomads going in the direction of what we think is Temuchin's main camp, and we want to meet them here. Join forces, practice our barbarian skills, and let them bring us into the camp without too much notice being taken of us."

Jason was up before dawn and had all the off-planet devices sealed into the lockbox before he woke the others. He had left out three self-heating meal packs but he would not let them be opened until the *escung* had been loaded. It was a clumsy, time-consuming job this first time, and he was relieved that his angry Pyrrans had been disarmed. The skin cover was pulled off the *camach* and the iron supporting poles were collapsed. These were tied onto the frame of the wheeled travois to act as a support for the rest of the luggage. The sun was well above the horizon and they were sweating, despite the lung-hurting chill air, before they were through loading everything aboard the *escung*.

The *moropes* were rumbling deep in their chests as they grazed, while the goats were spread out on all sides nibbling the scant grass. Meta looked pointedly at all this eating and Jason got the hint.

"Come and get it," he said. "We can harness up after we eat." He pulled the opening tab on his pack and steam rose at once from its contents. They broke off the attached plastic spoons and ate in hungry silence.

"Duty calls," Jason announced, scraping up the last morsel of meat. "Meta, use your knife and dig a nice deep hole to bury these meal packs. I'll saddle the *moropes* and harness the one that pulls the *escung*. Grif, take that basket, there on top, and pick up all the *morope* chips. We don't want to waste a natural resource."

"You want me to *what?*"

Jason smiled falsely and pointed to the ground near the big herbivores. "Dung. Those things there. We save them and dry them, and that is what we use from now on to heat and cook with." He swung the nearest saddle onto his back and made believe he did not hear the boy's answering remark.

They had observed how the nomads handled the big beasts and had had some practice themselves, but it was still difficult. The *moropes* were willing but incredibly stupid, and responded best only to the application of direct force. They were all almost exhausted by the time they moved out, Jason leading the way on one riding *morope* and Meta on the second. Grif, perched high on the loaded *escung*, trailed behind, riding backward to keep an eye on the goats. These animals trailed after, grabbing mouthfuls of grass as they went, conditioned to stay close to their owners who supplied the vital water and salt.

By early afternoon they were saddle-sore and weary, when they saw the cloud of dust moving diagonally across their front.

"Just sit quiet and keep your weapons handy," Jason said, "while I do the talking. Listen to the way they speak this simplified language so that later on you'll be able to do it yourself."

As they came closer, the dark blobs of *moropes* could be made out, with the scattered specks of the goat herds behind. Three *moropes* swung away from the larger group and headed their way at a dead run. Jason held up his hand for his party to halt, then cursed as he threw all of his weight on the reins to bring his hulking mount to a stop. Sensation penetrated its tiny brain and it shuddered to a halt and began instantly to graze. He loosened his knife in its sheath and noticed that Meta's right hand was unconsciously flexing, reaching for the gun that was not there. The riders thundered up, stopping just before them.

The leader had a dirty black beard and only one eye. The red, raw appearance of the empty socket suggested that the eyeball had been gouged out. He wore a dented metal helm that was crowned with the skull of some long-toothed rodent.

"Who are you, jongleur?" he asked, shifting a spiked mace from one hand to the other. "Where you go?"

"I am Jason, singer of songs, teller of tales, on my way to the camp of Temuchin. Who are you?"

The man grunted and picked at his teeth with one blackened nail.

"Shanin of the rat tribe. What do you say to rats?"

Jason had not the slightest idea what one said to rats, though he could think of a few possibly inappropriate remarks. He noticed now that the others had the same type of skull, rats' skulls undoubtedly, mounted on their helms. The symbol of their tribe, perhaps, different skulls for different tribes. But he remembered that Oraiel had no such decoration, and that the jongleurs were supposed to stay outside of tribal conflicts.

"I say hello to rats," he improvised. "Some of my best friends are rats."

"You fight feud with rats?"

"Never!" Jason answered, offended by the suggestion.

Shanin seemed satisfied and went back to picking his teeth. "We go to Temuchin, too," he said indistinctly around his finger. "I have heard Temuchin strikes against the mountain weasels so we join him. You ride with us. Sing for me tonight."

"I hate mountain weasels, too. I'll sing tonight."

At a grunted command the three men wheeled and galloped away. That was all there was to it. Jason's party followed and slowly caught up with the moving column of *moropes*, swinging in behind them so that their herd of goats did not mix with the others.

"That's what all the goat leads are for," Jason said,

coughing in the cloud of dust that hung heavy in the air. "As soon as we stop, I want you two to secure all our animals so they can't get lost in the other herd."

"Aren't you planning to help?" Meta asked coldly.

"Much as I would love to, this is a male-orientated, primitive society and that sort of thing just isn't done. I'll do my share of the work out of sight in the tent, but not in public."

It was a short day, which the disguised off-worlders appreciated, because the nomads reached their goal, a desert well, early in the afternoon. Jason, saddle-sore and stiff, slid to the ground and hobbled in small circles to work the circulation back into his numb legs. Meta and Grif were rounding up and tethering the protesting goats, which induced Jason to take a walk around the camp to escape her daggerlike glances. The well interested him: he came to look and stayed to help. Only men and boys were gathered here since there seemed to be a sexual taboo connected with the water. This was understandable, as water was as essential to life as hunting ability in this semiarid desert.

A rock cairn marked the well, which the men removed to disclose a beaten iron cover. This was heavily greased to retard its rusting, though the covering rocks had cut through the grease and streaks of oxidation were beginning to form. When the cover had been lifted aside, one of the men thoroughly greased it again on both sides. The well itself was about a meter in diameter and impressively deep, lined with stones so perfectly cut and set that they locked into place without mortar. They were ancient and much worn about the mouth, grooved by centuries of use. Jason wondered who the original builders had been.

Getting the water out of the well was done in the most primitive way possible—by dropping an iron bucket down the shaft, then pulling it up again with a braided leather rope. Only one man at a time could work at this, straddling the well head and pulling the rope up hand over hand. It was tiring work and the men changed position often, standing about to talk or to bring the filled waterskins back to their *camachs*. Jason took his turn at the well, then wandered back to see how the work was coming.

All the goats had been tethered, and Meta and Grif had the iron *camach* frame erected while they struggled to drag the cover into place. Jason contributed his mite by hauling their lockbox from the pile of gear and sitting on it. Its tattered leather cover disguised the alloy container inside, secured with a lock that could only be opened by the finger-print of one of the three of them. He plucked at the two-stringed lute that he had made in frank imitation of the one he had seen the jongleur use, and hummed a song to himself. A passing tribesman stopped and watched the *camach* being erected. Jason recognized the man as one of the riders who had intercepted them earlier and decided to take no notice of him. He plinked out a version of a space-man's drinking song.

"Good strong woman but stupid. Can't put up a *camach* right," the tribesman said suddenly, pointing with his thumb.

Jason had no idea what he should say, so he settled for a grunt. The man persisted, scratching in his beard while he openly admired Meta.

"I need a strong woman. I'll give you six goats for this one."

Jason saw that it was more than her strength that the man admired. Meta, working hard, had taken off her heavy outer furs, and her slim figure was far more attractive than the squat and solid ones of the nomad women. Her hair was neat, her teeth unbroken, her face unmarked or scarred.

"You wouldn't want her," Jason said. "She sleeps late, eats too much. Costs too much. I paid twelve goats for her."

"I'll give you ten," the warrior said, walking over and grabbing Meta by the arm and pulling her about so he could look at her.

Jason shuddered. Perhaps the tribeswomen were used to being treated like chattels, but Meta certainly wasn't. Jason waited for the explosion, but she surprised him by pulling her arm away and turning back to her work.

"Come here," Jason told the man. He had to break this up before it went too far. "Come have a drink. I have good *achadh.*"

It was too late. The warrior shouted in anger at being resisted by a mere woman and, with his bunched fist, struck her over the ear, then reached to pull her about again.

Meta stumbled from the force of the unexpected blow and shook her head. When he pulled at her this time, she did not resist but spun about, bringing up her arm at the same time. The stiffened outer edge of her hand caught him across the larynx, almost fracturing it, rendering him voiceless. She stood, ready now, while the man doubled over, coughing hoarsely and spitting up blood.

Jason tried to spring forward, but it was over before he had taken a single pace.

The warrior's fighting reflexes were good—but Meta's were even better. He came out of the crouch, blood streaming down his chin, with a knife in his hand, swinging it up underhand in a wicked knife-fighter's thrust.

Meta clutched his wrist with both her hands, twisting at the same instant so that the knife went by her. She continued to twist, levering the man's arm up behind his back, exerting bone-breaking pressure so that the knife dropped from his powerless fingers. She could have left it at this, but, because she was a Pyrran, she did not.

She caught the knife before it touched the ground, straightened and brought it slanting up into the man's back, below and inside his rib cage, sinking it to the hilt so the blade penetrated his lung and heart, killing him instantly. When she released him, he sank, unmoving, to the ground.

Jason sank back onto the lockbox and, as though by chance, his forefinger touched the keying plate and he felt the click as the bolt unlatched. A number of onlookers had watched the encounter and a hum of astonishment filled the air. One woman waddled over and picked up the man's arm, which dropped limply when she released it. "Dead!" she said in an astonished voice and looked wonderingly at Meta.

"You two—over here!" Jason called out, using their own "tribal" tongue that the crowd would not understand. "Keep your weapons handy and stand close. If this really gets rough, there are gas grenades and your guns in here. But once we use them, we'll have to wipe out or capture the entire tribe. So let's save that as a last resort."

Shanin, with a score of his warriors behind him, pushed through the crowd and looked unbelievingly at the dead man. "Your woman kill this man with his own knife?"

"She did—and it was his own fault. He pushed her around, started trouble, then attacked her. It was just self-defense. Ask anyone here." There was a mutter of agreement from the crowd.

The chief seemed more astonished than angry. He looked from the corpse to Meta, then swaggered over and took her by the chin, turning her head back and forth while he examined her. Jason could see her knuckles go white but she kept her control.

"What tribe she from?" Shanin asked.

"From far away, in the mountains, far north. Tribe called the . . . Pyrrans. Very tough fighters."

Shanin grunted. "I never heard of them." As though his encyclopedic knowledge ruled them out of existence. "What's their totem?"

What indeed, Jason thought? It couldn't be a rat or a weasel. What kind of animals had they seen in the mountains? "Eagle," he announced, with more firmness than he felt. He had seen something that looked like an eagle once, circling the high peaks.

"Very strong totem," Shanin said, obviously impressed. He looked down at the dead man and stirred him with his foot. "He has a *morope*, some furs. Woman can't have them." He looked up shrewdly at Jason, waiting for an answer.

The answer to that one was easy. Women, being property themselves, could not own property. And to the victor went the spoils. Don't let anyone ever say that dinAlt was not generous with secondhand *moropes* and used furs.

"The property is yours, of course, Shanin. That is only right. I would never think of taking them, oh no! And I shall beat the woman tonight for doing this."

It was the right answer and Shanin accepted the booty as his due. He started away, then called back over his shoulder. "He could not have been a good fighter if a woman killed him. But he has two brothers."

That meant something all right, and Jason gave it some thought as the people in the crowd dispersed, taking the dead man with them. Meta and Grif finished erecting the cover on the *camach* and carried all of their goods inside. Jason dragged in the lockbox himself, then sent Grif to tether the goats closer in, near their *moropes*. The killing could lead to trouble.

It did, and faster than Jason had imagined. There were some thuds and a shrill scream outside and he raced for the entrance. Most of the action was over by the time he reached it.

A half dozen boys, relatives perhaps of the dead man, had decided to exact a little revenge by attacking Grif. Most of them were older or bigger than he, so they must have planned on a quick attack, a beating and a hasty retreat. It did not work out quite as planned.

Three boys had grabbed him, to hold him securely while the others administered the drubbing. Two of these now lay unconscious on the ground, for the Pyrran boy had cracked their skulls together, while the third rolled in agony after having been kneed in the groin. Grif was kneeling on the neck of the fourth boy while attempting to break the leg of the fifth by twisting it up behind his back. The sixth boy was trying to get away and Grif was reaching for his knife to stop him before he made his escape.

"Not the knife!" Jason shouted, and helped the survivor on his way with a good boot in the coccyx. "We're in enough trouble without another killing."

Scowling, deprived of his pleasure, Grif elicited both a shrill scream, with an extra ankle twist, and a choked groan, from under his grinding knee. Then he stood and watched while the survivors limped and crawled from the area of combat. Except for a rapidly blackening eye and a torn sleeve, he himself was unhurt. Jason, speaking calmly, managed to get him inside the *camach,* where Meta put a cold compress on his eye.

Jason laced up the entrance and looked at his two Pyrrans, their tempers still aroused, stalking around as though still looking for trouble.

"Well," he said, shrugging his shoulders, "no one can say that you don't make a strong first impression."

8

Though they had the swords of lightning,
Die they did in countless numbers. Arrows' flight
Did speak to strangers,
Bidding them to leave our pastures . . .

"I speak with the voice of Temuchin, for I am Ahankk, his captain," the warrior said, throwing open the entrance to Shanin's *camach*.

Jason broke off his "Ballad of the Flying Strangers" and turned slowly to see who had caused the welcome interruption. His throat was getting sore and he was tired of singing the same song over and over. His account of the spaceship's defeat was the pop hit of the encampment.

The newcomer was a high-ranking officer, that was obvious. His breastplate and helm were shiny and undented, and even set with a few roughly cut jewels. He swaggered as he walked, planting his feet squarely as he stood before Shanin, his hand resting on his sword pommel.

"What does Temuchin want?" Shanin asked coldly, his hand on his own sword, not liking the newcomer's manner.

"He will hear the jongleur who is called Jason. He is to come at once."

Shanin's eyes narrowed to cold slits. "He sings for me now. When he is through, he will come to Temuchin. Finish the song," he said turning to Jason.

To a nomad chief all chiefs are equal and it is hard to convince them differently. Temuchin and his officers had plenty of experience and knew all the persuasive arguments. Ahankk whistled shrilly and a squad of heavily armed soldiers with drawn bows pushed into the *camach*. Shanin was convinced.

"I am bored with this croaking," he announced, yawning

and turning away. "I will now drink *achadh* with one of my women. All leave."

Jason went out with his honor guard and turned toward his *camach*. The officer stopped him with a broad hand against his chest. "Temuchin will hear you now. Turn that way."

"Take your hand from me," Jason said in a low voice that the nearby soldiers could not hear. "I go to put on my best jacket and to get a new string for this instrument because one of these is almost broken."

"Come now," Ahankk said loudly, leaving his hand where it was and giving Jason a shove.

"We will first visit my *camach*. It is just over there," Jason answered just as loudly. At the same time he reached up and took hold of the man's thumb. This is a good grip at any time, and his 2G-hardened muscles added the little extra something that made the thumb feel as if it were being torn from the hand. The officer writhed and resisted, pulling at his sword clumsily, crosswise, for it was his sword hand that Jason was slowly rending.

"I'll kill you with this knife that is pushed against your middle if you draw your sword," Jason said, holding the lute under his arm and pressing the bone pick into Ahankk's stomach. "Temuchin said to bring me, not kill me. He will be angry if we fight. Now—which do you choose?"

The man struggled for another moment, lips drawn back in anger, then released his sword. "We shall go to your *camach* first so you can dress in something more fitting than those rags," he ordered aloud.

Jason let go of the thumb and started off, turned slightly sideways so he could watch the officer. The man walked beside him calmly enough, rubbing his injured thumb, but the look he directed at Jason was pure hatred. Jason shrugged and went on. He had made an enemy, that was certain, yet it was imperative that he go to the tent first.

The trek with Shanin and his tribe had been exhausting but uneventful. There had been no more trouble from the relatives of the slain man. Jason had utilized the time well to practice his jongleur's art and to observe the customs and culture of the nomads. They had reached Temuchin's camp and settled in over a week ago.

"Camp" was not an apt designation, because the nomads

69

were spread out for miles along the polluted, refuse-laden stream they called a river, the biggest river apparently in the entire land. Because the animals had to compete for the scant forage, a good deal of territory was needed for each tribe. There was a purely military camp in the center of all these settlements but Jason had not yet been near it. Nor was he in a hurry to. There was enough for him to observe and record on the outskirts before he would be sure enough of himself to penetrate to the heart of the enemy. In addition, Temuchin had once seen him, face to face, and he appeared to be the kind of man who would have a good memory. Jason's skin was darker now, and he had used a pilating agent to hurry the growth of a thick and sinister mustache that hung almost to his chin on both sides of his mouth. Teca had inserted plugs that changed the shape of his nose. He hoped it would be enough. Yet he wondered how the war chief had heard—and what he had heard—about him.

"Rise, awake," he shouted throwing open the flap of his *camach*. "I shall go before the great Temuchin and I must dress accordingly." Meta and Grif looked coldly at Jason and the officer who had followed him and made no attempt to move.

"Get cracking," Jason said in Pyrran. "Rush around and look like you're impressed, offer this elegant slob a drink and stuff like that. Keep his attention off me."

Ahankk took a drink, but he still kept a wary eye on Jason.

"Here," Jason said, holding the lute out to Grif. "Put a new string on this thing, or make believe you are changing it if you can't find one. And *don't* lose your temper when I shove you. It's just part of the act."

Grif scowled and growled, but otherwise reacted well enough when Jason bullied him off to work with the lute. Jason shed his jacket, rubbed fresh grease into his face and a little onto his hair for good measure, then opened the lockbox. He reached in and took out his better jacket, palming a small object at the same time.

"Now hear this," he called out in Pyrran. "I'm being rushed to see Temuchin and there is no way out of it. I've taken one of the dentiphones and I've left two more on top. Put them on as soon as I've gone. Stay in touch and stay alert. I don't know how the interview is going to turn out, but if there is any trouble, I want us to be in contact at all times. We may have to move fast. Stick with it, gang, and don't despair. We'll lick them yet."

As he slipped into the jacket he screamed at them in in-between. "Give me the lute—and hurry! If anything is disturbed or there is any trouble while I am gone, I will beat you both." He stalked out.

They rode in a loose formation, and perhaps it was only accidental that there were soldiers on all sides of Jason. Perhaps. What had Temuchin heard and why did he want to see him? Speculation was useless and he tried to drop the train of thought and observe his surroundings, but it kept creeping back.

The afternoon sun was low behind the *camachs* when they approached the military camp. The herds were gone and the tents were arranged in neat rows. There were troops on all sides. A wide avenue opened up with a very large, black *camach* at the far end, guarded outside by a row of spearmen. Jason did not need any diagrams to know whose tent this was. He slid from his *morope*, tucked the lute under his arm, and followed his guiding officer with what he intended to be a proud but not haughty gait. Ahankk went in front of Jason to announce him, and as soon as his back was turned, Jason slipped the dentiphone into his mouth and pushed it into place with his tongue. It fitted neatly over an upper back molar, and the power would be turned on automatically by contact with his saliva. "Testing, testing, can you hear me?" he whispered under his breath. The microminiaturized device had an automatic volume control and could broadcast anything from a whisper to a shout.

"Loud and clear," Meta's voice rustled in his ear, in-audible to anyone but him. The output was fed as mechanical vibration into his tooth, thence to his skull and ear by bone conduction.

"Step forward!" Ahankk shouted, rudely jerking Jason from his radiophonic communication by grabbing his arm. Jason ignored him, pulling away and walking alone toward the man in the high-backed chair. Temuchin had his head turned as he talked to two of his officers, which was for the best, for Jason could not control a look of astonishment as he realized what the throne was made of. It was a tractor seat, supported and backed by recoilless rifles bound together. These were slung with leathern strings of desiccated thumbs, some of them just bone with a few black particles of flesh adhering. Temuchin, slayer of the invaders—and here was the proof.

Temuchin turned as Jason came close, fixing him with a cold, expressionless gaze. Jason bowed, more to escape those eyes than from any obsequious desires. Would Temuchin recognize him? Suddenly the nose plugs and drooping mustache seemed to him the flimsiest excuse for a disguise. He should have done better. Temuchin had stood this close to him once before. Surely he would recognize him. Jason straightened up slowly and found the man's chill eyes still fixed on him. Temuchin said nothing.

Jason knew he should stay quiet and let the other talk first. Or was that right? That is what he would do as Jason— attempt to outface and outpoint the other man. Stare him down and get the upper hand. But surely that was not to be expected of an itinerant jongleur? He must certainly feel a little ill at ease, no matter how snow-driven his conscience.

"You sent for me, great Temuchin. I am honored." He bowed again. "You will want me to sing for you."

"No," Temuchin said coldly. Jason allowed his eyebrows to rise in mild astonishment.

"No songs? What, then, will the leader of men have from a poor wanderer?"

Temuchin swept him with his frigid glance. Jason wondered how much was real, how much shrewd role-playing to impress the locals.

"Information," Temuchin said just as the dentiphone hummed to life inside Jason's mouth and Meta's voice spoke. "Jason—trouble. Armed men outside telling us to come out or they will kill us."

"That is a jongleur's duty, to tell and teach. What would you know?" Under his breath he whispered, "No guns! Fight them—I'll get help."

"What was that?" Temuchin asked, leaning forward threateningly. "What did you whisper."

"It was nothing, it was—" Damn, you couldn't say "nervous habit" in in-between. "It is a jongleur's . . . way. Speaking the words of a song quietly, so they will not be forgotten."

Temuchin leaned back, a frown cutting deep lines in his forehead. He apparently did not think much of Jason's rehearsing during an audience. Neither did Jason. But how could he help Meta and Grif?

"Men—breaking in!" her shouting voice whispered silently.

"Tell me about this Pyrran tribe," Temuchin said.

Jason was beginning to sweat. Temuchin must have a spy in the tribe, or Shanin had volunteered information. And the dead man's family seemed to be out for vengeance now, knowing he was away from the camp. "Pyrrans? They're just another tribe. Why do you want to know?"

"What?" Temuchin lunged to his feet pulling at his sword. "You dare to question me?"

"Jason!"

"Wait, no." Jason felt the perspiration beginning to form droplets under the layer of grease on his face. "I spoke wrong. Damn this in-between tongue. I meant to say, *What* do you want to know? I will tell you whatever I can."

"There are many of them. Swords and shields. They attack Grif, all together."

"I have never heard of this tribe. Where do they keep their flocks?"

"The mountains . . . in the north, valleys, remote, you know . . ."

"Grif is down, I cannot fight them all."

"What does that mean? What are you hiding? Perhaps you do not understand Temuchin's law. Rewards to those who are with me. Death to those who oppose me. The slow death for those who attempt to betray me."

"The slow death?" Jason said, listening for the words that did not come.

Temuchin was silent a moment. "You do not appear to know much, jongleur, and there is something about you that is not right. I will show you something that will encourage you to talk more freely." He clapped his hands and one of the attentive officers stepped forward. "Bring in Daei."

Was that a muffled breathing? Jason could not be sure. He brought his attention back to the *camach* and looked, astonished, at the man on the litter that was set down before them. The man was tied down by a tight noose about his neck. He did not try to loosen the rope and escape because there were just raw stumps where his fingers should have been. His bare, toeless feet had received the same treatment.

"The slow death," Temuchin said, staring fixedly at Jason. "Daei left me to fight with the weasel clans. Each day one joint is cut off each limb. He has been here many days. Now, today's justice." He raised his hand.

Soldiers held the man although he made no attempt to struggle. Thin strips of leather were sunk deep into the flesh of his wrists and ankles and knotted tight. His right arm was pressed against the ground and one soldier made a swift chop with an ax. The hand jumped off, spurting blood. The men methodically went to the other arm, then the legs.

"He has two more days to go, as you can see," Temuchin said. "If he is strong enough to live that long, I may be merciful on the third day. I may not be. I have heard of one man who lived a year before reaching his last day."

"Very interesting," Jason said. "I have heard of the custom but it slipped my mind." He had to do something quickly. He could hear the hammer of *moropes*' feet outside, and men's shouts. "Did you hear that? A whistle?"

"Have you gone mad?" Temuchin asked, annoyed. He waved angrily and the now unconcious man was carried out, the dismembered extremities kicked aside.

"It was a whistle," Jason said, starting toward the entrance. "I must step outside. I will return at once."

The officers in the tent, no less than Temuchin, were dumbfounded by this. Men did not leave his presence this way.

"Just a moment will do it."

"Stop!" Temuchin bellowed, but Jason was already at the entrance. The guard there barred his way, pulling out his sword. Jason gave him the shoulder, sending him spinning, and stepped outside.

The outer guards ignored him, unaware of what was happening inside. Walking casually but swiftly, Jason turned right and had reached the corner of the large *camach* before his pursuers burst out behind him. There was a roar and the chase was on. Jason turned the corner and raced full tilt along the side.

Unlike the smaller, circular *camachs*, this one was rectangular, and Jason reached and dived around the next corner before the angry horde could see where he had gone. Shouts and hoarse cries echoed behind as he raced full tilt around the structure. Only when he reached the front again did he slow to a walk as he turned the last corner.

The pursuit was all streaming off in the opposite direction, bellowing distantly like hounds. The two guards who had been at the entrance were gone and all the other nearby ones were looking in the opposite direction. Walking steadily Jason came to the entrance and went inside. Temuchin, who was pacing angrily, was aware that someone had come in.

"Well!" he shouted. "Did you catch—you!" He stepped back and drew his sword with a lightning slash.

"I am your loyal servant, Temuchin," Jason said flatly, folding his arms and not retreating. "I have come to report rebellion among your tribes."

Temuchin did not strike—nor did he lower his sword.

"Speak quickly. Your death is at hand."

"I know you have forbidden private feuds among those who serve you. There are some who would slay my servant because she killed a man who attacked her. I have been near her ever since this happened—until today. Therefore I asked a trusted man to watch and to report to me. I heard his whistle, because he dared not enter the *camach* of Temuchin. I have just talked to him. Armed men have attacked my *camach* in my absence and taken my servants. Yet I have heard that there is one law for all who follow Temuchin. I ask you now to declare about this."

There was the thud of feet behind Jason as his pursuers caught up and stormed through the entrance. They slid to a stop, piling up behind each other as they saw the two men facing each other—Temuchin with his sword still raised.

He glared at Jason, the sword quivering with the tension in his muscles. In the silence of the *camach* they could clearly hear his teeth grate together as he brought the sword down—point first into the dirt floor.

"Ahankk!" he shouted, and the officer ran forward, slapping his chest. "Take four hands of men and go to the tribe of Shanin of the rat clan—"

"I can show you—" Jason interrupted.

Temuchin wheeled on him, thrust his face so close that Jason could feel his breath on his cheek, and said, "Speak once again without my permission and you are dead."

Jason nodded, nothing more. He knew he had almost overplayed his hand. After a moment, Temuchin turned back to his officer.

"Ride at once to this Shanin and command him to take you to those who have taken the Pyrran servants. Bring all you find there here, as many alive as possible."

Ahankk saluted as he ran out: obedience counted before courtesy in Temuchin's horde.

Temuchin paced back and forth in a vile temper, and the officers and men withdrew silently, from the *camach* or back against its walls. Only Jason stood firm—even when the angry man stopped and shook his large fist just under Jason's nose.

"Why do I allow you to do this?" he said with cold fury. "Why?"

"May I answer?" Jason asked quietly.

"Speak!" Temuchin roared, hanging over him like a falling mountain.

"I left Temuchin's presence because it was the only way I could be sure that justice would be done. What enabled me to do this is a fact I have concealed from you."

Temuchin did not speak, though his eyes blazed with anger.

"Jongleurs know no tribe and wear no totem. This is the way it should be, for they go from tribe to tribe and should bear no allegiance. But I must tell you that I was born in the Pyrran tribe. They made me leave and that is why I became a jongleur."

Temuchin would not ask the obvious question and Jason did not allow the expectant silence to become too long.

"I had to leave because—this is very hard to say— compared to the other Pyrrans . . . I was so weak and cowardly."

Temuchin swayed slightly and his face suffused with blood. He bent and his mouth opened—and he roared with laughter. Still laughing, he went to his throne and dropped into it. None of the watchers knew what to make of this; therefore they were silent. Jason allowed himself the slightest smile but said nothing. Temuchin waved over the servant with a leathern blackjack of *achadh*, which he drained at a single swallow. The laughing died away to a chuckle, then to silence. He was his cold, controlled self once more.

"I enjoyed that," he said. "I find very little to laugh at. I think you are intelligent, perhaps too intelligent for your own good, and you may someday have to die for that. Now you will tell me about your Pyrrans."

"We live in the mountain valleys to the north and rarely go down to the plains." Jason had been working on this cover story since he had first joined the nomads; now was the time to put it to the test. "We believe in the rule of might, but also the rule of law. Therefore we seldom leave our valleys and we kill anyone who trespasses. We are the Pyrrans of the eagle totem, which is our strength, so that even one of our women can kill a plains warrior with her hands. We have heard that Temuchin is bringing law to the plains, so I was sent to find out if this were true. If it is true, the Pyrrans will join Temuchin—"

They both looked up at the sudden interruption—Temuchin because there were shouts and commands as a group of *moropes* reined up outside the *camach*, Jason because a weak voice had very clearly said "Jason" inside his head. He could not tell whether it was Meta or Grif.

Ahankk and his warriors came in through the entrance, half carrying, half pushing their prisoners. One wounded man, drenched with blood, and his unharmed companion, Jason recognized as two of the nomads from Shanin's tribe. Meta and Grif were brought in and dropped onto the ground, bloody, battered and unmoving. Grif opened his one uninjured eye and said "Jason . . . ," then slumped unconscious again. Jason started forward, then had enough self-control to halt, clenching his fists until his nails dug deep into his palms.

"Report," Temuchin ordered. Ahankk stepped forward.

"We did as you ordered, Temuchin. Rode fast to this tribe and the one Shanin took us to a *camach*. We entered and fought. None escaped, but we had to kill to subdue them. Two have been captured. The slaves breathe so I think they are alive."

Temuchin rubbed his jaw in obvious thought. Jason took a long chance and spoke.

"Do I have Temuchin's permission to ask a question?"

Temuchin gave him a long, hard look, then nodded agreement.

"What is the penalty for rebellion and private vengeance in your horde?"

"Death. Is there any other punishment?"

"Then I would like to answer a question that you asked earlier. You wanted to know what Pyrrans are like. I am the weakest of all the Pyrrans. I would like to kill the unwounded prisoner, with one hand, with a dagger alone, with one stroke—no matter how he is armed. Even with a sword. He looks to be a good warrior."

"He does," Temuchin said, looking at the big, burly man who was almost a head taller than Jason. "I think that will be a very good idea."

"Tie my hand," Jason ordered the nearest guard, placing his left arm behind his back. The prisoner was going to die in any case, and if his death could be put to a good use, that would probably be more than the man had contributed to any decent cause in his entire lifetime. Being a hypocrite, Jason? a tiny inner voice asked, and he did not answer because there was a great deal of truth in the charge. At one time he had disliked death and violence and sought to evade it. Now he appeared to be actively seeking it.

Then he looked at Meta, unconscious and curled in pain upon the ground, and his knife whispered from its sheath. A demonstration of unusual fighting ability would interest Temuchin. And that ignorant barbarian with the hint of a smug smile badly needed killing.

Or he would be killed himself if he hadn't planted the suggestion strongly enough. If they gave that brute a spear or a club, he would easily butcher Jason in a few minutes.

Jason did not change expression when the soldiers released the man and Ahankk handed him his own long two-handed officer's sword. Good old Ahankk: it sometimes helped to make an enemy. The man still remembered the thumb-twisting and was getting his own back. Jason slapped his broad-bladed knife against his side and let it hang straight down. It was an unusual knife that he had forged and tempered himself, after an ancient design called the "bowie." It was as broad as his hand, with one edge sharpened the length of the blade, the other for less than half. It could cut up or down and could stab, and it weighed more than two kilos. And it was made of the best tool steel.

The man with the sword shouted once and swung the sword high, running forward. One blow would do it, a swing with all of his weight behind it that no knife could possibly stop. Jason stood as calmly as he could and waited.

Only when the sword was swinging down did he move, stepping forward with his right foot and bracing his legs. He swung the knife up, with his arm held straight and his elbow locked, then took the force of the blow full on the edge of his knife. The strength of the swing almost knocked the knife from his hand and drove him to his knees. But there was a brittle clang as the mild steel struck the tool-steel edge, all of the impact coming suddenly on this small area, and the sword snapped in two.

Jason had the barest glimpse of the shocked expression on his face as the man's arms swung down, his hands still locked tightly about the hilt that supported the merest stub of a blade. The force of the blow had knocked Jason's arm down and he moved with the motion, letting the knife swing down and around—and up.

The point tore through the leather clothing and struck the man low in the abdomen, penetrating to the hilt. Bracing himself, Jason jerked upward with all his strength, cutting a deep and hideous wound through the man's internal organs until the blade grated against the clavicle in his chest. He held the knife there as the man's eyeballs rolled back into his head and Jason knew that he was dead.

Jason pulled the knife out and stepped back. The corpse slid to the floor at his feet.

"I will see that knife," Temuchin said.

"We have very good iron in our valley," Jason told him, bending to wipe the knife on the dead man's clothing. "It makes good steel." He flipped the knife in the air, catching it by the tip, and extended the hilt to Temuchin, who examined it for a moment, then called to the soldiers.

"Hold the wounded one's neck out," he said.

The man struggled for a moment, then sank into the apathy of one already dead. Two soldiers held him while a third clutched his long hair with both hands and pulled him forward, face downward, with his dirt-lined neck bare and straight. Temuchin walked over, balancing the knife in his hand, then raised it straight over his head.

With a single galvanic thrust of his muscles, he swung the knife down against the neck and a meaty *chunnk* filled the silent *camach*.

The tension released, the soldier moved back a step, the severed head swinging from his fingers. The blood-spurting body was unceremoniously dropped to the ground.

"I like this knife," Temuchin said. "I will keep it."

"I was about to present it to you," Jason said, bowing to hide his scowl. He should have realized that this would happen. Well, it was just a knife.

"Do your people know much of the old science?" Temuchin asked, dropping the knife for a servant to pick up and clean. Jason was instantly on his guard.

"No more or less than other tribes," he said.

"None of them can make iron like this."

"It is an old secret, passed on from father to son."

"There could be other old secrets." His voice was as hard and cold as the steel itself.

"Perhaps."

"There is a lost secret then that you may have heard of. Some call it 'flamepowder' and others, 'gunpowder.' What do you know of this?"

Indeed, what do I know of this? Jason thought, trying to read something from the other's fixed expression. What could a barbarian jongleur know of such things?

And if this was a trap, what should Jason tell him?

9

META MADE NO PROTEST as Jason washed the dirt from her cuts and sprayed them with dermafoam. The medikit had sewn 14 stitches into the cut on her skull, but he had done this while she was still unconscious and had covered the shaved area with a bandage. She had come to right after this, but had not moved or complained when he had put two more stitches in her split upper lip.

Grif breathed a hoarse snore from the mound of furs where Jason had placed him. The boy's wounds were mostly superficial and the medikit had advised sedation, which suggestion Jason had complied with.

"It's all over now," Jason said. "You had better get some rest."

"There were too many of them," Meta said, "but we did the best we could. Let me have a mirror. They surprised me, going for the boy first, but it was a wise plan. He went down at once. Then they came at me and I could not talk to you any more." She took the polished steel mirror from Jason, had one brief glance and handed it back. "I look terrible. It must have been a quick fight. I don't remember too clearly. Some of them had clubs, the women, and they tried to hit my legs. I know I killed at least three or four, one of the women, before I went down. What happened then?"

Jason took the *achadh* skin and worked the hidden valve on the mouthpiece that sealed off the fermented milk and opened the reservoir of spiced alcohol that the Pyrrans favored.

"Drink?" he asked, but she shook her head. He joined himself and had a long one. "Skipping the finer details for the moment, I managed to send some of the troopers after you. They brought back both of you, and a few rat survivors—all of whom are now dead. I killed the unwounded one myself in true Pyrran-vengeance fashion, for which I do not feel too ashamed. But I had to give my knife to Temuchin, who instantly spotted the advanced level of technology. I'm very glad now that I hand-forged it and that the tool marks can still be seen. Right away he asked me if we Pyrrans knew anything about gunpowder, which rocked me. I played it slippery, told him I knew nothing—just the name—but perhaps others in the tribe knew more. He bought that for the time being—I think. You just can't tell with that guy. But he wants us to move in. At dawn we have to truck our *camach* into the camp next to his, and say good-bye to Shanin and his rats, whom we shall not miss. And in case we should change our minds, there is a squad of Temuchin's boys waiting outside. I still haven't decided whether we are prisoners or not."

"I know I look terrible this way," she said, her head nodding.

"You'll always look good to me," Jason told her cheeringly, then realized that he meant it. He twisted the medikit to *full sedation* and pressed it to her arm. She did not protest. With more than a small amount of guilt, and the feeling that he alone was responsible for their danger and pain, Jason laid her down on the furs next to the boy and covered them both. What bit of insane stupidity was it that had permitted him to involve a woman and a child in this murderous business? Then he remembered that conditions here were still far better than they were on Pyrrus, and he had probably saved their lives by getting them away. He looked at their bruises and shuddered, and wondered if they would thank him for it.

In the morning the two wounded Pyrrans had just enough strength to stumble out of the *camach* so that Jason could supervise its dismantling by the soldiers. They grumbled about woman's work, but Jason would allow none of Shanin's tribespeople near any of his belongings. After all the recent deaths, he was sure that his feud had widened its boundaries until it took in a good portion of the tribe. It was only after Jason had lubricated their spirits with a large skin of high-proof *achadh* that the soldiers buckled down to finish the job and to load the *escung*. Jason strapped Meta and Grif in under the furs, in much the same way that he had been carried after his capture, and the small caravan set out, hurried on its way by many dark looks.

In Temuchin's own camp, there were enough females who could be drafted for the degrading labor so that the men could stand and watch, which was their normal contribution. Jason could not stay to supervise. He left this to Meta, because a message arrived demanding his instant appearance before Temuchin.

The two guards at the entrance to the warlord's *camach* stood aside when Jason approached. At least he had some prestige among the enlisted men. Temuchin was alone, holding Jason's knife, which was drenched with blood. Jason stopped, then relaxed when Temuchin seized the point and, with a quick snap of his wrist, sent it whistling through the air to sink deep into the carcass of a goat that he was using for a target.

"This knife has good balance," Temuchin said. "Throws well."

Jason nodded silently for he knew that he had not been summoned to an audience just to hear that.

"Tell me all you know about gunpowder," Temuchin said, bending over to retrieve the knife.

"There is very little to tell."

Temuchin straightened and his eyes caught Jason's as he tapped the hilt of the knife against the calloused palm of his hand. "Tell me everything you know. Instantly. If you had gunpowder, could you make it blow up with the big noise instead of burning with smoke?"

This was the clinch. If Temuchin thought that he were lying, that big knife would sink into his gut as easily as it went into the goat's. The warlord had some very specific ideas about the physical nature of gunpowder, so he was not bluffing. Time to take a chance.

"Though I have never seen gunpowder, I know what is said about it. I have heard how to make it explode."

"I thought you might." The knife thunked as it sank deep into the goat's flesh. "I think you know other things that you are not telling me."

"Men have secrets that they swear never to reveal. But Temuchin is my master and I will help him in every way that I can."

"Good. Don't forget that. Now tell me what you know about the people in the lowlands."

"Why—nothing," Jason said, astonished. The question had come as a complete surprise.

"You and everyone else. That is changing now. I know some things about the lowlanders and I am going to learn more. I am going to raid the lowlands and you are coming with me. I can use some of this gunpowder. Prepare yourself. We leave at midday. You are the only one who knows it is not a simple hunting expedition, so talk of the matter only at the risk of your life."

"I would rather die than speak a word of this to anyone."

Jason returned to his *camach*, deep in thought, and instantly told Meta everything he had just learned.

"This sounds very strange," she said, hobbling to the fire, her muscles stiff from the beating she had undergone. "I am hungry and cannot make this fire burn."

Jason fanned the fire, and coughed and averted his head

when he caught a lungful of pungent smoke. "I don't think you are using first-rate *morope* chips here. They have to be well dried to burn evenly. It sounded strange to me, too. How can he get down a vertical cliff over ten kilometers high? Yet he knows about gunpowder, and he certainly never found out about that here on the plateau." He coughed again then kicked sand over the fire. "Enough of that. You and Grif need something more nutritious than goat stew in any case. I'll crack out a couple of meal packs."

Meta picked up a war ax and stood by the entrance to make sure that Jason was not disturbed when he opened the lockbox. He took out the meal packs and unsealed them, then pointed to the radio.

"Report to Kerk at midnight. Let him know everything that is happening. You should be safe enough here, but if it looks like there will be any difficulty, tell him to pull you out."

"No. We will stay here until you return." She plunged her spoon into the food and ate hungrily. Grif took the other pack and Jason stood guard at the entrance during the meal.

"Put the empty cans into the lockbox until we find a safer spot to bury them. I wish there was more I could do."

"Don't worry about us. We know how to take care of ourselves," Meta told him firmly.

"Yes," Grif agreed, unsmiling. "This planet is very soft after Pyrrus. Only the food is bad."

Jason looked at them both, battered yet undefeated. He opened his mouth, then closed it because there was really nothing that he could say. He packed a leathern bag with the supplies he might need for the trip, extra clothing, and a microminiaturized transceiver that slipped into the hollow handle of his war ax. This and a short sword were his only weapons. He had tried using the laminated horn bows, but he was so improficient that he was better off not having one of the things around. Slinging a shield from his left arm, he waved good-bye and left.

When Jason rode up on his *morope,* he saw that a small force of less than 50 men had assembled for the expedition. They carried no extra equipment or supplies and it was obvious that it would not be a prolonged trip. Only after Jason had intercepted a number of cold glances did he realize that he was the only outsider there. All the others were either high-ranking officers and close associates of Temuchin or members of his own tribe.

"I can keep secrets, too," Jason told Ahankk, who rode close, scowling, but he received only a fine selection of grating curses in return. As soon as the warlord appeared, they rode off in a double column, following his lead.

It was hard riding and Jason was thankful for the weeks he had spent in the saddle. At first they started toward the foothills to the east, but as soon as they were hidden from sight of the camp and sure that they were not observed by stragglers, they turned and moved south at a ground-eating pace. The mountains rose up on all sides of them as they rode from valley to valley, climbing steadily. Jason, breathing through his fur neckpiece, could not believe that throat-hurting air could be so cold, yet it did not seem to bother anyone else.

They grabbed a quick, unheated meal at sunset, then kept on going. Jason could see the sense in this; he had almost frozen to the ground during their brief halt. They were in single file now. The trail was so narrow that Jason, like many of the others, dismounted to lead his *morope*, in an attempt to warm himself above the congealing point by the exertion. The cold light of the star-filled sky lit their way.

Coming to a junction of two valleys, Jason looked to his right, at the gray sea spreading out in the distance beyond the nearly vertical cliffs. Sea?! He stopped so suddenly that his *morope* trod on his heels and he had to jump aside to avoid being trampled.

No, it couldn't be the sea. They were in the middle of the continent. And too high up. Realization came late—he was looking at a sea rightly enough, the top of a sea of clouds. Jason watched until a turn in the trail took them from sight. The trail was dipping downward now as he knew it must. He halted his *morope* so that he could climb back into the saddle. Somewhere up ahead was the edge of the world.

Here the domain of the nomads ended at the continent-spanning cliff, a solid wall of rock reaching up from the plains below. Here, also, was where the weather ended. The warm southern winds blowing north struck the cliff, were forced upward and condensed as clouds, to then bring their burden of water back to the land below as rain. Jason wondered if they ever saw the sun at all this close to the escarpment. A glistening dusting of snow in the hollows showed that severe storms pushed even over the top of this natural barrier.

As the trail dropped it passed through a narrow pass and, once inside, Jason saw a stone hut under an overhang of rock, where guards stood and stoically watched them pass. Whatever their destination was, it must be close. A short while later they halted and word was passed back to Jason to wait on Temuchin. He shuffled to the head of the procession as fast as his numbed muscles would permit.

Temuchin was chewing steadily on a resistant piece of dried meat, and Jason had to wait until he had washed this morsel down with some of the half-frozen *achadh*. The sky was lightening in the east and, by the traditional nomad test, it was almost dawn, the moment when a black goat's hair could be told from a white.

"Bring my *morope*," Temuchin commanded as he strode away. Jason grabbed the reins of the tired, snapping beast and dragged it after the warlord. Three officers followed after him. The trail took two more sharp turnings and opened out onto a broad ledge, the farther side of which was the sheer edge of the cliff. Temuchin walked over and stared down at white-massed clouds not far below. But it was the rusty chunk of machinery that fascinated Jason.

The most impressive part was the massive A frame that was seated deep into the living rock at the cliff's edge, projecting outward and overhanging the abyss below. This had been hand-forged, all eight meters of its length, and what a prodigious labor that must have been. It was stabilized with cross-brace rods and rested against a ridge of rock at the lip of the drop that raised it to a 45-degree angle. The entire frame was pitted and scratched with rust, although some attempt had been made to keep it greased. A length of flexible black material led over a pulley wheel at the point of the A and back through a hole in a buttress of rock behind. Aroused now by curiosity, Jason went around the rock to admire the device behind it.

In its own way, this engine, though smaller, was more spectacular than the supporting frame on the cliff. The black ropelike material came through the hole and wound around a drum. This drum, on an arm-thick shaft, was held to the back of the vertical rock face by four sturdy legs. It could obviously take an immense strain as there was nothing to uproot: all of the pressure would be carried directly to the rock face, seating the legs even more firmly. A meter-wide gear wheel, fitted to the end of the drum, meshed with a smaller pinion gear that could be turned by a long crank handle. This was apparently made of wood, but Jason did not pay much attention to the fact. A number of pawls and ratchets made sure that nothing could slip.

It did not take a mechanical genius to understand what the device was for. Jason turned to Temuchin, forcefully controlling the tendency for one eyebrow to lift, and said: "Is this the mechanism by which we are supposed to descend to the lowlands?"

The warlord seemed about as impressed by the machine as Jason was himself.

"It is. It does not appear to be the sort of thing one would usually risk one's life with, but we have no choice. The tribe which built and operated it, a branch of the stoat clan, have sworn that they used it often to raid the lowlands. They told many tales, and had wood and gunpowder to prove it. The survivors are here and they will operate the thing. They will be killed if there is any trouble. We will go first."

"That won't help us very much if something goes wrong."

"Man is born to die. Life consists only of a daily putting off of the inevitable."

Jason had no answer to this one. He looked up as, with pained cries, a group of men and squat women were driven down the hill toward the winch.

"Stand back and let them do their work," Temuchin ordered, and the soldiers instantly withdrew. "Watch them closely and if there is treachery or mistakes, kill them at once."

Thus encouraged, the stoat clansmen turned to their jobs. They appeared to know what they were doing. Some turned the handle while others adjusted the clanking pawls.

One man even pulled himself out on the frame, far over the cliff's edge, to grease the pulley wheel on its end.

"I will go first," Temuchin said, slinging a heavy leather harness around his body under his arms.

"I hope that rope thing is long enough," Jason said, and instantly regretted it when Temuchin turned to glare at him.

"You will come next, after you have sent down my *morope*. See that it is blindfolded so it does not panic. Then you, then another *morope*, in that order. The *moropes* will be brought to the cliff only one at a time so they do not see what is happening to the others." He turned to the officers. "You have heard my orders."

Chanting in unison, the stoats turned the handle to wind the rope onto the drum, the pawls slowly clanking over. The pressure came on the harness but the rope stretched and thinned before Temuchin was lifted from the ground. Then his toes swung clear and he grabbed the rope as he swung out over the abyss, oscillating slowly up and down. When the bobbing had damped the operators reversed the motion and he slowly dropped from sight. Jason went to the lip and saw the warlord's figure get smaller and finally vanish into the woolly clouds below. A piece of rock broke loose under the pressure of Jason's toe and he stepped backward quickly.

Every hundred meters, more or less, the men slowed and worked cautiously as a blob appeared where two sections of the elastic rope were joined together. They turned the handle carefully until the knot had cleared the pulley, then went back to their normal operating speed. Men changed positions on the cranks without stopping so that the rope moved out and down continuously.

"What is this rope?" Jason asked one of the stoats who seemed to be supervising the operation, a greasy-haired individual whose only tooth appeared to be a yellowed fang that projected above his upper lip.

"Plant things, growing things—long with leaves. What you call them *mentri*—"

"Vines?" Jason guessed.

"Yah, vines. Big, hard to find. Grow down the cliff. Stretch and very strong."

"They had better be," Jason said, then pointed and grabbed the man as the vine rope suddenly began to bounce up and down. He wriggled in Jason's numbing grip and hurried to explain.

"All right, good. That means the man is down, let the vine go; it bounces up and down. Bring up!" he added, shouting at the crank operators.

Jason loosened his grip on the man, who moved quickly away rubbing the injured spot. It made sense; when Temuchin had let go of the rope, the sudden decrease in weight on the cable would have caused it to oscillate, though not too much. His weight was surely only a small part of the overall weight of that massive length of cable.

"The *morope* next," Jason ordered when the hook and sling were finally hauled up to the clifftop once more. The beast was led forward, blinking its red little eyes suspiciously at the brink ahead. The stoats efficiently fitted a broad harness about its body, then covered its eyes with a leather sack pulled down tight and tied under its jaw. After the hook had been attached, the *morope* stood patiently until it began to feel its weight coming off the ground. Then, panic-stricken, it began to struggle, its claws raking grooves in the dirt and cracking chips from the stone. But the operators had experience with this as well. The man whom Jason had been talking to ran up with a long-handled sledge-hammer and, with a practiced swing, hit a mark on the bag, which must have been right above the creature's eyes. It went instantly limp. With much shouting and heaving, the dead weight was swung clear of the ground and started over the edge.

"Hit just right," the man said. "Too hard, kill it. Not hard enough, it wake up soon and jump around, break rope."

"Well hit," Jason said, and hoped that Temuchin was not standing directly below.

Nothing appeared to be wrong and the rope vine clanked out endlessly. Jason found himself dozing off and stepped farther back from the edge. Suddenly there were shouts and he opened his eyes to see the rope jerking back and forth, heaving with great bounces. It even jumped from the pulley and one of the men had to climb up to reseat it.

"Did it break?" Jason asked the nearest operator.

"No, good, all fine. Just bounce big when the *morope* come off."

This was understandable. When the greater weight of the large beast was removed the elastic vine would do a great deal of heaving about. The motion had damped and they were bringing it up now. Jason realized that he was next and was aware of a definite dropping sensation in his stomach. He would have given a great deal not to suffer a descent on this iron-age elevator.

The beginning alone was bad enough. He realized that his feet were dragging free of the rock as the tension came on the vine and he automatically scratched with his toes, trying to stay on the solid mountaintop. He did not succeed. The wheel turned another clank and he was airborne, swinging out from the cliff and above the cloud-bottomed drop. He took one look down between his twirling feet, then riveted his attention straight ahead. The clifftop slowly rose above his head and the grim-faced nomads vanished from sight. He tried to think of something funny to say but, for once, was completely out of humorous ideas. Rotating slowly as he dropped, he could, for the first time, see the continent-spanning cliff sweeping away on both sides and could appreciate the incredible vastness of it. The air was clear and dry with the early-morning sun lighting up the rock face so that every detail could be plainly seen.

Below was the white sea of the clouds, washing and breaking against the base of the continentwide cliff. The jagged gray mountains that could be seen rising behind it were dwarfed by comparison. Against the immensity of this cliff, Jason felt like a spider on a thread, drifting down an endless wall, moving yet seemingly suspended forever at the same spot because the scale was so large. As he rotated, he looked first right, then left, and in each direction the grained escarpment ran straight to the horizon, still erect and sky-touching where it dimmed and vanished.

Jason could see now that the point on the cliff above, where the winch had been placed, was much lower than the rest of the stone barrier. He assumed that there was a matching rise in the ground below, for at any other spot along the cliff the length of the vine rope would not have been strong enough to support its own weight, exclusive of any added burden. The clouds rose up steadily below him until he felt he could almost reach out and kick them. Then the first damp tendrils of the fog touched him, and a few moments later the clouds closed around and he was alone in the gray world of nothingness.

The last thing that he expected to do, dangling at the end of the kilometer-long bobbing strand, was to fall asleep. But he did. The rocking motion, the fatigue of the day and night ride, and the blankness of his surroundings all contributed their bit. He relaxed, his head dropped, and in a few moments he was snoring lustily.

He awoke when the rain began trickling inside his collar and down his back. Though the air was much warmer he shivered and pulled his collar tight. It was one of those drizzling, dripping all-day rains that seem never to end. Through it he could make out the streaked face of the cliff still moving by, and when he bent and looked between his toes, something indeterminate was visible below. What? People? Friend or foe? If the locals knew about the winch that was out of sight in the clouds above, they might possibly keep a massacre party waiting here. He swung the war ax out of his belt and slipped the thong about his wrist. Individual boulders were standing out below, set in a drab field of rain-soaked grass. The air was humid and sticky.

"Unbuckle that harness and be ready to let go of it," Temuchin ordered, coming into sight as he stalked across the field below. "What is the ax for?"

"Anyone other than you who might be waiting," Jason answered, securing the ax in his belt again and working at the leather harness. A sudden stretch on the flexible rope lowered him to within feet of the grass.

"Let go!" Temuchin ordered, and Jason did, unfortunately just as the rope started up again. He rose a few feet and, for one instant, was suspended in midair, unmoving and unsupported, before he fell heavily. He rolled when he hit and jammed the hilt of his sword painfully into his ribs, but was otherwise undamaged. There was a quick *whoosh* above them as the rope, relieved of its burden, contracted and snapped upward.

"This way," Temuchin said, turning and walking off while Jason struggled to his feet. The grass was slippery and wet, and mud squelched up around his boots when he walked. Temuchin went around a pillar of rock and pointed up at its ten-meter-high summit.

"You can watch from there to see when your *morope* arrives. Wake me then. My beast is grazing on this side. Be sure it does not stray." Without waiting for an answer, Temuchin lay down in a relatively dry spot in the lee of the rock and pulled a flap of leather over his face.

Sure, Jason said to himself, just the job I wanted in the rain. A nice wet rock and a tremendous view of absolutely nothing. He pulled himself up the steeply slanted stone and sat down on its rounded peak.

Thoughts of sleep were gone now; even sitting comfortably was impossible on the knobby hardness, so Jason writhed and suffered. The silence was disturbed only by the endless susurration of the falling rain, broken by an occasional trumpet of satiated joy from the *morope* as it enjoyed the unaccustomed banquet. From time to time the sheets of rain shifted, opening up a view down the hillside of grass pastures, with quick rivulets and dark-stained stones pushing up through the greenery. Ages of rain and damp discomfort passed before Jason heard hoarse breathing overhead and could make out a dim form dropping down slowly through the haze. He slid to the ground and Temuchin was awake and alert the instant Jason touched his shoulder.

There was something awe-inspiringly impressive about the great bulk of the limp *morope,* apparently unsupported, that swung down over their heads. Its legs were beginning to twitch and its breathing grew faster.

"Quickly," Temuchin ordered. "It is beginning to awake."

A sudden bounce dropped the *morope* lower and they grabbed for it, but the return contraction pulled it out of reach again. It was beginning to turn its head and was attempting to lift its neck. The next drop brought it almost to the ground and Temuchin leaped for its neck, grabbing it and hanging on, his added weight pulling the foreparts of the creature to the damp ground.

"Unbuckle it!" he shouted.

Jason dived for the straps. The buckles were easy-opening, being released by throwing back an iron handle. It would have been impossible to open normal buckles against the tension of the taut, stretched cable. The *morope* was beginning to thrash about when Jason threw open the last buckle—and leaped clear. The contraction of the elastic cable pulled the harness out from under the *morope*, raking its flesh so that it bellowed with pain, half flipping it over. The jangling harness, with a departing hiss, instantly vanished from sight in the rain.

The rest of the day settled into routine. Now that Jason knew what to do, Temuchin proved himself an experienced field soldier by taking advantage of the lull to catch up on his sleep. Jason wished he could join him, but he had been left in charge and he knew better than to try and avoid the responsibility. Soldiers and mounts dropped out of the rain-filled sky at regular intervals and Jason organized the operation. Some of the soldiers watched the field of grazing *moropes* while others stood by to land the new arrivals. The rest slept, except for Ahankk, who, in Jason's opinion, seemed to have fine vision and who therefore occupied the lookout position. Twenty-five *moropes* and 26 men were down before the end suddenly came.

The work party were half dozing, depressed by the endless rain, when Ahankk's hoarse call jabbed them to instant awareness. Jason looked up and had a brief vision of a dark form hurtling down, apparently right at them. This was just an illusion of the mist for the *morope* grew in size and struck the landing spot, plunging to the ground like a falling rock and hitting with a sickening, explosive sound. A great length of rope fell on and around it, the end landing not far from Jason and the soldiers.

There was no need to call Temuchin. He had been awakened by the shout and the sound of impact. He turned away after a single glance at the bloody, deformed corpse of the beast.

"Tie four *moropes* to the harness. I want it dragged away from here, along with that rope." While his lieutenants jumped to obey him, he turned to Jason. "This is why I sent a man first, then a *morope*. Two of the men will have to ride double. The stoats warned me that the rope broke after use, and that there was no possible way to tell when this would be. It usually breaks under a heavy load."

"But has been known to snap when letting a man down. I can see why you went first. You'd make a good gambler, warlord," Jason said.

"I am a good gambler," Temuchin told him calmly,

running a scrap of oiled leather over his rusting sword. "There is just one rope in reserve, so I left orders to halt the drop if this one should break. A new rope will be in place by the time we return and a guard will be lowered and waiting for us. Now—we ride."

10

"Is IT PERMITTED to ask where we are going?" Jason said as the war party moved slowly down the grassy hillside. They were spread out in a wide crescent with Temuchin and Jason at the center, with the *moropes* dragging the carcass of their fellow close by.

"No," Temuchin said, which pretty well took care of that.

It was a smooth descent, as though the plains below were rising up to meet the escarpment, now invisible in the rain behind them. Grass and small shrubs covered the hill, cut through by streams and freshets. As they went lower, these joined to form good-sized brooks. The *moropes* splashed through them, snorting at the presence of such prodigious amounts of water. And the temperature rose. Jason and the others opened the ties that sealed their clothing, and he was happy to tilt his helm back so the fine drizzle fell onto his overheated face. He wiped away the layer of grease that had covered his skin and began to think about the possibilities of bathing again.

The hill ended suddenly in a ragged cliff above a foam-flecked river. Temuchin ordered the corpse of the fallen animal and the festoons of rope dragged forward to the brink, where a squad of soldiers heaved and tipped it over the edge. It hit the water with a showering splash and, with a last, almost flippant wave of one claw-studded paw, it was whirled away and vanished from sight. Without hesitation Temuchin turned their course southwest along the river's bank. It was obvious that he had been forewarned

94

of this obstacle, and the march continued at its kilometer-eating pace.

By late afternoon the rain had stopped and the character of the country had completely changed. Patches of brush and wood dotted the plain and, not far ahead, an extensive forest was visible under the lowering sky. As soon as Temuchin saw it, he halted the march.

"Sleep," he ordered. "We move again at nightfall."

Jason did not have to be ordered twice. He was off his mount while the others were still stopping; he curled up on the grass and closed his eyes. The *morope's* reins were tied about his ankle. After the skull-banging, the grazing, drinking and galloping, the creature was happy to rest, too. It stretched full length on the ground, its chin extended in the rich grass, from which it pulled a clump to hold in its mouth while it slept.

The sky was dark, but to Jason it felt as though he had just closed his eyes when the steel fingers sank into his leg and shook him awake.

"We ride," Ahankk said. Jason sat up, his stiff muscles creaking with the effort, and rubbed the granules of sleep from his eyes. He had washed out the dregs of *achadh* from his drinking skin earlier in the day and filled it with fresh stream water. He drank his fill and then sprayed a goodly quantity over his face and head. There was no water shortage in this land.

They rode out in a single file, Temuchin leading and Jason one but last from the rear. Ahankk rode as rearguard, and it was obvious from his hot gaze and ready sword that Jason was what he was guarding. The exploring party was now a war party and the nomads needed no aid and expected only interference from a wandering jongleur. He was safe in the rear, where he could not cause any trouble. If he did, he would be killed instantly. Jason rode quietly, trying to generate an aura of innocent compliance with the set of his shoulders.

There was no sound, even when they entered the woods. The padded feet of each *morope* fell in easy rhythm in the tracks of the preceding beast. Leather did not creak and metal did not rattle. They were spectral forms moving through rain-sodden silence. The trees opened up and Jason was aware that they had entered a clearing. A dim light

95

was visible in the near distance and, by glancing out of the corners of his eyes at it, Jason could make out the dark form of a building.

Still silent, the soldiers had made a smooth right turn and were moving on the building in a single line. They were no more than a few meters from the structure when a rectangle of light suddenly appeared as a door was opened. A man, silhouetted sharply against the light, stood in the opening.

"Save him—kill the rest!" Temuchin shouted, and the attackers leaped forward before the words were out of his mouth.

Chance put Jason near the man in the open doorway, yet everyone else seemed to get there first. The man leaped back with a hoarse cry, trying to close the door, but three men hit it at once, driving it open and sending him back. All three of them remained flat on the floor where they had fallen, and Jason, who had just slid from his *morope's* back, saw why. Five more of the men, two kneeling and three standing, had stopped at the open doorway with drawn bows. Two, three times they fired and the air hissed and thrummed from their bowstrings and the arrows' flight. Jason reached them as they stopped the firing and charged into the building. He was right behind them, but the fight was over.

The barnlike room, lit by a single spluttering candle, was filled to overflowing with death. Toppled tables and chairs made a ragged jumble into which were mixed the dead and dying. A gray-haired man with an arrow in his chest moaned and stirred; a soldier bent over and severed his throat with a chop of his ax. There were crashes as the building was broken into from the rear by the rest of the nomads, who had surrounded it. Escape was impossible.

One man was still alive, still fighting, the man who had stood in the doorway. He was tall and shock-headed, dressed in rough homespun, and he laid about him with an immense quarterstaff. It would have been simple enough to kill him—an arrow would have done it—but the nomads wanted to capture him and had never encountered this simple weapon before. One already sat on the floor, clutching his leg, and a second was disarmed even as Jason watched, his sword clanging into a corner. The lowlander

96

had his back to the wall and was unapproachable from the front.

Jason could do something about this. He looked around swiftly and saw a rack of simple farm implements against the wall. One of these was a long-handled shovel that looked as if it would do. He grabbed it in both hands and banged the center down hard against his knee. It bent but did not break. Well-seasoned wood.

"I'll take him!" Jason shouted, running to the fight. He was an instant late because the quarterstaff landed square on the swordsman's arm, snapping the bones and sending the man's weapon flying. Jason took his place and swung the shovel at the lowlander's ankles.

The man quickly spun the end of his staff down to counter the blow, and when the weapons crashed together, Jason used the force of impact to reverse his direction of motion, bringing the handle end of the shovel around toward the lowlander's neck. The man parried this blow in time as well, but in doing so he had to step aside, away from the wall, and this was all that was needed.

Ahankk, who had come in with Jason, swung the flat of his ax against the man's skull and he dropped, unconscious, to the floor. Jason threw away the shovel and picked up the fallen quarterstaff. It was a good two meters long, made of tough and flexible wood bound about with iron rings.

"What is that?" Temuchin asked. He had watched the end of the brief battle.

"A quarterstaff. A simple but effective weapon."

"And you know how to use it? You told me you knew nothing about the lowlands." His face was expressionless as he talked, but there was a glow like an inner fire in his eyes. Jason realized that he had better make the explanation good or he would join the rest of the corpses.

"I still know nothing about the lowlands. But I learned to handle this weapon when I was a child. Everyone in my . . . tribe uses them." He did not bother to add that the tribe he was talking about was not the Pyrrans, but the agrarian community on Porgorstorsaand, far across the galaxy, where he had grown up. With rigid class and social distinctions, the only real weapons were borne by the soldiers and the aristocracy. But you can't deny a man a stick when he lives in a forest, so quarterstaffs were in common use, and at one time Jason had been proficient in the use of this uncomplicated yet decisive weapon.

Temuchin turned away, satisfied for the moment, while Jason spun the staff experimentally. It was nicely weighted.

The nomads were efficiently looting the building, which appeared to be a farm of some kind. The livestock were kept under the same roof and all of the animals had been butchered when the soldiers had broken in. When Temuchin said kill, he meant kill. Jason looked at the carnage but would permit himself no change of expression, even when one of the men, looking for booty, turned over a wooden chest. There was a baby behind it, perhaps thrust there at the last minute by one of the women now dead upon the floor, and the soldier skewered it unemotionally with a quick stab of his sword.

"Bind that one and bring him," Temuchin ordered, brushing the dirt from a piece of cooked meat that had been knocked to the floor in the attack, then taking a bite from it.

Swift, tight turns of leather secured his wrists behind his back; then the prisoner was propped against the wall. When three buckets of water dashed into his face had failed to bring him around, Temuchin heated the tip of his dagger blade in a burning candle and pressed it into the soft flesh of the man's arm. He moaned and tried to pull away, then opened his eyes, which swam blearily with the aftereffects of the blow.

"Do you speak the in-between tongue?" Temuchin asked. When the man answered something incomprehensible, the warlord struck him, carefully, on the purple and enflamed wound made by the earlier blow. The farmer screamed and tried to get away, but still answered in the same unknown language.

"The fool cannot speak," Temuchin said.

"Let me," one of his officers said, stepping forward. "What he talks is not unlike the tongue of the hill-serpent clan in the far east near the sea."

Communication was established. With laborious rephrasings and repeatings, the message was communicated to the farmer that he would be killed if he did not help them. No promises were made for what would happen if he did, but the lowlander was not in the best of bargaining positions. He quickly agreed.

"Tell him we wish to go to the place of the soldiers," Temuchin said, and their prisoner bobbed his head in quick agreement. Understandable. A peasant in a primitive economy has little love for the tax-collecting, oppressing soldiers. He babbled in his hurry to convey information. The translator interpreted his words.

"He says that there are many soldiers there, two hands, perhaps five hands of them. They are armed and the place is strong. They have something else, some kinds of weapons, but I cannot make out what the creature is talking about."

"Five hands of men," Temuchin said, smiling and looking out of the corners of his eyes. "I am frightened."

The nomads nearby hooted with laughter and struck each other on the back, then hurried to tell the others. Jason did not think it a great witticism, but he could find no fault with the men's morale.

A sudden silence passed over them as two of the soldiers slowly approached, supporting and half dragging one of their comrades. The man hopped on one leg, fighting to keep the other foot clear of the ground, and when he raised his pain-twisted face to Temuchin, Jason recognized him as the one injured in the battle with the quarterstaff-wielding peasant.

"What has happened?" Temuchin asked, all traces of laughter gone from his voice.

"My leg, . . ." the man, a minor chieftain, answered hoarsely.

"Let me see," the warlord ordered, and the soldier's boot was quickly cut open.

The man's knee had been shattered brutally, the knee-cap fractured so badly that pieces of white bone had penetrated the skin. Slow trickles of blood seeped from the wound. The soldier must be suffering incredible pain, yet he made no outcry. Jason knew that it would take skilled surgery and bone replacement to enable the man to walk again, and wondered what his fate would be on this barbarian world. He found out quickly.

"You cannot walk, you cannot ride, you cannot be a soldier," Temuchin said.

"I know that," the man said, straightening and throwing off the hands of the men who helped him. "But if I am to die, I wish to die in combat and be buried with my thumbs.

99

I cannot hold a sword to fight the demons in the underworld if I have no thumbs."

"That is the way it will be," Temuchin said, drawing his sword. "You have been a good soldier and a good friend and I wish you success in your battles to come. I will fight you myself for it is an honor to be sent below by a warlord."

The battle was no ritual, and the wounded man did well despite his injured leg. But Temuchin fought so that the other had to turn toward his wounded side, but he could not, so a quick thrust caught him under the ribs and he died.

"There was another wounded man," Temuchin said, still holding his bloody sword. The soldier with the broken arm stepped forward, the arm in a sling.

"The arm will get better," he said. "The skin did not break. I can fight and ride, though I cannot shoot a bow."

Temuchin hesitated a moment before he answered. "We need every man that we have. Do those things and you will return with us to the camp. We will ride as soon as this man is buried." He turned to Jason.

"Ride in front with me," he ordered, "and do not make any stupid noise." He apparently did not think much of Jason's soldiering ability, and Jason did not feel like correcting him. "This place of the soldiers is what we are looking for. The stoat clan has raided this country in the past, but with no more than two or three men at a time as to send more *moropes* down is dangerous. They avoid the soldiers and attack these farms. But they have fought the soldiers and it is from them that I learned of the gunpowder. They killed one soldier and took his gunpowder, but when I put fire to it, it merely burned. Yet the stoats swear that it blew up, and others have said the same and I do not doubt them. We will capture the gunpowder and you will make it blow up."

"Take me to it," Jason said, "and I'll show you how it's done."

They blundered through the forest until well after midnight before their prisoner tearfully admitted that he had lost his way in the darkness. Temuchin beat him until he howled with pain then, reluctantly, ordered the men to rest until morning. The rain had begun again and they sought what comfort they could find under the dripping trees.

Jason had a bad taste in his mouth. It wasn't the dung-cooked food this time or the filthy *achadh,* but the massacre at the farm. Get close to the trees and you don't see the forest. He had been living with the nomads, living like a nomad, and had become part of their culture. They were interesting people and, since moving to Temuchin's camp, he had found them a warm, if not exactly the galaxy's most humorous, people, and at least it was possible to get along with them. They were honest in their own way and respected their own code of laws. They were also cold-blooded murderers and killers. It did not matter that they killed according to their own sets of values. This did not change the situation. Jason could still see the sword thrusting into the infant and he moved uncomfortably on the sodden leaves.

He had been among the trees and forgotten the forest. He had forgotten that these people had slaughtered the first mining expedition and would relish nothing better than doing the same to any other off-worlders that they met. He was a spy in their midst and he was working for their complete downfall.

That was more like it. He could live with himself as long as it was constantly clear that he was just playing a role, not enjoying himself, and that all this masquerading had some purpose. He had to wreck the social structure of these nomads and see to it that the Pyrrans opened their mines in safety.

Alone in the wet night, chilled and depressed, it looked like a very dim possibility. The hell with that. He twisted and attempted to get comfortable and go to sleep but the images of the massacre kept interfering.

In your own way, Temuchin, you are a great man, he thought. But I am going to have to destroy you. The rain fell remorselessly.

At first light they moved out again, a silent column through the fog-shrouded forest. The captive peasant chattered his teeth in fear until he recognized a clearing and a path. Smiling and happy now, he showed them the correct way. A wad of his clothing was stuffed into his mouth so that he could not give any alarm.

A crackling of broken twigs sounded ahead and there was the sound of voices.

The column stopped with instant silence and a sword was pressed against the prisoner's neck. Nothing moved. The voices ahead grew louder and two men came around a turning of the trail. They walked two, three paces before they were aware of the motionless, silent forms so close to them in the fog. Before they could act, a half dozen arrows had snuffed out their lives.

"What are those stick things they carry?" Temuchin said to Jason.

Jason slid to the ground and turned the nearest corpse over with his boot. The man wore a lightweight steel breastplate and a steel helm; other than that, he was unarmored, dressed in coarse cloth and leather. He had a short sword in his belt and still clutched in his hand what could only have been a primitive musket.

"It is what is called a 'gun,'" Jason said, picking it up. "It uses gunpowder to throw a piece of metal that can kill. The gunpowder and metal are put down this tube here. When this little lever on the bottom is pulled, this stone throws a spark down into the gunpowder, which blows up and shoots the metal out."

When Jason looked up, he saw that every man within hearing had his bow and arrow aimed at his throat. He put the weapon down carefully and pulled two leather bags from the dead soldier's belt and looked inside of them. "Just what I thought. Bullets and cloth patches here—and this is gunpowder." He handed the second bag up to Temuchin, who looked into and smelt it.

"There is not very much here," he said.

"It doesn't take very much, not for these guns. But there is sure to be a bigger supply in the place where these men came from."

"That is what I thought," Temuchin said, and he waved the raiding party on as soon as the arrows had been retrieved and the bodies relieved of their thumbs and rolled aside. He took both muskets himself.

Less than a ten-minute ride along the trail brought them to the edge of a clearing, a large meadow that flanked a smoothly flowing river. At the water's edge stood a squat and solid stone building with a high tower in its center. Two figures were visible at the top of the tower.

"The prisoner says that this is the place of the soldiers," said the officer who had been translating.

"Ask him if he knows how many entrances there are," Temuchin ordered.

"He says that he does not know."

"Kill him."

A swift sword thrust eliminated the prisoner and his corpse was dumped into the brush.

"There is only that one small door on this side and the narrow holes through which bows and the gun things may be fired," Temuchin said. "I do not like it. I want two men to look at the other sides of this building and tell me what they see. What is that round thing above the wall?" he asked Jason.

"I don't know—but I can guess. It could be a gun, the same as these only much bigger, that would throw a large piece of metal."

"I thought so, too," Temuchin said, and narrowed his eyes in thought. He issued orders to two men, who turned and rode back along the trail.

The scouts dismounted and vanished silently into the underbrush. These men, who had learned to conceal themselves in the apparently barren plains, could disappear completely in the wooded cover. With a predator's patience, the warriors, still mounted, waited silently for the scouts to come back.

"It is as I thought," Temuchin said when they had returned and reported to him. "This place is well made and is built only for fighting. There is one more door, the same size, on the other side by the water. If we wait until nightfall, we can take the place easily, but I do not wish to wait. Can you fire this gun?" he asked Jason.

Jason nodded reluctantly, because he already had a very good idea what Temuchin had in mind—even before he saw the two men returning with one of the dead soldiers. Everyone fought in Temuchin's horde, even lute-playing gunpowder experts. Jason tried to think of a way out of this fix, but he could not, so he volunteered before he was drafted. It made no difference at all to Temuchin. He wanted the gate open and Jason was the best man for the job.

By rearranging the soldier's uniform, he managed to

103

conceal the arrow holes and most of the blood, then he rubbed mud over the rest of the bloodstains to disguise them. A fine rain was beginning to fall and this would be a help. While he was putting on the uniform, Jason called for the officer who had been translating and had him repeat over and over again the simple phrase "Open—quickly!" in the local tongue, until Jason felt he had it right. Nothing complicated. If they insisted on conversation before they let him in, he was as good as dead.

"You understand what you are to do?" Temuchin asked.

"Simple enough. I come up to that gate from downriver, while the rest of you wait at the edge of the forest upriver. I tell them to open up. They open up. I go in and do my best to see that the gate stays open until you and the rest arrive."

"We will be very quick."

"I know that, but I'm going to be very alone." Jason had one of the soldiers hold his helmet over the pan of the musket while Jason blew out the possibly damp gunpowder. He did not want a misfire with his single shot. He shook fresh powder into the pan, then wrapped a piece of leather around to keep it dry. He pointed to the gun.

"This thing will fire only once for I'll have no time to reload. And I don't think much of this government-issue short sword. So, if you don't mind too much, I would like to borrow back my Pyrran knife."

Temuchin merely nodded and passed it over. Jason threw away the sword and slipped the knife into his belt in its place. The helmet smelled of rank sweat, but it rode low on his head, which was fine. He wanted his face concealed as much as possible.

"Go now," Temuchin ordered, irritated at the delay the donning of the disguise had caused. Jason smiled coldly and turned and walked away into the woods.

Before he had gone 50 meters he was soaked to the waist by the dense, waterlogged underbrush. This was the least of his troubles. Pushing his way through the sodden forest, he wondered how he had become involved in this latest bit of madness. Gunpowder, that was the reason. He cursed loudly and fluently, then peered out at the fortified building, now barely visible through the falling rain. Another 20 meters should do it. He pushed on, then left the

104

shelter of the trees and walked ahead until he reached the riverbank. The water swirled by, laden with mud, and the rain spattered onto its surface, making an endless series of conjoining rings. He wanted to check the powder in the pan, but knew it was wiser not to. Do it, that's all, do it. Lowering his head he trudged toward the building, just visible through the rain.

If the men in the watchtower were looking at him, they gave no sign. Jason plodded closer, looking up under the edge of the helmet, the gun clutched across his chest. Now he was close enough to see the crumbled mortar between the roughly cut stones and the heavy bolts that studded the wood of the door ahead. He was close to the wall when one of the soldiers leaned out of the tower and called down to him incomprehensible words. Jason waved and trudged on.

When the man called again, Jason waved and shouted "Open!" in what he hoped was the correct accent. He made his voice as harsh as possible to disguise any inaccuracies. Then he was against the wall and out of sight of the men in the tower, who were still calling out to him. The door, solid and unmoving was just before him. Nothing happened, and the tension tightened another notch. There was a scratching sound and he saw a gun barrel coming out of a narrow window to the right of the door.

"Open—quickly!" he shouted and hammered on the door. "Open!" He pressed flat against the door so the gun could not bear on him and hammered again with the butt of the musket.

There were sounds inside the fortified building, voices and moving about, but the pulse of Jason's blood sounded even louder in his ears, thudding like a hidden drum, with a measureless time between each beat. Could he get away? Both sides would shoot him if he tried. But he could not stay here, powerless and trapped. As he raised his musket to hammer on the door again, he heard the rattle of heavy chains inside and a grating sound remarkably like that made by the sliding of an iron bolt. He cocked the flintlock through the protecting cover and released one side so that the leather could be pulled quickly away. The instant the door started to open he crashed his shoulder against it with all of his weight and pushed through, slamming it wide as hard as he could.

He kept moving, through the short archway and into the open square that the building was built around. Out of the corner of his eye he was barely aware of the man who had opened the door, now crushed by it, slumping to the ground. That was all he had time to notice because he saw that he was about to be killed.

Strike hard and fast and do not stop—that was what the nomads did and they were right. One soldier with a sword in his hand stood to the side, while directly in front of Jason were a number of others with guns leveled and ready to fire. Before the surprised men could shoot, Jason shouted and dived into their midst. Just before he hit them he pulled the trigger and was pleasantly surprised when the musket went off with a hollow boom and one of the men clutched his chest and fell. That was the last fact that Jason remembered clearly. He left the ground in a blocking dive, swinging the gun barrel and butt as he did, and crashed into them.

It was very confusing. After the first impact, he threw the gun at a soldier, kicked another one as he pulled out the heavy knife and swung it wildly. One man fell on him, dead or wounded, and Jason clutched his body for protection and lunged out with the knife again and again.

There was a sharp pain in his leg, then in his side and arm, and a loud ringing sounded in his head. He swung the knife in an arc and realized that he was falling. The ground felt good and so did the weight of the man lying, unmoving, on top of him. Above him the officer appeared, wild-eyed and raging, stabbing down with his sword. Jason parried it almost contemptuously with the knife, then stabbed upward to sink his blade in just above the man's groin. Blood spurted and the officer screamed and fell, and Jason had to push the body aside to see. By the time he did this, the quick battle had been decided.

The first of Temuchin's soldiers arrived, plunging headlong through the gate. He must have ridden at full speed toward the opening and dived from his saddle as the beast turned away. It was Temuchin himself, Jason realized, as the red-maned barbarian roared and swung his sword to cut down two attacking soldiers. After that, it was all over but the mopping up.

Once the immediate dangers had been cleared from

around him, Jason stumbled over and dropped with his back against the wall. The ringing in his head ebbed away to a dull buzzing, and when he took his helmet off, he found an immense dent in its side. But at least there seemed to be no matching dent in his head. He touched his fingers to the sore spot on his skull, then examined them carefully. No blood. But there was enough on his side and dripping down his leg to make up for it. A shallow cut in his hip, just under the half armor, had produced a sopping amount of blood, though the wound itself was superficial, as was the slice in his arm. The wound in his leg had bled only slightly, although it was the more serious of the two, a deep stab wound in his thigh muscles. It hurt, yet he could walk; he had no intention of being exterminated for being found wanting like the soldier at the farm. There were some strips of sterilized suede in his saddlebags, for bandaging, but the blood would just have to drip until he got to them.

From the moment when Temuchin dived through the doorway there had been no slightest doubt as to the outcome of the battle. The garrison soldiers had never before faced an enemy to match the barbarous fiends who now fell upon them. The muskets were more of a hindrance than a help, because the bows fired far faster and more accurately than the clumsy, sightless muzzle-loaders. Some soldiers fled and some stood and fought, but the outcome was the same in either case. They were slaughtered. The screams grew fainter and more distant as the survivors tried to escape into the building.

Blood mixed with rain in the sodden courtyard and there were bodies heaped on every side. A single nomad lay slumped in the doorway where a bullet had stopped him, and he appeared to be the only casualty suffered by the raiders. A motion caught Jason's eye and he saw a soldier raise his head above the top of the watchtower where he had been hiding. Something twanged sharply and an arrow sank into the man's eyesocket; he dropped back out of sight more permanently this time.

There were no more groans or appeals for mercy: the fort had been taken. The nomads moved silently among the corpses, bending to their grisly amputation ritual. Temuchin came from one of the doorways, his sword red and dripping, and waved one of his men to the huddled collection of bodies near the gate that they had forced.

"Three of these belong to the jongleur," he said. "The rest of the thumbs are mine." The soldier bowed and took out his dagger. Temuchin turned to Jason. "There are rooms in here with many things. Find the gunpowder."

Jason stood up, a lot faster than he really wanted to, and realized that he still held the bloody knife. He wiped it on the clothing of the nearest corpse and held it out to Temuchin, who took it without a word, then turned and went back into the building. Jason followed, trying vainly to walk without hobbling.

Ahankk and another officer were guarding the door of a low-ceilinged storeroom. The nomads were looting the bodies and the rest of the fortress, but were not permitted here. Jason pushed by and stopped just inside the doorway. There were baskets of lead bullets, fist-sized cannon balls, extra muskets and swords, and a number of squat barrels sealed with wooden plugs.

"Those have the right look," Jason said, pointing, then put up his arm to stop Temuchin when he started forward. "Don't walk in here. See those gray grains on the floor near the open keg? That looks very much like spilled gunpowder and it can catch fire when you walk on it. Let me sweep it up before anyone else comes in here."

Bending over sent a dagger of pain through his side and leg which Jason did his best to ignore. Using a bunched-up piece of cloth, he made a clean path across the room. The open barrel did contain gunpowder. He let the rough granules slide back through the hole, then pushed home the bung. Picking the barrel up as gently as he could, he carried it over and gave it to Ahankk. "Don't drop this, bang it, set fire to it or let it get wet. And send down"— he counted quickly—"nine men for the rest of the gunpowder. Tell them what I just told you."

Ahankk turned away and there was a crashing explosion outside followed by a distant boom. Jason jumped to the window and saw that a big bite had been taken out of the watchtower. Fragments of stone dropped into the mud and a cloud of dust was soaked up by the rain. The walls vibrated with the impact and the distant explosion sounded again. A nomad ran in through the gate, shouting loudly in his own tongue.

"What is he saying?" Jason asked.

Temuchin clenched his fists. "Many soldiers coming. They are firing a large gun that makes that noise. Many hands of soldiers, more than he can count."

11

THERE WAS no panic and scarcely any excitement. War was war, and the strange environment, the rain, the novel weapons—none of this could affect either the barbarians' calm or their fighting ability. Men who attack spaceships have only contempt for muzzle-loading cannon.

Ahankk took charge of the detail to carry the gunpowder, while Temuchin himself went to the battered watchtower to see what kind of force was attacking. Another cannon ball hit the wall and bullets hummed by like lethal bees while he stood there, unmoving, until he had seen enough. He leaned over and shouted orders down to his men.

Jason trailed after the men who were carrying the gunpowder, and when he emerged, he discovered that the warlord was the only other living person left inside the fort.

"Through that door," Temuchin ordered, pointing to the gate that opened onto the riverbank. "The ones who come cannot see that side yet, and all the *moropes* are there and behind this building. All of you with the gunpowder mount up and, when I signal the charge, you will go at once to the trees. The rest of us will delay the soldiers and then join you."

"How many men do you think are attacking?" Jason asked, as the gunpowder bearers hurried out.

"Many. Two hands times the count of a man, perhaps more. Go with the gunpowder, the attack is close." It was, too. Bullets splattered against the wall and spanged in through the firing slits. The roar of attacking voices sounded just outside.

The count of a man, Jason thought, hopping and hobbling to his *morope,* which was being held outside. All of a man's fingers and toes, twenty. And a hand times that would be a hundred, two hands two hundred. And their party numbered 23 at the most, if no more of the men had been killed during the last attack. Ten men, each to carry a barrel of gunpowder, with Jason along as technical adviser, left 13 lancers for the attack. Thirteen against a couple of hundred. Good barbarian odds.

Events moved fast after that. Jason barely had time to haul himself into the saddle before the gunpowder party wheeled away, and he made a tardy rearguard. They reached the back of the building just as the first attackers appeared. The remaining 13 riders charged out and the victorious roar of the foot soldiers turned instantly into mingled cries of shock and pain. Jason stole one glance over his shoulder and saw the cannon upended, men fleeing in all directions, while the *moropes* and their bloodthirsty riders cut a swathe of death through the ranks. Then the trees were before him and he had to avoid the whipping branches.

They waited just inside the screen of the woods. Within a minute there was the *thud-thud* of galloping *moropes* and seven of them plunged through the sodden brush. One of the beasts was carrying two riders. Their numbers were decreasing with every encounter.

"Go on," Temuchin ordered. "Follow the trail back the way we came. We will stay here and slow down any who try to follow."

As Jason and the powder team left, the survivors were dismounting and taking cover at the edge of the open field. It would take a determined attack to press home against the deadly arrows that would emerge from the obscuring forest.

Jason did not enjoy the ride. He had not dared to bring his medikit, though he wished now that he had taken this risk. Neither had he ever before tried to bandage two slippery wounds on himself, with cardboard-stiff chamois, while charging along a twisting trail on a hump-backed *morope.* It was his fond hope that he would never have to do it again. Before they reached the sacked farmhouse, the other riders caught up with them and the entire party galloped on in exhausted silence. Jason was hopelessly lost on the foggy, tree-shrouded paths, which all looked alike to him. But the nomads had far better eyes for the terrain and rode steadily toward their objective. The *moropes* were faltering and could be kept moving only by constant application of the prickspurs. Blood streamed down their sides and soaked into their damp fur.

When they reached the river, Temuchin signaled a stop.

"Dismount," he ordered, "and take only what you must have from your saddlebags. We leave the beasts here. One at a time now, over that rise to the river." He moved off first, leading his own mount.

Jason was too foggy from exhaustion and pain to realize what was happening. When he finally pulled his mount forward, he was surprised to see a knot of men on the riverbank with not a single *morope* in sight.

"Do you have everything you want?" Temuchin asked, taking Jason's bridle and pulling the *morope* close to the bank. As Jason nodded, he whipped the bowie knife across in a wicked, backhand slash that cut the creature's throat and almost severed its head from its body. He moved quickly to avoid the pulsing gout of blood, then put his foot against the swaying animal and pushed it sideways into the river. The swift current carried it quickly from sight.

"The machine cannot lift a *morope* up the cliff," Temuchin said. "And we do not want their bodies near the landing spot or the place will be known and soldiers will wait there. We walk." He looked at Jason's wounded leg. "You can walk, can't you?"

"Great," Jason said. "Never felt better. A little hike after a couple of nights without sleep and a thousand-kilometer ride is just what I need. Here we go." He walked off as swiftly as he could, trying not to limp. "We'll get this gunpowder back and I'll show you just how to use it," he reminded, just in case the warlord had forgotten.

It was not a very nice walk. They did not stop, but instead, to relieve each other, passed the barrels from one to another without halting. At least Jason and the other three walking wounded missed this assignment. Trudging uphill on the slippery grass was not easy. Jason's leg was a pillar of pain that bled a steady trickle of blood down into his boot top. He kept falling behind, and the march was endless. All of the others had passed him and, at one point, they were out of sight over a ridge ahead. He wiped the rain and sweat from his eyes and limped on, trying to follow their vague path in the tall grass, which was already straightening up and blurring the signs. Temuchin appeared on the hilltop above and looked back at him, fingering his sword hilt, and Jason put on a lung-destroying burst of speed. If he faltered, he would join the *moropes*.

An indeterminate period of time later, it came as a complete shock when he stumbled into the small group of men sitting on the grass, their backs to a familiar tower of rock.

"Temuchin has gone," Ahankk said. "You will go next. Each of the first ten men on the rope will carry up a barrel of this gunpowder."

"That's a great idea," Jason said collapsing inertly onto the soggy grass. It was an unconscionably long time before he could even struggle to a sitting position to do what he could to fix his crude bandages. One of the men carried over a barrel of gunpowder that had been secured in a harness of leather straps, with a loop to go around Jason's neck. The rope came down soon after this and he allowed himself to be strapped into it. This time the possibility of falling did not trouble him in the slightest. He rested his head on the gunpowder and fell asleep as soon as the lift began, nor did he awake until they pulled him to the clifftop and his forehead banged against the rock. Fresh *moropes* were waiting and he was permitted to return alone to the camp, without the gunpowder. He allowed the animal to go at its slowest pace so that the ride was not unbearable, but when he reached his own *camach*, he found that he did not possess the strength to dismount.

"Meta," he croaked. "Help a wounded veteran of the wars." He swayed when she poked her head out of the flap, then let go. She caught him before he hit the ground and carried him in her arms into the tent. It was a pleasant experience.

"You should eat something," Meta said sternly. "You have had enough to drink."

"Nonsense," he said, sipping from the iron cup and

smacking his lips. "I don't have tired blood—I have no blood. The medikit said that I was partially exsanguinated and gave me a stiff iron injection to make up for it. Besides, I'm too tired to eat."

"The readings also said that you needed a transfusion."

"A little hard to do that here. I'll drink plenty of water and have goat's liver for dinner every night."

"Open!" someone shouted, pulling at the laced and knotted entrance flap of the *camach*. "I speak with the voice of Temuchin."

Meta put the medikit under a fur and went to the entrance. Grif, who had been fanning the fire, picked up a lance and balanced it in his hand. A soldier poked his head in.

"You will come to Temuchin now."

"I come at once, tell him that."

The soldier started to argue, but Meta twisted his nose and pushed him back through the opening. She laced it shut again.

"You cannot go," she said.

"I have no choice. We've sutured the wounds by hand with gut, that's acceptable, and the antibiotics are not detectable. The iron is already seeping into my bone marrow."

"That is not what I meant," Meta said angrily.

"I know what you meant, but there is very little we can do about it." He pulled out the medikit and twisted the control dial. "Pain killer in the leg so I can walk on it, and a nice big shot of stimulant. I'm taking years off my life with this drug addiction, and I hope someone appreciates it."

When he stood up, Meta grabbed him by the arms. "No, you cannot," she said.

He used a gentler warfare, taking her face in his hands and kissing her. Grif snorted with contempt and turned back to his fire. Her hands relaxed.

"Jason," she said haltingly. "I don't like this. There is nothing I can do to help."

"There's plenty, but not at this moment. Just hold the fort for a while longer. I'm going to show Temuchin how to make his big bang, and then we're going to get out of here, back to the ship. I'll tell him I am going to bring the

Pyrran tribe in, which is just what I intend to do. Along with some other things. The wheels are turning and plans are being made, and there is a new day coming soon to Felicity." The drugs were making him light-headed and elated, and he believed every word he said. Meta, who had spent too long a time bent over a dung fire in this frozen campsite, was not quite so enthusiastic. But she let him go. Duty comes first—that is a lesson every Pyrran learns in the nursery.

Temuchin was waiting, showing no sign of the strain of the past days, pointing to the barrels of gunpowder on the floor of his *camach*.

"Make it explode," he commanded.

"Not in here and not all at once, unless you are planning a mass suicide. What I need is some sort of container that I can seal, and not too big a one either."

"Speak your needs. What you must have will be brought in here."

The warlord obviously wanted his explosive experiments classified Top Secret, which was all right with Jason. The *camach* was warm and relatively comfortable, with food and drink close at hand. He sank into the furs and worried a baked goat's leg until his materials had been assembled; then, after wiping his hands on his jacket, he set to work.

A number of clay pots had been assembled and Jason chose the smallest one, little more than a cup in size. Then he worked out the plug from one of the barrels and carefully shook some of the gunpowder out onto a sheet of leather. The grains were not very uniform, but he doubted if this would affect the speed of burning very much. This stuff had certainly worked well enough in the muskets. Using a scoop formed of stiff leather, he carefully loaded the pot until it was half full. A trimmed piece of chamois fitted on top of the granules and he tamped it down gently with the rounded end of a worn thighbone. Temuchin stood behind him watching every step of the process closely. Jason explained.

"The granules should be close together for even burning, for smooth burning makes the best banging. Or so I have been told by the men in the tribe who know about this sort of thing. This is all as new to me as it is to you. Then the leather goes in to hold the gunpowder in place and to

114

act as a waterproof shield." Jason had ready a mixture of water, dirt from the *camach* floor and crumbled dung. This made a damp, claylike substance that he now pushed into the pot to seal it. He patted it smooth and pointed.

"It is said that in order to explode, the gunpowder must be completely contained. If there are any openings, the fire rushes out through them and the substance simply burns."

"How does the fire reach it now?" Temuchin asked, frowning in concentration as he forced himself to follow the unaccustomed technical explanations. For an illiterate who couldn't count very well and did not have a shard of technical knowledge, he was doing all right. Jason took up one of the heavy iron needles that were used for sewing the *camach* covers.

"You've asked the right question. The plug is dry enough now, so I can poke a hole through it with this, through the mud and the leather, right down to the powder. Then, using the other end of the needle, I'll push this piece of cloth all the way down into the hole. I liberated the cloth from one of your men who liberated it from a lowlander's back. I have soaked the cloth in oil so that it will burn easily." He hefted the pot-grenade in his hand. "So I think that we are ready to go."

Temuchin stalked out and Jason, with the bomb in one hand and the flickering oil lamp in the other, followed at a suitable distance. A large area had been cleared before the warlord's *camach* and the soldiers held the curious at a suitable distance. The word had been quickly passed that something strange and dangerous was going to happen, so men had come flocking from all parts of the sprawling camp. They were packed solidly into the spaces between the surrounding *camachs*. Jason placed the bomb carefully in the ground and raised his voice.

"If this works there should be a loud noise, smoke and flame. Some of you here know what I mean. So—here goes."

He bent and applied the lamp to the fuse, holding it there until the cloth smoldered and burst into flame. It was burning slowly enough so that he could stand for a few seconds to make sure that it was going well. It was. Only then did he turn and stroll back to the *camach* next to Temuchin.

Even Jason's drug-induced confidence did not survive the anticlimax. The fuse burned, smoked, gave off some sparks and then apparently went out. Jason made himself wait a long time, in spite of the impatient murmurs and occasional angry shouts. He had no desire to bend over the bomb and have it blow up in his face. Only when Temuchin began to finger his knife in a suggestive manner did Jason walk out, hoping that he appeared to be more relaxed than he felt, to look down at the charred fuse opening. He nodded once sagely, then headed back to the *camach*.

"The fuse went out before it reached the gunpowder. We need a bigger hole or a better fuse—and I have just remembered another stanza of the 'Song of the Bomb' that speaks about that. I will do it now. Do not let anyone approach it until I return." Before he could get any arguments, he went back into the *camach*.

The best fuses contained gunpowder, so they could burn even without a supply of air. He needed a gunpowder fuse to get down through that layer of mud. There was plenty of powder here—but what could he roll it in? Paper was best, but in short supply at the present moment. Or was it? He made sure that the entrance was well secured and that he was alone in the tent. Then he rooted in the bottom of his waist wallet and dug out his medikit. He had brought it despite the risk, because he had no idea how long this session would take and had not wanted to run any risk of passing out before it was over.

It took just a second to press, twist and pull open the recharging chamber. Folded above the ampules was the inspection and recharge sheet, just big enough for his needs. He slipped the medikit out of sight again.

Making the fuse was simple enough, though he practically had to twist each grain of powder into the paper separately to make sure they didn't lump together and burn too fast. When the job was done, he rubbed oil and lampblack into the paper to disguise its pristine whiteness. "This should do it," he said, taking the fuse and the needle and going back to the demonstration.

It almost did a lot more than he had bargained for. The nomads were jeering openly now and making rude noises, and Temuchin was white with rage. The bomb was

116

still sitting innocently where he had left it. Pretending not to hear the unflattering remarks, Jason bent over the bomb and made a new hole in the clay seal. He was taking no chances of poking a smoldering fragment of rag down into the gunpowder. It was a chancy business, and the sweat on his forehead had nothing to do with the chilling temperature of the morning air as he pushed home the new fuse.

"This is the one that works," he said as he applied the flame.

The paper smoked lustily and crackled as a shower of sparks flew into the air. Jason had one brief, horrified glimpse of the flame streaking down the oily gunpowder fuse, then he turned and dived for safety.

This time the results were very impressive. The bomb exploded with a highly satisfactory roar and pieces of jagged pottery whistled away in every direction, ripping holes in a score of *camachs* and inflicting minor wounds on some of the spectators. Jason was so close to the blast that it rolled him over and over on the ground.

Temuchin still stood unmoving at the opening of the *camach*, but he did look a slight bit more pleased now. The few shouts of pain from the audience were drowned out in the enthusiastic cries and happy back-slapping. Jason sat up shakily and felt himself all over, but could find nothing broken that had not been broken before.

"Can you make them bigger?" Temuchin asked, an anticipatory gleam of destruction in his eye.

"They come in all sizes. Though I could give you a more exact idea if you would let me know just what use you have in mind for them."

A stir on the other side of the field distracted Temuchin before he could answer. A number of men on *moropes* were trying to force their way through the crowd and the bystanders did not like the idea. There were angry shouts and at least one broken-off scream.

"Who approaches without permission?" Temuchin said, and when he reached for his sword, his personal guard drew their weapons and formed up close to him. The first row of onlookers jumped aside rather than be trampled and a *morope* and rider came through.

"What made that noise?" the rider asked, his voice just as used to automatic command as was Temuchin's.

It was a voice that was very familiar to Jason.

It was Kerk.

Temuchin went striding forward in cold anger, his men grouped around him, while Kerk dismounted and was joined by Rhes and the other Pyrrans. A really beautiful battle was in the making.

"Wait!" Jason shouted, and ran to get between the two groups, who were on obvious collision course. "These are the Pyrrans!" he shouted. "My tribe. Warriors who have come to join the forces of Temuchin." Out of the corner of his mouth he hissed at Kerk. "Relax! Bend the knee a bit before we all get massacred."

Kerk did nothing of the sort. He stopped, looking just as irritated as Temuchin, and fingered his sword hilt in the same threatening manner. Temuchin came on like an avalanche and Jason had to step back or he would have been crushed between the two men. When Temuchin stopped his toes were touching Kerk's and they glared at each other with almost eyeball-to-eyeball contact.

They were very much alike. The warlord was taller, but the solid breadth of the Pyrran could never be mistaken for fat. Their apparel was just as impressive, as Kerk had followed Jason's radioed instructions. His breastplate sported a multicolored and severely two-dimensional design of an eagle, while the eagle's skull itself crowned his helm.

"I am Kerk, leader of the Pyrrans," he said, slipping his sword up and down with an irritating, grating sound.

"I am Temuchin, warlord of the tribes. You will bow to me."

"Pyrrans bow to no man."

Temuchin rumbled deep in his throat like an infuriated carnivore and began to draw his sword. Jason resisted an impulse to cover his eyes and flee. This would be bloody murder.

Kerk knew what he was doing. He had not come here to depose Temuchin—at least not right now—so he did not reach for his own sword. Instead, his hand moved with the cracking speed that only Pyrrans have developed, and he seized the wrist of Temuchin's sword arm.

"I do not come to fight you," he said calmly. "I come as an equal to side with you in your cause. We will talk."

His voice did not waver—nor did Temuchin's sword

come one centimeter more out of the loops. The warlord had a massive strength and resiliency, but Kerk was an unmoving boulder. He neither moved nor showed any sign of strain, but the veins stood out on Temuchin's forehead. The silent struggle continued for ten, fifteen seconds, until Temuchin suffused red under the darkness of his skin, every muscle of his body rock hard with the effort of his exertions.

When it appeared that human muscle and sinew could stand no more, Kerk smiled. Just the barest turning up of the corners of his mouth, visible only to Temuchin and Jason, who stood close by. Then, slowly and steadily, the warlord's arm was forced down until his sword was secure in its loops and could go no farther.

"I did not come here to fight you," Kerk said in a barely audible voice. "The young men may wrestle with each other. We are leaders who talk."

He released his grip so suddenly that Temuchin swayed with the reaction, as his tensed muscles no longer had anything to battle against. The decision was his once again, and the intelligent man was warring in his body against the brute reactions of the born barbarian.

For long seconds this silent impasse continued, then Temuchin began to chuckle, the laughter rising quickly to a full-throated roar. He threw his head back and laughed defiance of the universe, then swung his arm and clapped Kerk on the shoulder with a blow that would have stunned a *morope* or killed a lesser man. Kerk just swayed slightly and returned the smile.

"You are a man I might like!" Temuchin shouted. "If I do not kill you first. Come into my *camach*." He turned away and Kerk went with him. They passed Jason without deigning to notice him. Jason rolled his eyes upward, happy to see that the skies had not fallen nor the sun gone nova, then turned and followed them.

"Stay here," Temuchin ordered when they reached the *camach,* spearing Jason with a look of cold fury as though he alone were responsible for the ill events. Temuchin waved the guards to position, then followed Kerk inside. Jason did not complain. He preferred waiting here in the wind, chill as it was, to witnessing the confrontation in the tent. If Temuchin were killed, how would they escape?

Fatigue and pain were beginning to creep back, and he swayed in the wind and wondered if he could risk a quick stab with his medikit. The answer was obviously no, so he swayed and waited.

Angry voices sounded loudly inside and Jason cringed and waited for the end. Nothing happened. He swayed again and decided that it would be easier to sit down, so he dropped. The ground was chill against his bottom. The voices rose once more inside, then were followed by an ominous silence. Jason noticed that even the guards were exchanging concerned glances.

There was a sharp ripping sound and they jumped and turned, raising their lances. Kerk had opened the entrance flap by pulling on it—hard. But he had neglected to unlace it first. The thick leather thongs were snapped, or torn loose from their heavy supports, and the supporting iron rod was bent at a sharp angle. Kerk apparently noticed none of this. He stalked by the guards, nodded at Jason, and kept on walking. Jason had a quick look at Temuchin's face, swollen with anger, in the opening. This glimpse was enough. He turned and hurried after Kerk.

"What happened in there?" he asked.

"Nothing. We just talked and felt each other out and neither of us would give way. He would not answer my questions so I did not bother to answer his. It is a draw—for the moment."

Jason was worried. "You should have waited until I returned. Why did you come like this?" He knew the answer even as he asked, and Kerk confirmed it.

"Why shouldn't we? Pyrrans do not enjoy sitting on a mountain and acting as jailers. We came to see for ourselves. There was some fighting on the way here and the morale has improved."

"I'm sure of that," Jason said fervently, and wished he were lying down back in his *camach*.

12

Back they came from the land of wetness,
Back they came, with thumbs in bunches,
Telling tales of the glorious killing
In the lands below the clifftops.

Though the wind hissed around the *camach* and occasionally blew a scattering of fine snowflakes in through the smokehole, the interior was warm and comfortable. The atomic heater generated enough BTU's to defeat all the drafts and leaks, while the strong drink Kerk had brought sat in Jason's stomach far better than the vile *achadh*. Rhes had supplied a case of meal packs and Meta was opening them. The rest of the Pyrrans were setting up their *camachs* nearby or were unobtrusively on guard near the entrance. For a rare instance, in the heart of the barbarian camp, they were free from observation and safe from sudden violence.

"Pig," Meta said when Jason reached for a steaming and nose-captivating meal pack, "you've already had one."

"First one was for me. This one's for my shattered tissues and drained blood." While he chewed a warming and succulent mouthful, he pointed at Kerk's helm. "I see that you joined the eagle clan all right, but where did you get so many skulls? They sure impressed the locals. I didn't know there were that many eagles on the entire planet."

"There probably aren't," Kerk said, running his finger over the hook-beaked and eyeless skull. "We managed to shoot this one and make a mould. All of the others are plastic castings. Now tell us what these plans are that you have formulated, because, as enjoyable as this childish masquerade is, we want an end to it. And a beginning to the mining operation."

"Patience," Jason said. "This operation is going to have to take a little time, but I guarantee that there will be plenty of fighting so it will have its high spots. Let me fill in some of the things I have discovered since I talked to you last.

"Temuchin has most of the plains tribes behind him, at least all of the ones that count. He is a damn intelligent man and a shrewd leader. He intuitively knows most of the military-textbook axioms. Keep the troops occupied, that's a basic one. As soon as they chased the first expedition away, he talked around among the clans and found the one or two tribes that the majority were feuding with. They wiped these out and split up the loot. This has been the process ever since. You're either with him or against him, and no one is neutral. All this in spite of the nomads' natural tendency to align and realign and go their own way. The few leaders who have tried to get out from under the new regime have met such violent deaths that all the others are very impressed."

Kerk shook his head. "If he has united all of these people, then there is nothing we can do."

"Kill him?" Meta suggested.

"See what a few weeks among the barbarians will do for a girl?" Jason said. "I can't say that I'm not tempted. The alliance would fall apart—but we would be back to square one. If we tried to open the mines, some other leader would appear and the attacks would start again. No, we have to do better than that. If it is possible, I would like to take over his organization and turn it to our own ends. And, Kerk, you're not quite right. He has not united all the tribes, just the strongest ones on the plains. There are a number of smaller ones around the edges that he is not bothering about; they pose no threat. But there are a lot of hairy-necked mountain tribes in the north who pride themselves on their independence, most of them from the weasel clan. They fight each other, but they will work together against any threat from the outside. Temuchin is that threat—and that will be our big chance to take over."

"How?" Rhes asked.

"By being better at the job than he is. By covering ourselves with glory and doing better than he does in the mountain campaign. And arranging it so that he makes a

122

couple of mistakes. If we work it right, we should come back from the campaign with Kerk either in the highest councils or an equal of Temuchin. This is a rough society and nobody cares how great you were last year, but what you have done for them lately. A real barnyard pecking order is in operation, and we are going to arrange it so that Kerk is top pecker. All of us except Rhes, that is."

"Why not me?" Rhes asked.

"You are going to organize the second part of the plan. We never paid much attention to the lowlands, below the cliffs, because there are no heavy metal deposits. However, there appears to be a fairly advanced agrarian culture at work down there. Temuchin found a way of sending down a raiding party, an expedition I do not wish to try again, to get some gunpowder. I'm sure he wants to use it against the hill tribes, an ace in the hole to assure victory. Those mountain passes must be hard to attack. I helped Temuchin bring the gunpowder back—and kept my eyes open at the same time. Aside from the gunpowder, I saw flintlocks, cannon, military uniforms and bags of flour. That's strong evidence."

"Evidence of what?" Kerk was irritated. He preferred to work with simpler, more familiar chains of logic.

"Isn't it obvious? Proof that a fairly advanced culture is in operation here. Chemistry, single-crop culture, central government, taxes, forging, large casting, weaving, dyeing . . ."

"How do you know all that?" Meta asked, astonished.

"I'll tell you tonight, dear, when we're alone. It would just appear like bragging now. But I know that my conclusions are correct. There is a rising middle class down there in the lowlands, and I'll wager that the bankers and the merchants are rising the fastest. Rhes is going to buy his way in. As an agrarian himself, he has the right background for the job. Look at this, the key to his success."

He took a small metal disk from his pouch and tossed it into the air, then handed it to Rhes. "What is it?" Rhes asked.

"Money. Coin of the lower realm. I took it from one of the dead soldiers. This is the axle on which the commercial world rotates, or is the lubrication on the axle, or whatever other metaphor you prefer. We can analyze this and forge

123

up a batch that will not only be as good, but will be richer and better than the original. You'll take them to buy yourself in, set up shop as a merchant and get ready for the next move."

Rhes looked at the coin distastefully. "And now I'm supposed to play this wide-mouthed question game like everyone else here and ask you what is next move?"

"Correct. You catch on quick. When Jason talks, everyone listens."

"You talk too much," Meta said primly.

"Agreed, but it's my only vice. The next move will be to unite the tribes here, with Kerk in control or close to it, to welcome Rhes when he sails north with his trade goods. This continent may be bisected by a cliff that normally prevents contact between the nomads and the lowlanders, but you can't convince me that I won't find a place somewhere here in the north where it might be possible to land a ship or small boats. One little bit of beach is all we need. I'm sure that seagoing contact has been ruled out in the past because it takes an advanced technology to make floating ships out of iron. Hide- and bone-framed coracles are a possibility, but I doubt if the nomads have ever even considered the possibility of traveling on water. The lowlanders must surely have ships, but there is nothing up here to tempt them into exploration. Quite the opposite, if anything. But we're going to change all that. Under Kerk's leadership the tribes will give a peaceful welcome to traders from the south. Trade will enter the picture and a new era will begin. For a few tired furs, the tribesmen will be able to gather the products of civilization and will be seduced. Maybe we can hook them on tobacco, booze or glass beads. There must be something they like that the lowlands can supply. And this will be the thin end of the wedge. First a landing on the beach with trade goods, then a few tents to keep the snow off. Then a permanent settlement. Then a trading center and market—right over the spot where our mine is going to be. The next step should be obvious."

There was plenty of discussion, but only about the details. No one could fault Jason's plan; in fact, they rather approved of it. It sounded simple and workable, and assigned parts to all of them that they enjoyed playing. All except Meta, that is. She had had enough of dung fires and menial manual labor to last for the rest of her life. But she was too good a Pyrran to complain about her assignment, so she remained silent.

It was very late before the meeting broke up; the boy, Grif, had been asleep for hours. The atomic heater had been turned off and locked away, but the aura of its warmth remained. Jason collapsed into the fur sleeping bag and let out an exhausted sigh. Meta rolled over and put her chin against his chest.

"What is going to happen after we win?" she asked.

"Don't know," Jason said tiredly, letting his hand run through her short-cropped hair. "Haven't thought about it. Get the job done first."

"I've thought about it. It should mean the end of the fighting for us, forever I mean. If we stay here and build a new city. What will you do then?"

"Hadn't thought," he said blurredly, holding her close and enjoying the sensation.

"I think I would like to stop fighting. I think there must be other things to do with a person's life. Did you notice that all the women here take care of their own children, instead of putting them into the nursery and never seeing them again as on Pyrrus? I think that might be a nice thing."

Jason jerked his hand away from her hair as from molten metal and his eyes sprang wide open. Dimly, in the far distance, he could hear the harsh ringing of wedding bells, a sound he had fled from more than once in his life, a sound that brought out an instant running reflex.

"Well," he said with what he hoped was due deliberation, "that sort of thing might be nice for *barbarian* women, but it certainly isn't the sort of fate to be wished on an intelligent, civilized girl." He waited tensely for an answer, until he realized from the evenness of her breathing that she had fallen asleep. That took care of that, at least for the time being.

Then he held the solid warmth of her body in his arm and he wondered what exactly it was he was running from and, while he wondered, the drugs and exhaustion hit and he fell asleep.

In the morning the new campaign began. Temuchin had issued his orders and the march got under way at dawn,

125

with a freezing, bone-chilling wind sweeping down from the mountains in the north. The *camachs,* the *escungs,* even carrier *moropes* were left behind. Every warrior brought his own weapons and rations, and was expected to take care of himself and his mount. At first the movement was very unimpressive, a scattering of soldiers working their way through the *camachs,* among the shouting women and the ragged children running in the dust. Then two men joined together, and a third, until an entire squad rode together, the riders bobbing up and down in response to the undulating motion of their mounts.

Jason rode next to Kerk, with the 94 Pyrran warriors following in a double column. He turned in his saddle to look at them. The women could not ride with them, and eight men had gone to the lowlands with Rhes, while the remainder were on guard duty at the ship. That left 96 men in all to accomplish the mission—to gain control of the barbarian army and this occupied portion of the planet. On the surface it looked impossible, but the bearing of the tiny Pyrran force did not reflect that. They were solemn and ready to take on anything that came their way. It gave Jason an immense feeling of security to have them riding behind him.

Once clear of the campsite, they could see other columns of men paralleling their course across the rolling sweep of the steppe. Messengers had gone out to all the tribes camped along the river to tell them that they were to ride today. The horde was gathering. From all sides they came, drifting toward the line of march, until there were riding men visible on all sides, clear to the horizon. There was a marked sense of organization now, with different clans falling in behind their captains and forming into squadrons. In the distance Jason saw the black banners of Temuchin's household guards and pointed them out to Kerk.

"Temuchin has two *moropes* loaded with our gunpowder bombs, and he wants me to ride with him to supervise the operation. He pointedly did *not* mention the rest of the Pyrrans, but we're all going to stay with him whether he likes it or not. He needs me for the gunpowder—and I ride with my tribe. It's a winning argument that I'm sure he can't beat."

"Then we shall put it to the test," Kerk said, spurring

his beast into a gallop. The Pyrran column sliced through the galloping horde toward their leader.

They swung in from the right flank until they were riding level with Temuchin's men, then slacked back to the same pace. Jason started forward, ready with his foolproof arguments, but found them unnecessary. Temuchin took one slow, cold look at the Pyrrans, then turned his eyes forward again. He was like a chess master who sees a mate 12 moves ahead and resigns without playing the game out. Jason's arguments were obvious to him and he did not bother to listen to them.

"Examine the lashings on the gunpowder bombs," he ordered. "They are your responsibility."

From his vantage point near the warlord, Jason witnessed the smooth organization of the barbarian army and began to realize that Temuchin must be a military genius. Illiterate and untutored, with no authorities to rely on, he had reinvented all of the basic principles of army maneuvers and large-scale warfare. His captains were more than just leaders of independent commands. They acted as a staff, taking messages and relaying orders on their own initiative. A simple system of horn signals and arm motions controlled the troops, so that the thousands of men formed a flexible and dangerous weapon.

Also an intensely rugged one. When all the troops had joined up, Temuchin formed them into a kilometer-wide line and advanced on the entire front at once. Without stopping. The advance, which had begun before dawn, continued into the early afternoon without a halt for any reason. The rested and well-fed *moropes* did not like the continuous ride, but they were capable of it when goaded on by the spurs. They shrieked protest, but the advance went on. The endless jogging did not seem to bother the nomads, who had been in the saddle almost since birth, but Jason, in spite of his recent riding experience, was soon battered and sore. If the ride was affecting the Pyrrans in any way, it was not noticeable.

Squadrons of riders scouted out ahead of the main company of troops, and by late afternoon the invading army came across their handiwork. Slaughtered nomads, first a single rider, his blood mixed with that of his butchered *morope*, then a family unit that had been unlucky enough

127

to cross the path of the army. The *escungs* and folded *camachs* were still smoldering, surrounded by a ghastly array of dead bodies. Men, women and children, even the *moropes* and flocks, had been brutally slain. Temuchin fought total war and where he had passed nothing remained alive. He was brutally pragmatic in his thinking. War is fought to be won. Anything that assures victory is sensible. It is sensible to make a three-day ride in a single day if it means the enemy can be surprised. It is sensible to kill everyone you meet so that no alarm can be given, just as it is sensible to destroy all their goods so your warriors will not be burdened by booty.

The truth of Temuchin's tactics was proved when, just before dark, the racing army swooped down upon a large-sized village of the weasel clan in the foothills of the mountains.

As the great line of riders topped the last ridge, the alarm was given in the camp, but it was too late for escape. The ends of the line swung in and met behind the camp, though it looked as though some hard-ridden *moropes* had slipped through before the forces joined. Sloppy, Jason thought, surprised that Temuchin had not done a better job.

After this it was just slaughter. First by overwhelming flights of arrows that drove back and decimated the defenders, then by a lance charge at full gallop. Jason hung back, not out of cowardice, but from simple hatred of the bloodshed. The Pyrrans attacked with the rest. Through constant practice they were all now proficient with the short bow, though they still could not fire as fast as the nomads, but it was in shock tactics that they proved what they could do. If they had any qualms about killing the nomad tribe, they did not show it. They struck like lightning and tore through the defenders and overrode them. With their speed and weight they did not parry or attempt to defend themselves. Instead, they hit like battering rams, slashed, killed and kept on without slowing. Jason could not join them in this. He remained with the two disgruntled men who had been detailed to guard the gunpowder bombs, picking out chords on his lute as he composed a new song to describe this great occasion. It was dark before the pillage was over and Jason rode slowly into the ravished encampment. He met a rider who was searching for him.

"Temuchin would see you. Come now," the man ordered. Jason was too tired and sickened to think of any sharp comebacks.

They made their way through the conquered encampment, with their *moropes* stepping carefully over the sprawled and piled corpses. Jason kept his eyes straight ahead, but could not close his nose to the slaughterhouse stench. Surprisingly, very few of the *camachs* had been damaged or burned, and Temuchin was holding an officers' council in the largest of them. It had undoubtedly belonged to the former leader of the clan; in fact, the chieftain himself lay gutted, dead and unnoticed, against the far side of the tent. All of the officers were assembled—though Kerk was not present—when Jason entered.

"We begin," Temuchin said, and squatted cross-legged on a fur robe. The others waited until he sat, then did the same. "Here is the plan. What we did today was nothing, but it is the beginning, To the east of this place is a very large encampment of the weasel tribes, and tomorrow we march to attack this place. I want your men to think we go to this camp, and I want those who watch from the hills to think the same. Some were permitted to escape to observe our movements."

That for my theory about sloppy soldiering, Jason thought. I should have known better. Temuchin must have this campaign planned down to the last arrowhead.

"Today your men have ridden hard and fought well. Tonight the soldiers not on guard will drink the *achadh* they find here and eat the food and will be very late arising in the morning. We will take the undamaged *camachs* and destroy the rest. It will be a short day and we will camp early. The *camachs* will be set up, many cooking fires lit and kept burning, while patrols will sweep as far as the foothills so that the watchers will not get too close."

"And it is all a trick," Ahankk said, grinning behind his hand. "We will not attack to the east after all?!"

"You are correct." The warlord had their complete attention, the officers leaning forward unconsciously so as not to miss a word. "As soon as it is dark, the horde will ride west, a day's and a night's ride should bring us to The Slash, the valley that leads to the weasel's heartland. We will attack the defenders, with the gunpowder bombs against their forts, and seize control before reinforcements can arrive."

"Bad fighting there," one of the officers grumbled, fingering an old wound. "Nothing there to fight for."

"No, nothing *there*, you brainless fool," Temuchin said in such a cold and angry tone that the man recoiled, "nothing at all. But it is the gateway to their homeland. A few hundred can stop an army in The Slash, but once we are through they are lost. We will destroy their tribes one by one until the weasel clan will be only a memory for the jongleurs to sing about. Now issue your orders and sleep. Tomorrow night the long ride and the attack begins."

As the others filed out, Temuchin took Jason by the arm.

"The gunpowder bombs," he said. "They will blow up each time they are used?"

"Of course," Jason answered, with far more enthusiasm than he felt. "You have my word on that."

It wasn't the bombs that were worrying him—he had already taken precautions to assure satisfactory explosions —but the prospect of another nonstop ride even longer than the first. The nomads would do it, there was no doubt about that, and the Pyrrans could make it as well. But could he?

The night air was bitterly cold when he emerged from the heat of the *camach*. His breath made a sudden silver fog against the stars before it vanished. The plains were still, cut through by the occasional snort of a tired *morope* or the drunken shouts of the soldiers.

Yes, he would make the ride all right. He might have to be tied to the saddle and hopped up with drugs, but he was going to make it. What really concerned him was the shape he would arrive in at the other end of the ride. This did not bear thinking about.

13

"HOLD ON for just a short while longer. The Slash is in sight ahead," Kerk shouted.

Jason nodded, then realized that his head was bobbing continuously with the *morope's* canter and his nodding was indistinguishable from this motion. He tried to answer, but started coughing at the cracked dryness of his throat, filled and caked with the dust stirred up by the running animals. In the end he released his cramped grip on the saddle pommel long enough to wave, then clutched at it again. The army rode on.

It was a nightmare journey. It had started soon after dark on the previous night, when company after company of riders had slipped away to the west. After the first few hours, fatigue and pain had blended together for Jason into a misty unreality that, with the darkness and the countless rows of running shapes, soon resembled a dream more than reality. A particularly loathsome dream. They had galloped, without stopping, until dawn, when Temuchin had permitted a short halt to feed and water the *moropes* for the balance of the journey. This stop may have helped their mounts, but it had almost finished Jason.

Instead of dismounting, he had fallen from his *morope*, and when he tried to stand, his legs had failed him. Kerk had dragged him to his feet and walked him in a circle while another Pyrran cared for both their mounts. Feeling had finally returned to his numb legs and with it excruciating pain. His thighs were soaked with blood where the continual friction of the saddle had chafed away the skin. He had permitted himself a light injection of painkiller and some stimulant, then the ride had begun again. One fact he knew and hated was that he had to be sparing with the drugs. When this ride was over, the real battle would begin, and that would be the time when he would need all of his wits and strength. So the strongest drugs would have to be saved until then.

In an inverse way he could be proud of himself. More than one rider and *morope* had been lost during this insane ride, and he, the off-worlder who had never seen one of the creatures until a few months ago, was still going on. Barely. Some of the mounts had stumbled and fallen. Other riders had apparently gone to sleep or passed out, had slipped from their saddles and been trampled. It was certain death to drop beneath those running claws.

If The Slash was up ahead, the time had finally come to utilize the drugs he had been hoarding. Squinting against the late-afternoon sun and the blinding clouds of dust, he saw a dark cut against the gray white of the mountains ahead. The Slash. The valley they hoped to capture that would lead them to certain victory. Right now the drugs were more important than any number of victories. He dialed the medikit with clumsy fingers and jammed it against the heel of his hand.

As the drugs cleared the haze of fatigue and drew numbing layers over the pain, Jason realized that Temuchin was insane.

"He's calling for a charge!" Jason shouted across to Kerk as the signal horns sounded on all sides. "After all this riding . . ."

"Of course," Kerk said. "It is the correct way."

The correct way. It wins wars and kills men. An angry *morope,* squealing at the pain of ruthlessly applied spurs, reared up and threw its rider under the running feet of the others. This was not the only death. Still, the attack was pressed home.

Across the plains the army swept and into the mouth of the valley. Picked bowmen dismounted and clambered along the walls of The Slash to add their fire to the attack of the solid column streaming by below them. The leaders vanished into the valley and still others followed. A cloud of dust obscured the entrance. The Pyrrans pressed forward to the attack with the others while Jason turned off and headed for Temuchin's standard as he had been ordered. The personal guardsmen opened to let him through.

Temuchin took a report from a rider, then turned to Jason. "Get your bombs," he ordered.

"Why?" Jason asked, then hurried on as the light of instant anger burst in the other man's eyes. "What do you want me to do with them? Order, great Temuchin, and I shall obey. Only please give me some idea what you want me for."

The anger vanished as quickly as it had come. "The battle has gone as did all the others," the warlord said. "We have taken them by surprise and only the normal garrison is here. The lower redoubts have been taken and we now press on the higher ones. These are rock-walled and set into the cliff. Arrows cannot reach the defenders. They must be attacked on foot, slowly, from behind shields, if we are not to lose half an army. They cannot be stormed. Each time before it has been this way. One by one we take the redoubts and work our way up The Slash. Before we reach the other end the reinforcements have arrived and further battle is useless. But this time it will be different."

"I can just guess. You think that a gunpowder bomb in each position would take the fight out of the defenders and speed the attack?"

"You speak correctly."

"Then here I go, the First Felicitian Grenadiers to the attack. I will want some of my people to help me. They can throw farther and better than I can."

"The order will be issued."

By the time Jason had found the pack animals and unloaded the first of the bombs, the Pyrrans had arrived—Kerk and two others, sweaty and dusty from the fight, with that look of grim pleasure Pyrrans have only during battle.

"Ready to throw some bombs?" Jason asked Kerk.

"Of course. What is the mechanism?"

"Improved. I had a feeling that excuses are not much good with Temuchin and I wanted grenades that would go off every time." He held up one of the pot-bombs and pointed to the cloth wick. "There's gunpowder in these things all right, but mostly for the smoke and the stink. The wick is a dummy. You'll have to light it. I've made punk pots from grass for this, but that is just for effect. Let the wick smolder a bit, then pull up on it sharply. There is a microgrenade embedded in each one of these things, with the cloth wick tied to the trip pin. After you pull, you have three seconds to toss and duck."

Taking a flint and steel from his wallet, Jason bent over the pot of shredded punk and began to scratch away industriously. As the sparks smoldered and died, he looked out of the corners of his eyes to be sure he wasn't observed, then quickly actuated the lighter he had palmed. The tongue of flame flicked out and fired the punk.

"Here you are," he said, handing the smoldering pot to Kerk. "I suggest you carry this and throw the grenades, as you can undoubtedly toss them farther than I can."

"Farther and much more accurately."

"Yes, there is that, too. I and the others will carry the bombs for you and act as guards in case of a counterattack. Here we go."

They left their mounts and proceeded on foot into The Slash. The attacking troops were still moving up, so they worked their way along the sloping wall of the valley to avoid being trampled. As they went farther in, they met the first debris of battle—wounded soldiers who had crawled to the side out of the path of the still attacking army. The ones who had not made it were just red smears in the dust below. There were occasional dead *moropes* as well, their massive bodies standing up like bloodstained boulders. Now The Slash narrowed and the walls grew steeper. They found themselves following a goat path, their hands pressed against the stone for support. In this manner they reached the first redoubt. This was a crude but effective wall of piled rocks that fortified a narrow ledge. Jason clambered up the boulders to peer inside. He would need some idea of how these things were built up in order to blow them down. The defenders, stocky men in dusty furs, each with a weasel's skull lashed above his forehead, lay where they had fallen. Their bodies bristled with arrows; their thumbs were missing. Hard-carapaced death beetles had appeared out of the ground and were already at work.

"If they're all like this, we won't have any trouble," Jason said, sliding down to rejoin the others. "The boulders are just piled up, with no sign of any mortar. A grenade, if it doesn't knock out all the soldiers, should blow a gap in the wall big enough to let Temuchin's lads through."

"You are optimistic," Kerk said, taking the lead again. "These are merely outposts. The main defenses must lie ahead."

"Well, that's better than being pessimistic. I'm trying to talk myself into believing I'll live through this barbarian war and actually be warm again some time."

It was no longer possible to walk on the valley side and they had to drop down and push their way through the soldiers. As the rock walls became more vertical, The Slash narrowed, and Jason could appreciate the difficulties of capturing it when it was stoutly defended. All of the *moropes* had been sent back and the attackers were now on foot. An arrow cracked into the stone above Jason's head and clattered down at their feet.

"We're at the front lines," Jason said. "Hold the advance here while I take a look." He pulled himself up the sloping side of one of the massive boulders that filled the gorge and, with his helm pulled low, slowly raised his head above the top. An arrow instantly clanged off of it and he quickly tilted his head forward until he was peering through the merest slit between the helm and the stone.

The advance had stopped ahead, where two redoubts, on opposite sides of The Slash, could sweep the entire floor of the valley with their accurate arrow fire. The defenders were firing from slits between the rocks and were almost impregnable to any return fire. Temuchin's forces were suffering losses in order to take the defended points the hard way. Protected slightly by their shields, moving in quick rushes from boulder to boulder, they crept forward. And died.

"The range is about 40 meters," Jason said, sliding back to the ground. "Do you think you can toss one of these things that far?"

Kerk bounced the homemade bomb on the palm of his broad hand and estimated its weight. "Easily," he said. "Let me look first so I will know what the distance is." He moved up to the position Jason had vacated, took one look, then dropped back down.

"That defended position is bigger than the others. It will take at least two bombs. I will light this one, hand you the smudge pot, then step out and throw the bomb. In the meantime you will have lit a second one—do not arm it—which you will give to me as soon as I have thrown the first. Is that clear?"

"Crystalline. Here we go."

Jason slipped off the sling of bombs and kept only one in his hand. The nearby soldiers (they had all heard about the gunpowder experiments) were watching closely. Kerk lit the false fuse, blew it into smoking life, then stepped out from the shelter of the rock. Jason hurriedly lit the bomb he carried and stood ready to pass it on.

With infuriating calm Kerk drew his arm back as one arrow zinged close by him and another shattered on his breastplate. Then he lowered the bomb, wet his finger and raised it to check the direction of the wind. Jason hopped from one foot to the other and clamped his teeth tightly together to stop from shouting at the Pyrran to throw.

More arrows arrived before Kerk was satisfied with the wind and drew his arm back again. Jason saw his thumb and index finger give the smoldering fuse a quick tug before, with a single contraction of all his muscles, he threw the bomb. It was a good, classic grenade throw, straight-armed and overhand, sending the bomb on a high arc toward the defended position. Jason reached out and slapped the second bomb into Kerk's waiting hand. This one followed the first so closely that both were in the air at the same time.

Kerk stood where he was and Jason, dismaying his own cowardly survival instincts, remained exposed as well, watching the two black spots soar high and down behind the wall.

There was an instant of waiting—then the entire stone-walled position leaped out into the air and crashed down in fragments below. Jason had a quick vision of bodies tossed high before he dodged behind the boulder to avoid the chunks of falling rock.

"Very satisfactory," Kerk said, pressed against the stone face close to Jason while stone shards rattled down around them.

"I hope the others are all this easy."

Of course, they weren't. The watchful defenders saw quickly enough that one man, throwing something, was responsible for the disaster, and the next time Kerk emerged he had to withdraw swiftly as a solid flight of arrows smashed down on his position.

"This is going to take some planning," Kerk said, automatically snuffing out the sputtering fuse.

136

"Are you afraid? Why do you stop?" an angry voice asked, and Kerk wheeled around to face Temuchin, who had come up to the front under the protective shields of his personal guard.

"Caution wins battles, fear loses them. I shall win this battle for you." Kerk's voice was as coldly angry as the warlord's.

"Is it caution or cowardice that keeps you behind this boulder after I have ordered you to destroy the redoubts?"

"Is it caution or cowardice that puts you here beside me instead of leading your men into battle?"

Temuchin made an animal-like noise deep in his throat and pulled out his sword. Kerk raised the gunpowder bomb, apparently eager to stuff it down the other's throat. Jason drew in a deep breath and stepped between the two furious men.

"The death of either of you would aid the enemy," he said, facing Temuchin for he was fairly sure that Kerk would not strike him from behind. "The sun is already behind the hills, and if the redoubts are not knocked out by dark, it may be too late. Their reinforcements could arrive during the night and that would be the end of this campaign."

Temuchin swung his sword back to cut Jason out of the way, while Kerk clutched his arm to pull him aside, his fingers steel clamps penetrating to the bone. Jason controlled the impulse to howl with pain and said, "Order the rest of the Pyrrans here and have them, and other soldiers, throw rocks at the defended points. They won't do much harm—but the bowmen will not be able to pick out the real bomb throwers." The sword hesitated, the grinding fingers relaxed the slightest amount—and Jason hurried on.

"It is sure death for one man to stand up to the concentrated fire. But if we can divide the fire, we can march up this valley just as fast as we can walk and clean them out. We'll be past the defenses by dark."

For one instant Temuchin's attention wavered back to his army and the darkening sky—and the tension was broken. Winning this battle was the only important thing, and personal intrigues would have to wait. He began to issue orders, unaware of the sword still grasped in his hand. Kerk's taloned grip finally relaxed and Jason stretched his bruised muscles.

The advance could not be stopped now. Stone-throwing figures bobbed up on all sides, and the baffled enemy had no way of telling which one was the lightning hurler. While the nomads just lobbed their stones and darted back to safety, the Pyrrans, with years of grenade-throwing experience, took careful aim and planted their small boulders behind the barricaded walls, breaking more than one skull in the process. They marched forward relentlessly and, one by one, the resisting strong points were demolished.

"We're coming to the end!" Jason shouted, pounding Kerk on the shoulder to get his attention and pointing ahead.

At this place The Slash was less than a hundred meters wide, pinched in by two tall spires of solid rock that rose straight up from the valley floor. Through this narrow gap could be seen the red of the sunset sky—and the plain beyond. The almost vertical walls ended at the spires. Once the horde passed them, it could not be stopped.

As Jason and Kerk pushed forward with a fresh supply of bombs, they realized that most of the soldiers were running back toward them. From up ahead came the shrill rise and fall of the iron horns.

"What is happening?" Kerk asked, grabbing one of the running men. "What do the horns mean?"

"Retreat!" the man said, pointing upward. "Look at that." He pulled free and was gone.

A large boulder bounced down among the fleeing soldiers, squashing one of them like an insect. Jason and Kerk looked up and saw men clambering on the valley's rim high above. They were clearly outlined against the sky, heaving and pulling at a rounded pile.

"On the other side, too!" Jason called out. "They've got boulders heaped up on both sides, ready to be rolled down on our heads. Pull back!" Reluctantly they retreated as more of the stones rumbled down.

Only the fact that this last-resort weapon had never been used before saved the attacking forces. The rocks and boulders had been piled higher generation after generation, until the supporting props were wedged firmly against the cliff edge. Warriors with long rods pushed at them, but they would not budge. Finally, one brave, or fool-hardy, tribesman swung down on a rope and hammered the supports where they sank into the stone. He must have succeeded because in an eyeblink he was gone, swept away by the falling boulders that, for a fleeting instant, appeared to hang suspended in the air before they fell. A short while after this the supports on the opposite cliff gave way as well.

Jason and Kerk ran with the others.

The loss of life was not great, for most of the men had been warned in time. In addition, the narrowness of The Slash at this point acted as a choke, piling up the falling stone behind the gateway higher and higher.

When the last boulder had rattled into silence, The Slash was walled shut, completely plugged by the barrier of rock.

The campaign was obviously lost.

14

"I DO NOT like it," Kerk said. "I do not think that it can be done."

"Kindly keep your doubts to yourself," Jason whispered as they came up to Temuchin. "I'll have enough of a job selling him this in any case. If you can't help, at least stand there and nod your head once in a while as if you agreed with me."

"Madness," Kerk grumbled.

"Greetings, oh warlord," Jason intoned. "I have come bringing aid that will turn this moment of disaster into victory."

If Temuchin heard, he gave no sign. He sat on a boulder with his hands over the pommel of his sword, which stood upright on the ground before him, looking straight ahead at the sealed pass that had stopped his dream of conquest. The last rays of the setting sun lit up the sheer, vertical faces of the towers of rock that formed the gate.

"The pass is now a trap," Jason said. "If we try to climb the rubble blocking it, or clear it away, we will be shot down by the men concealed behind it. Long before we can have forced passage, the reinforcements will have arrived. However, there is one thing that can be done. If we were to stand on the top of the higher spire of rock, on the left there, we could drop the gunpowder bombs down on the enemy, keeping them at bay until your soldiers had climbed the rockfall."

Temuchin's eyes went slowly up the smooth fall of rock to the summit high above. "That stone can not be climbed," he said without turning his head.

Kerk nodded and opened his mouth to agree, then made an oofing sound instead as Jason planted an elbow in the pit of his stomach.

"You are right. Most men cannot climb that rock. But we Pyrrans are mountain men and can climb that tower with ease. Do we have your permission?"

The warlord turned deliberately and examined Jason as though he were more than a little mad. "Begin then. I will watch."

"It must be done during daylight. We will need to see in order to throw the bombs. Then there is special equipment in our saddlebags that we must make ready. Therefore the climb will begin at dawn and by afternoon The Slash will be yours."

They could feel Temuchin's eyes burning into their backs as they returned to the others. Kerk was baffled.

"What equipment are you talking about? None of this makes sense."

"Only because you have never been exposed to accepted rock-climbing techniques. The piece of equipment I will need first is your radio, because I have to call the ship and have the other equipment made. If they work hard, it can be done and delivered before dawn. See that our men set up camp as far from the others as possible. We want to be able to slip away without being noticed."

While the others unrolled the fur sleeping bags and dug the fire pits, Jason used the radio. The *moropes* were arranged in a rough circle while he crouched in the center

140

behind the concealing bulk of their bodies. The duty officer aboard the *Pugnacious* sent a messenger to awaken and call in all the men, then copied down Jason's instructions. There were no complaints or excuses as a war emergency is a normal part of Pyrran life, and delivery of the equipment was promised for well before dawn. Jason listened to a repeat of his instructions, then signed off. He ate some of the hot stew and left orders to be awakened when the completion call came through. It had been a long day, he was on the verge of exhaustion, and tomorrow promised to be even worse. Settling down in his sleeping bag, boots and all, he pulled a flap of fur over his face to keep the ice from forming in his nostrils and fell instantly to sleep.

"Go away," he muttered, and tried to pull away from the clutching hand that was crushing his already well crushed arm.

"Get up," Kerk said. "The call came through ten minutes ago. The launch is leaving now with the cargo and we must ride to meet it. The *moropes* are already saddled." Jason groaned at the thought and sat up. All of the heat was instantly sucked from his body and he began to shiver.

"M-medikit-t," he rattled. "Give me a good jolt of stimulants and painkillers because I have a feeling that it is going to be a very long day."

"Wait here," Kerk said. "I will meet the launch myself."

"I would like to, but I can't. I have to check the items before the launch returns to the ship. Everything must be perfect."

They carried him to his *morope* and put him into the saddle. Kerk took his reins and led the beast while Jason dozed, clutching the pommel so he would not fall. They trotted through the predawn darkness and, by the time they had reached the appointed spot, the medication had taken hold and Jason felt remotely human.

"The launch is touching down," Kerk said, holding the radio to his ear. There was the faintest rumble on the eastern horizon, a sound that would never be heard back at the camp.

"Do you have the flashlight?" Jason asked.

"Of course, wasn't that part of the instructions?" Jason

141

could imagine the big man scowling into the darkness. It was inconceivable for a Pyrran to forget instructions. "It has a photon store of 18,000 lumen-hours, and at full output can put out 1,200 LF."

"Throttle it down, we don't need a tenth of that. The verticapsule is phototropic and has been set to home on any light source twice as radiant as the brightest star—"

"Capsule launched, on this radio bearing, distance approximately ten kilometers."

"Right. It does about 120 an hour wide open so you can turn the light on now on the same bearing. Give it something to look for."

"Wait, the pilot's saying something. Take the light."

Jason took the finger-sized tube and switched it on, turning the intensity ring until a narrow beam of light spiked away into the darkness. He pointed it in the direction of the grounded launch.

"The pilot reports that they had some trouble making a stain take on the nylon rope. It's on now, but they can't guarantee that it will be waterproof, and it is very blotchy."

"The blotchier the better. Just as long as it resembles leather from a distance. And I'm not expecting any rain. Did you hear that?"

A rising hum sounded from the sky and they could make out a faint red light dropping down toward them. A moment later the beam glinted from the silvery hull of the verticapsule and Jason turned down the light's intensity. There was a faint whistle of jets as the meter-long shape came into sight, dropping straight down, slowing as its radar altimeter sensed the ground. When it was low enough, Kerk reached up and threw the landing switch, and it settled with a dying hum to the ground. Jason flipped open the cargo hatch and drew out the coil of brown rope.

"Perfect," he said, handing it to Kerk. He burrowed deeper and produced a steel hammer that had been hand-forged from a single lump of metal. It balanced nicely in his palm: the leather wrappings on the handle gave it a good grip. It had been acid-etched and rubbed with dirt to simulate age.

"What is this?" Kerk asked, pulling a metal spike out of the compartment and turning it over in the light.

"A piton, a solid one. Half of them should be like that,

and half with clips—like this one." He held up a similar spike that had a hole drilled in its broad end through which a ringlike clip had been passed.

"These things mean nothing to me," Kerk said.

"They don't have to." Jason emptied the cargo compartment while he spoke. "I'm climbing the spire and I know how to use them. I only wish that I could take along some of the more modern climbing equipment, but that would give me away at once. If we had any in the ship, which we don't. There are explosive piton setters that will drive a spike into the hardest rock, and instant-adhesive pitons that set in less than a second and the join is tougher than the rock around it. But I'm not using any of them. But I have had this rope wrapped around one of those monofilaments of grown ceramic fiber, the ones we use instead of barbed wire. With a breaking strength of more than 2,000 kilos. But what I have here will get me up the spire. I'll just climb until I run out of handholds, then I'll stop and drive in a piton and climb on it. For overhangs, or any other place where I need a rope, I use the ones with the rings. And these are for use close to the ground." He held up a crude-looking piton marred by hand-forged hammer blows and pitted with age. "All of these are made from bar-steel stock, which is a little rare in this part of the world. So the ones Temuchin and his men will see have been made into artificial antiques. Everything's here. You can tell the launch to take the verticapsule back."

The jets blew sand in their faces as the capsule rose and vanished. Jason held the light while Kerk tied the plaited leather rope to the end of the stained nylon line, then stowed this in the backpack, along with the rest of the equipment that Jason would use during the climb. Behind them, as they rode back to the encampment, the first light of dawn touched the horizon.

When the Pyrrans marched up The Slash, they saw that a desperate battle had been fought during the night. The dam of rubble and rock still sealed the neck of the valley —but now it was sprinkled darkly with corpses. Soldiers slept on the ground, out of bowshot of the enemy above, many of them wounded. A bloodstained nomad, with the

143

totem of the lizard clan on his helm, sat impassively while a fellow clansman cut at the bone shaft of the arrow that had penetrated his arm.

"What happened here?" Jason asked him.

"We attacked at night," the wounded soldier said. "We could not be quiet because the rocks slipped and rolled away while we climbed, and many were hurt in this way. When we were close to the top, the weasels threw bundles of burning grass on our heads and they were above us on the clifftop in the darkness. We could not fight back and only those who were not high on the rocks lived to come down again. It was very bad."

"But very good for us," Kerk said as they moved on. "Temuchin will have lost prestige with this defeat, and we will gain it when we climb the rock. If we can—"

"Don't start the doubting act again," Jason said. "Just stand by at the base here and pretend that you know exactly what is going on."

Jason took off his heavy outer clothing and shivered. Well, he would warm up quickly enough as soon as he started his ascent. From below the tower looked as unclimbable as the side of a spaceship. He was tying the piton hammer's thong around his wrist when Ahankk walked up, his face working as he tried both to sneer and to look dubious at the same time.

"I have been told, jongleur, that you are so stupid you think you can climb straight up rock."

"That is not all you have been told," Jason said, slipping his arms through the pack straps and settling the pack on his back. "Lord Temuchin told you to come here to see what happens. So get comfortable and rest your legs for the moment when you must run to your master with the glad news of my success."

Kerk looked up dubiously at the vertical face of rock, then down at Jason. "Let me climb," he said. "I am stronger than you and in far better condition."

"That you are," Jason agreed. "And as soon as I get to the top, I'll throw down the rope and you can climb up with all the bombs. But you can't go first. Rock climbing is a skilled sport, and you are not going to learn it in a few minutes. Thanks for the offer, but I'm the only one who can do this job. So here we go. I would appreciate a lift so

I can get a grip on that small ledge right over your head."

There was no nonsense about climbing up onto the Pyrran's shoulders. Kerk just bent and seized Jason by the ankles and lifted him straight up into the air. Jason walked his hands up the stone face as he rose and grabbed onto the narrow ledge while Kerk steadied his feet. Then his toes scrabbled and caught on a protruding hump and the climb had begun.

Jason was at least ten meters above the ground before he had to drive his first piton. A good bit of ledge, wide enough to lie down on, was well beyond the reach of his outstretched fingertips. The rock surface here was interlaced with cracks, so he picked a transverse one at the right height before him. The first piton was one of the disguised ones; he jammed it into the crack. Four sharp blows with the hammer wedged it in solidly. Slowly and carefully—it had been a good ten years since he had done any real climbing—he stepped out and eased his weight onto the piton. It held. He straightened his leg, sliding up the rough surface of the rock until he could reach the ledge. Then he pulled himself up to a sitting position and, breathing heavily, looked down at the upturned faces below. All of the soldiers were looking at him now, and even Temuchin had appeared to watch the climb. The enemy was surely taking an interest in what was happening, but the swell of the rock face cut them off from sight and arrowshot. They could come to the edge of the canyon's wall, but they could not reach him unless they climbed the tower as well.

The rock was cold and he had better keep moving.

There was no way to estimate the height accurately, but he thought he must now be at least as high as the rim of the canyon. He had his toes jammed into a wide crack and was trying to drive a piton at an awkward angle off to one side when he heard the shouting below.

He bent as much as he could and called down, "What? I can't hear what you are saying." As he did this an arrow cracked into the rock at the place where his head had been and spun away and fell.

Jason almost fell after it, keeping his grip only by a convulsive clutch at the ribbed surface of the rock. When he turned his head, he saw a weasel tribesman hanging from a leather strap that was tied tightly about his body. He had a second arrow notched and ready to fire. The men holding the other end of the strap were out of sight on the rim of The Slash, but by lowering the bowman below the bulging outcropping they had put him within bowshot of Jason.

The warrior carefully drew the arrow back to the point of his jaw and took aim. The hammer was tied by its thong to Jason's wrist so he would not lose it, but he still clutched the piton in his left hand. With a reflexive motion, he hurled it at the bowman. The blunt end caught him in the shoulder. It did not injure him, but it deflected his aim enough so that the second arrow missed as well. He pulled a third from his belt and notched it to the bowstring.

Down below the soldiers were also shooting their bows, but the range was long and the overhead aim difficult. One arrow, almost spent, sank into the bowman's thigh, but he ignored it.

Jason let go of the hammer and took out a piton. It was tempered steel, well weighted and needle sharp. And he had had one try already so he knew the range. Taking the pointed end in his fingertips he drew well back beyond his head, then threw it with all the strength of his arm.

The point caught the bowman in the side of the neck and sank deep. He let go of his bow, scratched for the weapon with his fingers, shuddered and died. His body vanished from sight as the others pulled him up.

Someone had quieted the men below and he heard Kerk's voice cutting through the sudden silence.

"Hold on and brace yourself!" he shouted.

Jason looked down slowly and saw that the Pyrran had moved back from the base of the cliff and was holding one of their bombs, bent over and lighting it. Frantically, Jason kicked his toes in farther and, making fists of both hands, he jammed them deep into a vertical crack in the stone face.

Below him, the soldiers retreated from the base of the cliff. The foreshortened figure of Kerk reached back and back, until his knuckles appeared to be touching the ground. Then, in a single, spasmodic contraction of all his muscles, he hurled the bomb almost straight up into the air.

For a heart-stopping instant Jason thought it was coming right at him—then he realized it was going off to one side. It seemed to slow as it reached the summit of its arc, before it disappeared behind the curve of rock. Jason pushed hard against the cold stone.

The boom of the explosion was transmitted to him through the stone, a shuddering vibration. Fragments of rock and bodies blew out into space behind him and he knew his flank was safe. Kerk would be ready if the same trick were tried again. Yet there was still a feeling of unease."

"Kerk!" Jason shouted. "The piton!" He spoke in Pyrran. "What happened to the piton I dropped? If Temuchin should see it . . ."

One glimpse would be enough to reveal that they were off-worlders. The nomads were familiar enough with the appearance of alien artifacts.

One, two thudding heartbeats of time Jason waited before Kerk called back to him.

"All . . . right. . . . I saw it drop . . . picked it up while they were all looking at you. Are you hurt?"

"Fine," Jason whispered, then drew a deep breath. "Fine!" he shouted. "I'm going on now."

After this it was just work. Twice Jason had to sling a loop of rope through the carabiner of a piton and sit in it to rest. His strength was giving out and he had used the most potent stimulants in the medikit by the time he reached the foot of a chimney that went right to the top of the tower. It looked to be about ten meters high and the two faces appeared to be parallel all the way up.

"One last try," he said, spitting on his hands and instantly regretting it as the saliva chilled and froze. He brushed the ice from his palms and took off the pack. The less weight, the better; even the hammer had to be left behind now. He piled the discarded items at the foot of the chimney and slung the coil of rope around his neck so that it rested on his chest.

Wedging his back against one wall he walked up the other until his body was parallel to the ground, held up by the friction of his shoulders and his feet. He pushed higher with his arms, then walked upward with his feet. Centimeter by centimeter he worked his way up the chimney.

Before he reached the top he knew he would not make it.

Yet, at the same time, he knew he had to make it. Going back down would be just as hard as keeping on upward. And if he fell, he would break at least an arm or a leg at the foot of the chimney. Where he would simply lie and die of thirst. There was no chance of anyone else's getting up here to help him. It would be better to keep on.

With infinite slowness the sky appeared above, closer and closer, and slower and slower as the strength ebbed from his limbs.

When he finally reached the spot where his toes were actually at the lip of the rock, he had no strength left to pull himself over the edge. For a few seconds he rested, took a deep breath and straightened his legs. He twisted as he did so and clutched at the crumbling edge of rock. For a moment of time he hung there, neither falling nor able to pull himself out of the chimney. Then, ever so slowly, he pulled and scraped with bloody fingertips until he dragged himself out and lay exhausted on the tilted summit of the pinnacle.

The top was amazingly small; he saw that as he lay gasping for air. No bigger than a large-sized bed. When he was able to, he crawled to the edge and waved at the waiting men below. They saw him and a ragged and spontaneous cheer went up.

Was there anything to cheer about? He went to the far side and looked, moving back as the waiting bowmen on the cliff top below fired at him. Only two arrows rose high enough to hit him, but these were badly aimed. He looked again and saw the enemy position spread out like a model below him. Everything was visible and within easy range, both the men on the rim of The Slash and the rows of bowmen protecting the top of the rockslide.

He had done it.

"Good man, Jason," he said aloud. "You're a credit to any world."

Sitting cross-legged, he made a large loop in the end of the line and passed it around the summit of the rock itself, making an immovable anchor. Then he let the leather-tipped end over the edge and paid it out slowly, until a signaling tug told him that it had reached the ground. He shortened the rope with a quickly knotted sheepshank and gave the agreed upon signal—three tugs on the line—to show that it was secured. Then he sat down to wait.

Only when the rope began to jerk violently and stand out from the cliff did he get up. Kerk was right below, looking unwinded and fresh, with an immense load of bombs slung on his back. He had taken the rope in both hands and walked straight up the face of the cliff.

"Can you reach down to help me over the edge of the cliff?" Kerk asked.

"Absolutely. Just don't squeeze or break anything."

Jason lay face down, with the rock rim in his armpit, and reached over. Kerk let go with one hand and they seized each other's wrists in an acrobat's hold. Jason did not try to pull—he probably could not have lifted Kerk's weight if he had tried—but instead he spread-eagled and anchored himself as well as he could against the stone. Kerk pulled himself up, threw an arm over the edge, then heaved his body over.

"Very good," he said, looking down at the enemy below. "They do not stand a chance. I have extra microgrenades that we can use. Shall we begin?"

"You're letting me throw out the first bomb of the season? How nice."

As the explosions roared and rumbled into a continuous thunder, Temuchin's army shouted a victorious echo and started up the rocky slope. The battle was decided and would soon be won, and after it, the war would be won as well.

Jason sat down and watched Kerk happily bombing the natives below.

This part of the plan was complete. If the next step worked as well, the Pyrrans would have their mines and their planet. *Their* last battle would be won.

Jason sincerely hoped so. He was getting very tired.

15

Strike like lightning, magic thunder
Slew the weasels, cleansed the mountains.
Piled high, the thumbs of conquest
Reached above a tall man's head.
Then the word of strangers coming
To his land reached Lord Temuchin.
With sword and bow and fearless army
Rode he out to slay invaders . . .

from THE SONG OF TEMUCHIN

Jason dinAlt reined his *morope* to a stop at the top of the broad slope and searched for a path down through the tumbled boulders. The wind, damp and cold, funneled up through this single gap in the high cliffs, struck him full in the face. Far below, the ocean was gray steel, flecked with the spray-blown tops of waves. The sky was dark, cloud-covered from horizon to horizon, and somewhere out to sea thunder rumbled heavily.

A faintly marked path was visible, threading down the rock-covered slope; Jason spurred his mount forward. Once he had started down he saw that the path was well-worn and old. The nomads must come here regularly, for salt perhaps. An aerial survey from the spaceship had shown that this was the only spot for thousands of kilometers where there was a break in the palisade of cliffs. As he descended, the air became a little warmer, but the dampness after the dust-dry plateau cut into him. A final turn brought him out in a circular bay, with great cliffs rising on both sides and a beach of black sand below. Two small boats were drawn up on the shore with yellow cloth tents set up beside them. Farther out in the bay a squat two-master, with a smoke-stained funnel aft, lay with furled sails, swinging at anchor. Jason's approach was seen and, from the knot of men around the boats, a tall figure emerged and strode purposefully across the sand. Jason halted the *morope* and slid down to meet him.

"That's a great outfit you're wearing, Rhes," he said as he shook the other man's hand.

"No more exotic than yours," the Pyrran said, smiling and running his fingers through the purple ruffles that covered his chest. He wore crotch-high boots of yellow suede and a polished helmet with a golden spike. It was most impressive. "This is what the well-dressed Master Merchant of Ammh wears," he added.

"From the reports I hear that you made out very well in the lowlands."

"I've never enjoyed myself more. Ammh is basically an agrarian society that is working very hard to enter a primitive machine age. The classes are completely separate, with the merchant and the military at the top, along with a small priest class to keep the peasants quiet. I had the capital to enter the merchant class and I made the most of it. The operation is going so well that it is self-financing now. I have a warehouse in Camar, the seaport closest to the barrier mountains, and I have just been waiting for the word to sail north. Would you care for a glass of wine?"

"And some food. Trot out your best for me."

They had reached the open-sided tent which contained a trestle table loaded with bottles and cuts of smoked meat. Rhes picked up a long-necked green bottle and handed it to Jason. "Try this," he said. "A six-year-old vintage, very good. I'll get a knife to cut the seal."

"Don't bother," Jason said, cracking the neck off the bottle with a sharp blow against the edge of the table. He drank deeply from the golden wine that bubbled out, then wiped his mouth on the back of his sleeve. "I'm a barbarian, remember? This will convince your guards of my rough-shod character." He nodded toward the soldiers who stood about, frowning and fingering their weapons.

"You've developed some vile habits," Rhes said, wiping the broken neck of the bottle with a cloth before he poured a glassful for himself. "What's the plan?"

Jason chewed hungrily at a fatty chop. "Temuchin is on

the way here with an army. Not a big one—most of the tribes went home after the weasels were wiped out. But all of them first swore fealty to him and agreed to join him whenever he ordered. When he heard about your landing here, he called in the nearest tribes and started his march. He's about a day away now, but Kerk and the Pyrrans are camped right across his trail. We should join up tonight. I rode on here alone just to check the setup before contact is made."

"Does everything meet your approval?"

"Just about. I would keep your armed thugs close by, but don't make it look so obvious. Let a couple of them lounge around and stuff the rest into a tent. Do you have the trade goods we talked about?"

"Everything. Knives, steel arrowheads, wooden shafts for arrows, iron pots, plus a lot more. Sugar, salt, some spices. They should find something they like out of this lot."

"That's our hope." Jason looked unhappily at the empty bottle, then tossed it away.

"Would you like another one?" Rhes asked.

"Yes, but I'm not going to take it. No contact with the enemy—not yet. I'll get back to the camp so I can be there when we have the meet with Temuchin. This is the one that counts. We have to get the tribes on our side, start peaceful trade and squeeze the warlord out into the cold. Keep a bottle on ice until I get back."

By the time Jason's mount had climbed up to the high plains again the sky was lower and darker, and the wind threw a fine shrapnel of sleet against the back of his neck. He crouched low and used his spurs to move the *morope* at its best speed. By late afternoon he came up to the Pyrran camp just as they were starting to move out.

"You're just in time," Kerk said, riding over to join him. "I have the ship's launch up high in a satellite orbit, tracking Temuchin's force. Earlier this afternoon he turned off the direct route to the beach and headed for Hell's Doorway. He'll probably stop there for the night."

"I never thought of him as being much of a religious man."

"I am sure that he isn't," Kerk said. "But he is a good enough leader to keep his men happy. This pit, or whatever it is, appears to be one of the few holy places they have. Supposed to be a backdoor leading directly to hell. Temuchin will make a sacrifice there."

"It's as good a place as any to meet him. Let's ride."

The dark afternoon blended imperceptibly into evening as the sky pressed down and the wind hurled granular blizzard snow at them. It collected in the folds of their clothing and on the *moropes'* fur until they were all streaked and coated with it. It was almost fully dark before they came to the *camachs* of Temuchin's followers. There were welcome shouts of greetings from all sides as they rode toward the large *camach* where the chieftains were meeting. Kerk and Jason dismounted and pushed by the guards at the entrance flap. The circle of men turned to look as they came in. Temuchin glared pure hatred at them.

"Who is this that dares come uninvited to Temuchin's meeting of his captains?"

Kerk drew himself up and gave as well as he had received. "Who is this Temuchin who would bar Kerk of the Pyrrans, conqueror of The Slash, from a meeting of the chiefs of the plains?"

The battle was joined and everyone there knew it. The absolute silence was broken only by the rustle of wind-driven snow against the outside of the *camach*.

Temuchin was the first warlord to have brought all of the tribes together under one banner. Yet he ruled nothing without the agreement of his tribal chieftains. Some of them were already displeased with the severity of his orders and would have preferred a new warlord—or no warlord at all. They followed the contest with close attention.

"You fought well at The Slash," Temuchin said. "As did all here. We greet you and you may now leave. What we do here today does not concern that battle nor does it concern you."

"Why?" Kerk asked with icy calmness, seating himself at the same time. "What are you trying to conceal from me?"

"You accuse me . . ." Temuchin was white with anger, his hand on his sword.

"I accuse no one." Kerk yawned broadly. "You seem to accuse yourself. You meet in secret, you refuse a chieftain entrance, you attempt insult rather than speaking the truth. I ask you again what you conceal?"

"It is a matter of small importance. Some lowlanders have arrived on our shores, to invade, to build cities. We will destroy them."

"Why? They are harmless traders," Kerk said.

"Why?" Temuchin was burning with anger now and could not stand still; he paced back and forth. "Have you never heard of 'The Song of the Freemen'?"

"As well as you have—or better. The song says to destroy the buildings of those who will trap us. Are there buildings to be destroyed?"

"No, but they will come next. Already the lowlanders have put up tents—"

One of the chieftains broke in, singing a line from "The Song of the Freemen":

"Knowing no home, other than our tents."

Temuchin controlled his rage and ignored the interruption. The words of the song were against him, but he knew where the truth lay.

"These traders are like the point of the sword that makes but a scratch. They are in tents and they trade today—but soon they will be ashore with bigger tents, then buildings in order to trade better. First the tip of the sword, then the entire blade to run us through and destroy us. They must be wiped out now."

What Temuchin said was absolutely true. It was very important that the other chieftains should not realize that. Kerk was silent for an instant and Jason stepped into the gap.

" 'The Song of Freemen' must be our guide in this matter. This is the song that tells us—"

"Why are you here, jongleur?" Temuchin said in a voice of stern command. "I see no other jongleurs or common soldiers. You may leave."

Jason opened his mouth, but could think of nothing to say. Temuchin was unarguably right. Jason, he thought, you should have kept your big mouth shut. He bowed to the warlord, and as he did he whispered to Kerk:

"I'll be close by and I'll listen in on the dentiphone. If I can think of anything that will help, I will tell you."

Kerk did not turn around, but he murmured agreement and his voice was transmitted clearly to the tiny radio in Jason's mouth. After this, there was nothing Jason could do except leave.

Bad luck. He had hoped to be in on the showdown. As he pushed through the flap, one of the guards stationed there bent to lace it behind him. The other one dropped his lance.

Jason looked at it surprised, even as the man reached out with both hands and grabbed him by the wrists. What was this?! Jason twisted upward with his forearms against the other's thumbs, to break the simple hold, while at the same time aiming a knee at the man's groin as a note of disapproval. But before he could free himself or connect, the guard behind him slipped a leather strap over his head and jerked it tight about his throat.

Jason could neither fight nor cry out. He writhed and struggled ineffectively as he quickly slipped into black unconsciousness.

16

SOMEONE WAS GRINDING snow into Jason's face, forcing it into his nostrils and mouth, effectively dragging him back to consciousness. He coughed and spluttered, pushing himself away from the offending hands. When he had wiped the snow from his eyes, he looked around, blinking, trying to place himself.

He was kneeling between two of Temuchin's men. Their swords were drawn and ready, and one of them held a guttering torch. It illuminated a small patch of drifted snow and the black lip of a chasm. Red-lit snowflakes rushed by him and vanished into this pit of darkness.

"Do you know this man?" a voice asked, and Jason recognized it as Temuchin's. Two men appeared out of the night and stood before him.

"I do, great Lord Temuchin," the second man said. "It is the other-world man from the great flying thing, the one who was captured and escaped."

Jason looked closer at the muffled face and, as the

155

torch flared up, he recognized the sharp nose and sadistic smile of Oraiel, the jongleur.

"I never saw this person before. He is a liar," Jason said, ignoring the hoarseness of his voice and the pain in his throat when he spoke.

"I remember him when he was captured, great lord, and later he attacked and beat me. You saw him yourself there."

"Yes, I did." Temuchin stepped forward and looked down at Jason's upturned face, his own cold and impassive. "Of course. He is the one. That is why he looked familiar."

"What are these lies . . ." Jason said, struggling to his feet.

Temuchin seized him by the forearms in an implacable grip, pushing him backward until his heels were on the crumbling edge of the abyss.

"Tell the truth now, whoever you are. You stand at the edge of Hell's Doorway and in one moment you shall be hurled down it. You cannot escape. But I might let you go if you tell me the truth."

As he talked, Temuchin bent Jason's body back, farther and farther over the blackness, until only the grip on his wrists prevented him from falling. Jason could not see the warlord's face: it was a black outline against the torches. Yet he knew there was no hope of mercy there. This was the end. The best he could do now was to protect the Pyrrans.

"Release me and I shall tell you the truth. I am from another world. I came here alone to help you. I found the jongleur Jason, and he was dying, so I took his name. He had been gone from his people many years and they no longer remembered him. And I have helped you. Release me and I will help you more."

A weak voice, filled with static, buzzed in his head. "Jason, is that you? Kerk here. Where are you?" The dentiphone was still operating—he had a chance.

"Why are you here?" Temuchin asked. "Are you helping the lowlanders to bring their cities to our lands?"

"Release me. Do not drop me now into Hell's Doorway and I will tell you."

Temuchin hesitated a long moment before he spoke again.

156

"You are a liar. Everything you say is a lie. I do not know what to believe." His head turned and for an instant the torchlight lit the humorless smile on his lips.

"I release you," he said, and opened his hands.

Jason clawed at empty air, tried to twist so he could clutch at the cliff's edge, but he could do nothing. He fell into the blackness.

A rush of air.

A blow on his shoulder, his back. Then he was scraping along the side of the cliff, struggling to keep his face and hands away from the abrasive dirt and stone. The cliffside tore at the leather of his garments as he plummeted down the outward-slanting surface.

Then it ended and he fell free in the blackness once again. Falling for an unmeasurable moment of time, seconds or minutes—forever—until a crushing impact enfolded him.

He did not die, and that surprised him very much. He wiped something from his face and realized that it was snow. A snowbank, a drift, here at the bottom of Hell's Doorway. A snowbank in hell and he had fallen into it.

"Where there's life, there's still hope, Jason," he told himself unconvincingly. What hope was there at the bottom of this inaccessible pit? Kerk and the Pyrrans would get him out, that was a morale-building hope. Yet, even as he thought this, his tongue contacted a jagged end of metal in his mouth. With restored fear he groped out the crushed remains of the dentiphone. Some time during the fall, he had unknowingly ground it between his teeth and destroyed it.

"You're on your own again, Jason," he said aloud, and did not enjoy in the slightest the tiny sound of his voice in the immense blackness. What were his assets? He floundered about in the drift until he could reach back for his medikit. It was gone. Well, his wallet was still on his belt, though his knife was gone from his boot. His fingers searched through the assorted junk in the wallet until they touched an unfamiliar tube. What? The photon-store flashlight, of course. Dropped in here and forgotten since the night they had picked up the climbing equipment.

But was it broken? The way his luck was running it probably was. He switched it on and groaned aloud when nothing happened. Then he turned the intensity ring and the brilliant beam slashed through the darkness. Light! Even though his situation was not materially changed, Jason felt a lift in his morale. He broadened the beam and flashed it around his prison. The air was still and the snowflakes fell silently through the light and vanished. Snow covered the flat valley floor below and piled in drifts against the walls. Black rock rose up on both sides, pushed out above his head where a ledge of rock projected. The sky was invisible, cut off by the jutting rock. He must have slid down that rocky angle and been shot off like a projectile into this snowbank. Pure chance had saved him.

There was a moaning cry and something black plunged down from above and through the beam of light, striking the valley bottom no more than ten meters from Jason.

The vertical rocks there were coated with only a thin layer of snow and the man had struck full across them. His eyes were open and staring, a trickle of blood ran from the gaping mouth. It was his betrayer, the jongleur Oraiel.

"What's this? Temuchin eliminating eyewitnesses? That's not like him." The mouth still gaped open but Oraiel had finished forever with speaking.

Jason floundered out of his drift and started across the floor of the narrow valley. The ground was smooth in the center, smooth and very flat. He did not consider why until there was an ominous creaking beneath his feet. Even as he tried to throw himself backward the ice broke, splintering and cracking in every direction, and he fell into the dark waters beneath.

The sudden shock of the frigid water almost drove the air from his lungs, but he clamped his mouth shut, sinking his teeth hard into his lower lip. At the same time his fingers tightened convulsively on the flashlight. Without this he would not be able to find the opening in the ice again.

Almost at the same instant his feet touched the rocky bottom, the water was not deep, and he kicked upward. The light shone on a mirror above as he rose and his hand went out to press, palm to palm, against his imaged hand. It was ice, solid and unbroken above him. Only when he felt his fingers being dragged across its surface did he realize that he was being pulled swiftly along by a current. The hole in the ice must already be far behind him.

If Jason dinAlt had been prone to despair, this was the moment when he would have died. Trapped beneath the ice at the bottom of this inaccessible valley, this was indeed the time to give up. He never considered it. He held the burning lungful of air; he tried to swim to the side where he could get some footing, perhaps press up through the ice; he waved the light upward looking for a break.

The current was too swift. It threw him numbingly against the rocks, then hurtled him back into the swift-flowing current. He pointed down stream and kicked to stay in the center, looking down at the smooth rocks that flew by an arm's length beneath his face.

The water was cold; it numbed his skin and carried him along with it. But it was the fire in his lungs that could not be ignored. Logically he knew that he had enough oxygen in his body cells and his bloodstream to live for many minutes. The breathing reflex in his chest was not interested in logic. *Dying!* it screamed. *Air, breathe,* until he could deny it no longer. Numbly he drifted upward to the mirrored surface and broke through into blackness and sucked in a shuddering, life-giving breath.

It took a long time for the reality of what had occurred to penetrate his numbed senses. He dragged himself to a dark, stony shore and lay half in and half out of the water like some form of beached marine life. Moving seemed completely out of the question, but as the shuddering cold bit deep he realized it was either that or die here. And where was *here?* With pained slowness he pulled himself clear of the water and moved the light up the rocky wall, across the rock above and back down the rock to the water again. No snow? The meaning of this forced through his chilled and sluggish synapses.

"A cave."

It was obvious enough by hindsight. The narrow valley, Hell's Doorway, must have been cut by water, slowly eroded out through the centuries by the small stream. It had no visible outlet because it plunged underground—and it had taken him with it. That meant he wasn't finished yet. The water had to have an outlet, and if it did he would find it. For a moment he considered the fact that it might sink lower and lower into the rock strata and vanish, but he swiftly rejected this defeatist idea.

"Carry on!" he shouted aloud as he stumbled to his feet, and the echoes called back "On . . . on . . . on. . . ."

"Good idea, on, onwards. Just what I shall do."

He shivered and squelched forward through the fine sand at the edge of the water, and the next thing he saw were the footprints emerging from the stream and going on ahead of him.

Was someone else here?! The footprints were sharp and clear, obviously recently made. There must be an entrance to these caverns that was well known. All he had to do was follow the footprints and he would be out. And as long as he kept walking he would not freeze in his sodden clothing. The cave air was cool, but not so cold as the plateau outside.

When the trail left the sand beside the stream and ventured into an adjoining cavern, it became more difficult to follow, but not impossible. Small stalagmites growing from the limestone floor had been kicked down, and there were occasional marks gouged into the soft stone of the walls. The tunnels branched and one went back to the water where it ended abruptly at a rocky bank. The shore was gone and the water filled the cave here, coming close to the smooth ceiling. Jason retraced his steps and picked up the trail again at the next branch.

It was a long walk.

Jason rested once and fell asleep without realizing it. He awoke, shivering uncontrollably, and forced himself to go on. As far as he knew, the watch concealed in his belt buckle was still operating, but he never looked at it. Somehow the measuring of time could not be considered in these endless, timeless caverns.

Walking down one of them, no different from all the others, he found the man he had been following. He was sleeping on the cave floor ahead, a barbarian, in furs very much like Jason's.

"Hello," he called in the in-between tongue, then fell silent as he came closer. The sleep was for eternity and the man had been dead a very long time. Years, centuries perhaps, in these dry, cold, and bacteria-free caverns. There was no way to tell. His flesh and skin were brown and mummified, leather lips shriveled back from yellow teeth. One outstretched hand lay, pointing ahead, a knife just

160

beyond the splayed fingers. When Jason picked it up, he saw that it was tarnished only by the thinnest patina of rust.

What Jason did next was not easy, but it was essential for survival. With careful motions he removed the fur outer garments from the corpse. It crackled and rustled when he was forced to move the stiff limbs, but made no other protest. When he had the furs, he moved farther down the cavern, stripped himself bare and donned the dry clothes. There was no repugnance; this was survival.

He stretched his own clothes out to dry, bunched the fur under his head, turned the light to a dim yellow glow—he could not bear the thought of total darkness—and fell instantly into a troubled sleep.

17

"THEY SAY that if everything is the same for a long time, you can't tell how long the time is because everything is the same. So I wonder how long I have been down here." He trudged a few steps more and considered it. "A long time, I guess."

The cavern branched ahead and he made a careful mark with the knife, at shoulder height, before taking the right-hand turning. This tunnel dead-ended at the water, a familiar occurrence, and he knelt and drank his stomach full before turning back. At the junction he scratched the slash that meant "water" and turned down the other branch.

"One thousand eight hundred and three . . . one thousand eight hundred and four . . ." He had to count every third step of his left foot now because the number was so large. It was also meaningless, but it gave him something to say and he found the sound of his voice to be less trying than the everlasting silence.

At least his stomach had stopped hurting. The rumblings

and cramps had been very annoying in the beginning, but that had passed. There was always enough water to drink, and he should have thought of measuring the time by the number of notches he took in his belt.

"I've seen you before, you evil crossway you." He spat dryly in the direction of the three marks on the wall at the junction. Then he scratched a fourth below them with the knife. He would not be coming back here again. Now he knew the right sequence of turns to take in the maze ahead.

He hoped.

"Cuglio, he only has one sphere. . . . Fletter has two but very queer. . . . Harmill . . ." He pondered as he marched. Just what was it that Harmill had? It escaped him now. He had been singing all the old marching songs that he remembered, but for some reason he was beginning to forget the words.

Some reason! Hah. He laughed dirtily at himself. The reason was obvious. He was getting very hungry and very tired. A human body can live a long time with water and without food. But how long can it go on walking?

"Time to rest?" he asked himself.

"Time to rest," he answered himself.

In a little while. This tunnel was slanted downward and there was the smell of water ahead. He was getting very good with his nose lately. Many times there was sand next to the water on which he could sleep, and this was far better than the bare rock. There was very little flesh over his bones now and they pressed through and hurt.

Good. There was sand here, a luxurious, wide band of it. The water was wider and must be deeper, almost a pool. It still tasted the same. He squirmed out a hollow in the unmarked sand, turned the flashlight out, put it into his pouch and went to sleep.

He used to leave it on when he slept, but this did not seem to make any difference any more.

As always, he slept briefly, woke up, then slept again. But there was something wrong. With his eyes open he lay staring up into the velvety darkness. Then he turned to look at the water.

162

Far out. Deep down. Faint, ever so faint, was a shimmer of blue light.

For a long time he lay there thinking about it. He was tired and weak, starved, probably feverish. Which meant he was probably imagining it. The dying man's fantasy, the mirage for the thirsty. He closed his eyes and dozed, yet when he looked again the light was still there. What could it mean?

"I should do something about this," he said, and turned his flashlight on. In the greater light the glow in the water was gone. He stood the flashlight up in the sand and took out his knife. The tip was still sharp. He raked it along the inside of his arm, drawing a shallow slice that oozed thick drops of blood.

"That hurts!" he said, then, "That's better."

The sudden pain had jarred him from his lethargy, released adrenalin into his bloodstream and forced him into unaccustomed alertness.

"If there's light down there, it must be an exit to the outside. It has to be. And if it is, it may be my only chance to get out of this trap. Now. While I still think I can make it."

After that, he shut up and took breath after breath, filling his lungs again and again until his head began to swim with hyperventilation. Then, with a last breath, he turned the light to full intensity and put the end in his mouth so that he could direct it forward by tilting his head. One, two, hands together and dive.

The water was a cold shock, but he had expected that. He dove deep and swam as hard as he could toward the spot where he had seen the light. The water was wonderfully transparent. Rock, just solid rock on the other side of the pool. Perhaps lower then. The water soaked into his clothes and helped pull him down, almost to the bottom, where a ledge cut across the pool. Below it, the current quickened and moved outward. Headfirst, pushing against the rock above, he went under, bumped along a short channel and was in the clear again.

Above him now was more light, far above, inaccessible. He kicked and stroked but it seemed to come no closer. The flashlight fell from his mouth and spun down to oblivion. Higher, higher. Though he was going toward the light, it seemed to be getting darker. In a panic he thrashed his arms, although they seemed to be pushing against mercury or some medium far thicker than water. One hand struck something hard and round. He seized it and pulled and his head was thrust above the surface of the water.

For the first minute all he could do was hang from the tree root and suck in great, rasping breaths of air. When his head began to clear, he saw that he was at the edge of a pond almost completely surrounded by trees and undergrowth. Behind him the pool ended at the base of a towering cliff that stretched upward until it vanished in the haze and clouds above. This was the outlet of the underground stream from the plateau.

He was in the lowlands.

Pulling himself out of the water was an effort, and when he was out, he just lay on the grass and steamed until some small fraction of his strength had returned. The sight of some berries on the nearby bushes finally stirred him into motion. There were not many of them, which was probably for the best, for even these few caused racking stomach pains after he had wolfed them down. He lay on the grass then, his face stained with purple juice, and wondered what to do next. He slept, without wanting to, and when he awoke, his head was clearer.

"Defense. Every man's hand turned against the other. The first local who sees me will probably try to brain me just to get these antique furs that I'm wearing. Defense."

His knife had vanished along with his flashlight, so a sharp fragment of split rock had to do. A straight sapling was raw material and he worried it off close to the ground with the chip of stone. Taking off the branches was easier, and within the hour he had a rough but usable quarterstaff. It served first as a walking stick as he hobbled eastward on a forest path that appeared to go in the right direction.

Toward evening, when his head was starting to swim again, he met a stranger on the path. A tall, erect man in semimilitary uniform, armed with a bow and a very efficient-looking halberd. The man snapped some questions at Jason in an unknown language, in answer to which Jason simply shrugged and made mumbling noises. He tried to appear innocent and weak, which was easy enough to do. With his drawn skin, tangled beard and filthy furs, he certainly

164

couldn't have looked very ominous or appetizing. The stranger must have thought so too, for he did not use his bow and came forward with his halberd only indifferently at the defense.

Jason knew that he had only one good—or halfhearted—blow in him, and he had to make it count. This efficient looking young man would eat him alive if he missed.

"Umble, umble," Jason muttered, and shrank back, both hands on the length of stick.

"Frmblebrmble!" the man said, shaking his halberd menacingly as he came close.

Jason pushed down with his right hand, pivoting the quarterstaff with his left so that the end whipped up. Then he lunged it forward into the other's midriff in the region of the solar plexus ganglion. The stranger let out a single, mighty whoosh of air and folded, unmoving, to the ground.

"My fortunes change!" Jason chortled as he fell on the other's bulging purse. Food perhaps? Saliva dampened his mouth as he tore it open.

18

RHES WAS in his inner office, finishing up with his bookkeeping, when he heard the loud shouts in the courtyard. It sounded as though someone were trying to force his way in. He ignored it; the other two Pyrrans had gone, and he had a lot of work to finish up before he left. His guard, Riclan, was a good man and knew how to take care of himself. He would turn any unwanted visitors away. The shouting stopped suddenly, and a moment later there was a noise that sounded suspiciously like Riclan's armor and weapons falling onto the cobbles.

For two days Rhes had not slept, and there was still much to be done before he went away for good. His temper was therefore not of the best. It is very unhealthy to be around a Pyrran when he feels this way. When the door opened, he stood prepared to destroy the interloper.

Preferably with his bare hands so that he could hear the bones crunch. A man with an ugly black beard, wearing the uniform of a freelance soldier, entered, and Rhes flexed his fingers and stepped forward.

"What's the trouble? You look ready to kill me," the soldier said in fluent Pyrran.

"Jason!" Rhes was across the room and pounding his friend on the back with excitement.

"Easy," Jason said, escaping the embrace and dropping onto the couch. "A Pyrran greeting can maim, and I haven't been feeling that good lately."

"We thought you were dead! What happened?"

"I'll be happy to explain, but would prefer to do it over food and drink. And I would like to hear a report myself. The last time I heard about Felicitian politics was just before I was pushed off a cliff. How does the trade go?"

"It doesn't," Rhes said glumly, taking meat and bread from a locker and fishing a cobwebbed bottle of wine from its straw bed. "After you were killed—or we thought you were killed—everything came to pieces. Kerk heard you on his dentiphone and almost destroyed his *morope* getting there. But he was too late—you had gone over the edge of Hell's Doorway. There was some jongleur who had betrayed you, and he tried to accuse Kerk of being an off-worlder as well. Kerk kicked him off the cliff before he could say very much. Temuchin was apparently just as angry as Kerk and the whole thing almost blew up right there. But you were gone and that was that. Kerk felt the most he could do for you was to try and complete your plans."

"Did you?"

"I'm sorry to report that we failed. Temuchin convinced most of the tribal leaders that they should fight, not trade. Kerk aided us, but it was a lost cause. I eventually had to retreat back here. I'm closing out this operation, leaving it in good enough shape for my assistants to carry on, and the Pyrran 'tribe' is on its way back to the ship. This plan is over, and if we can't come up with another one, we have agreed to return to Pyrrus."

"You can't!" Jason said in the loudest mumble he could manage around the mouthful of food.

"We have no choice. Now tell me, please, how did you

get here? We had men down in Hell's Doorway later the same night. They found no trace of you at all, though there were plenty of other corpses and skeletons. They thought you must have gone through the ice and that your body had been swept away."

"Indeed swept away, but not as a body. I hit a snowbank when I landed and I would have been waiting for you, cold but alive, if I had not fallen through the ice as you guessed. The stream leads to a series of caverns. I had a light and more patience than I realized. It was nasty, but I finally came out below the cliffs in this country. I knocked a number of citizens on the head and had an adventurous trip to reach you here."

"A lucky arrival. Tomorrow would have been too late. The ship's launch is to pick me up just after dark and I have a ten-kilometer row to reach the rendezvous point."

"Well, you've got a second oar now. I'm ready to go anytime after I get this food and drink under my belt."

"I'll radio about your arrival so that word can be relayed to Kerk and the others."

They left quietly in one of Rhes's own boats and reached the rocky offshore islet before the sun touched the horizon. Rhes chopped a hole in the boat's planking and they put in some heavy rocks. It sank nicely, and after that, all they could do was wait and admire the guano deposits and listen to the cries of the disturbed seabirds until the launch picked them up.

The flight was a brief one after the pilot, Clon, had nodded recognition at Jason—which was about all the enthusiastic Pyrran welcome he expected. At the grounded *Felicity*, the off watch was asleep, and the on watch, at their duty stations, so Jason saw no one. He preferred it this way because he was still tired from his journey. The Pyrran tribesmen were to arrive some time the following day and socializing could wait until then.

His cabin was just as he had left it, with the expensive library leering at him metallically from one corner. What had ever prompted him to buy it in the first place? A complete waste of money. He kicked at it as he passed, but his foot only skidded off the polished metal ovoid.

"Useless," he said, and stabbed the *on* button. "What good are you, after all?"

"Is that a question?" the library intoned. "If so, re-state and indicate the precise meaning of 'good' in this context."

"Big mouth. All talk now—but where were you when I needed you?"

"I am where I am placed. I answer whatever questions are asked of me. Your question is therefore meaningless."

"Don't insult your superiors, machine. That is an order."

"Yes, sir."

"That's better. I maketh and I can breaketh just as well."

Jason dialed a strong drink from the wall dispenser and flopped into the armchair. The library flickered its little lights and hummed electronically to itself. He drank deep, then addressed the machine.

"I'll bet you don't think much of my plan to lick the natives and open the mine?"

"I do not know your plan; therefore I cannot give a judged opinion."

"Well, I'm not asking you. I bet you think that you could think of a better plan yourself?"

"In which area do you wish a plan?"

"In the area of changing a culture, that's where. But I'm not asking."

"Culture-changing references will be found under 'history' and 'anthropology.' If you are not asking, I withdraw the reference."

Jason sipped and brooded, and finally spoke.

"Well, I am asking. Tell me about cultures."

Jason pressed the *off* button and settled back in his chair. The lights went out on the library and the hum faded into silence.

So it could be done after all. The answer had been right there in the history books all the time, if he had only had the brains to look. There were no excuses for the stupidity of his actions. He should have consulted the library but he had not. Yet—it still might be possible to make amends.

"Why not?!"

He paced the room, hitting his fist into the palm of his hand. The pieces might still be put back together if he played it right. He doubted if he could convince the Pyrrans that the new plan would succeed, or even that it was a good idea. They would probably be completely against it. Then he would have to work without them. He looked at his watch. The launch was not due to leave for the first pickup of Kerk and the others for at least another hour. Time enough to get ready. Write a friendly note to Meta and be deliberately vague about his plans. Then have Clon drop him off near Temuchin's camp. The unimaginative pilot would do as he was told without asking questions.

Yes, it could be done, and by the stars he was going to do it.

19

Lord was he of all the mountains,
Ruled the plains and all the valleys.
Nothing passed without his knowledge.
Many died with his displeasure.

Temuchin sprang suddenly into the *camach*, his drawn sword ready in his hand.

"Reveal yourself!" he cried. "My guard lies outside, struck down. Reveal yourself, spy, so that I may kill you."

A hooded figure stepped from the darkness into the flickering light of the oil lamp and Temuchin raised his sword. Jason threw back the fur so his face could be seen.

"You!" Temuchin said in a hollow voice, and the sword slipped from his fingers to the ground. "You cannot be here. I killed you with these hands. Are you ghost or demon?"

"I have returned to help you, Temuchin. To open an entire new world to your conquest."

"A demon, that you must be, and instead of dying, you returned home through Hell's Doorway and gained new strength. A demon of a thousand guises—that explains how you could trick and betray so many people. The jongleur thought you were an off-worlder. The Pyrrans thought you were one of their tribe. I thought you a loyal comrade who would help me."

"That's a fine theory. You believe what you want. Then listen to what I have to tell you."

"*No!* If I listen, I am damned." He grabbed up the sword. Jason talked fast before he had to battle for his life.

"There are caves opening from the valley you call Hell's Doorway. They don't go to hell—but they lead down to the lowlands. I went there and returned by boat to tell you this. I can show you the way. You can lead an army through those caves and invade the lowlands. You rule here now— and you can rule there as well. A new continent to conquer. And you are the only man who could possibly do it."

Temuchin lowered the sword slowly and his eyes blazed in the firelight. When he spoke, his voice was hushed, as though he were speaking only to himself.

"You must be a demon, and I cannot kill that which is already dead. I could drive you from me, but I cannot drive your words from my head. You know, as no living man knows, that I am empty. I rule these plains and that is the end of it. What pleasure in ruling? No wars, no conquests, no joy of seeing one's enemy fall and marching on. Alone, by day and night I have dreamed about those rich meadows and towns below the cliffs. How even gunpowder and great armies could not stand against my warriors. How we would surprise them, flank them, besiege their cities. Conquer."

"Yes, you could have all that, Temuchin. Lord of all this world."

In the silence the lamp sputtered, tossing shadows of the two men to and fro. When Temuchin spoke again, there was resolve in his voice.

"I will have that, even though I know the price. You want me, demon, to take me to your hell below the mountains. But you shall not have me until I have conquered all."

"I'm no demon, Temuchin."

"Do not mock me. I know the truth. What the jongleurs sing is true, though I never believed it before. You have tempted me, I have accepted, I am damned. Tell me the hour and manner of my death."

"I can't tell you that."

"Of course not. You are bound as I am bound."

"I didn't mean it that way."

"I know how it was meant. By accepting all, I lose all. There is no other way. But I will have it like that. I will win first. That is true, demon, you will allow that?"

"Of course, you will win, and—"

"Tell me no more. I have changed my mind. I do not wish to know the manner of my end." He shook his shoulders as though to remove some unseen weight, then thrust his sword back into the slings at his waist.

"All right, believe what you will. Just give me some good men and I'll open up the passage to the lowlands. A rope ladder will get us into the valley. I'll mark the route and take them through the caves to prove that it can be done. Then the next time we do it, the army will follow. Will they go—down there?"

Temuchin laughed. "They have sworn to follow me to hell if I order it and now so they will. They will follow."

"Good. Shall we shake on that?"

"Of course! I will take the world and win eternity in hell, so I have no fear of your cold dead flesh now, my demon."

He crushed Jason's hand in his and, despite himself, Jason could not help but admire the giant courage of the man.

20

"LET ME TALK to him, please," Meta asked.

Kerk waved her away and clutched the microphone, almost swallowing it in his giant hand.

"Listen to me now, Jason," he said coldly. "None of us is with you in this adventure. You will not explain your purpose and you will gain nothing except destruction. If

171

Temuchin controls the lowlands, too, we will never replace him and open the mines. Rhes has returned to Ammh and is organizing resistance to your invasion. Some here have voted to join him. I am going to ask you for the last time. Stop what you are doing before it is too late."

When Jason's voice sounded from the radio, it had a curious flat quality, whether the fault of the transmission or that of the speaker it was hard to say.

"Kerk, I hear what you say and, believe me, I understand it. But it is too late now to turn back. Most of the army has gone through the caves and we've captured a number of *moropes* from the villages. Nothing I say could stop Temuchin now. This thing will have to be seen through to its conclusion. The lowlanders may win, though I doubt it. Temuchin is going to rule, above and below the cliffs, and in the end this will all be for the best."

"No!" Meta shouted, pulling at the microphone. "Jason, listen to me. You cannot do this. You came to us and helped us, and we believed in you. You showed us that life is not only kill and be killed. We know now that the war on Pyrrus was wrong because you showed us, and we only came to this planet because you asked us to. Now it seems, I think, it is as though you were betraying us. You have tried to teach us how not to kill and, believe me, we have tried to learn. Yet what you are doing now is worse than anything we ever did on Pyrrus. There, at least, we were fighting for our lives. You don't have that excuse. You have shown that monster, Temuchin, a way to make new wars and to kill more people. How can you justify that?"

Static rustled hoarsely in the speaker while they waited the long moments for Jason to speak. When he did he sounded suddenly very tired.

"Meta . . . I'm sorry. I wish I could tell you, but it is too late. They're looking for me and I have to hide this radio before they get here. What I'm doing is right. Try to believe that. Someone a long time ago said that you cannot make an omelet without breaking eggs. Meaning you cannot bring about social change without hurting someone. People are being hurt and are dying because of me and don't think I'm not aware of it. But . . . listen, I can't talk any more. They're right outside." His voice dropped to a whisper. "Meta, if I never see you again, just remember one thing. It's an old-fashioned word, but it is in a lot of languages. The library can translate it for you and give you the meaning.

"This is better by radio. I doubt if I could say it right to your face. You're stronger than I am, Meta, and your reflexes are a lot better, but you are still a woman. And, hell, I want to say that I . . . love you. Good luck. Signing off."

The speaker clicked and the room was silent.

"What was that word he used?" Kerk asked.

"I think I know," she answered, and she turned her face away so he could not see it.

"Hello, control!" a voice shouted. "Radio room here. A sub-space message coming in from Pyrrus with an emergency classification."

"Put it through," Kerk ordered.

There was the rustle of interstellar static, then the familiar drumbeat warble of the jump-space carrier wave. Superimposed on top of it was the quick, worried voice of a Pyrran.

"Attention, all stations within zeta radius. Emergency message for planet Felicity, ship's receiver *Pugnacious,* code Ama Rona Pi, 290-633-087. Message follows. Kerk, anyone there. Trouble hit. All the quadrants. We've shortened the perimeter, abandoned most of the city. Don't know if we can hold. Brucco says this is something new and that conventional weapons won't stop it. We can use the fire power of your ship. If you can return, come at once. Message ends."

The radio room had put the sub-space message through to all compartments of the ship and, in the horrified silence that followed its ending, running footsteps sounded from both connecting passageways. As the first men burst in, Kerk came to life and shouted his commands.

"All men to stations. We blast as soon as we're secured. Call in the outside guards. Release all the prisoners. We're leaving."

There was absolutely no doubt about that. It was inconceivable that any Pyrran could have acted otherwise.

Their home, their city, was on the verge of destruction, perhaps already gone. They ran to their posts.

"Rhes," Meta said. "He's with the army. How can we reach him?"

Kerk thought for a moment, then shook his head. "We cannot, that is the only answer. We'll leave the launch for him on the same island where we make the contacts. Record a broadcast telling him what has happened and set it on automatic to broadcast every hour. When he gets back to a radio, he will pick it up. The launch will be locked so no one else can get in. There is medicine in it, even a jump-space communicator. He will be all right."

"He won't like it."

"It's the best we can do. Now we have to ready for blast off."

They worked as a team driven by a common urge. Back. Return to Pyrrus. Their city was in danger. The ship lifted at 17G's, and Meta would have used more power if the structure of the ship could have withstood it. Their course through jump-space was the quickest and the most dangerous that could be computed. There were no complaints about the time the journey took: they accepted this period with stoic resignation. But weapons were readied and there was little or no conversation. Each Pyrran held, locked within him, the knowledge that their world and their life faced extinction, and these things cannot be discussed.

Hours before the *Pugnacious* was scheduled to break out of jump-space, every man and woman aboard was armed and waiting. Even nine-year-old Grif was there, a Pyrran like all the others.

From the eye-hurting otherness of jump-space to the black of interstellar space to the high atmosphere of Pyrrus the ship sped. Downward in a screaming ballistic orbit, where the hull heated to just below its melting point and the coolers labored against the overtaxing load. Their bodies reacted, sweat dripped from their faces and soaked their clothes, but the Pyrrans were unaware of the heat. The picture from the bow pickup was put on every screen in the ship. Jungle flashed by, then a high column of smoke climbed up on the distant horizon. Diving swiftly, like a striking bird of prey, the ship swooped down.

The jungle now occupied the city. A circular mound,

covered with plants and tough growth, was the only trace of the once impregnable perimeter wall. As they came low, they could see thornlike creepers bursting through the windows of the buildings. Animals moved slowly through the streets that had once been crowded with people, while a clawhawk perched on the tower of the central warehouse, the masonry crumbling under its weight.

As they flew on, they could see that the smoke was coming from the crushed ruin of their spaceship. It appeared to have been caught on the ground at the spaceport and was held down by a now blackened net of giant vines.

There were no signs of activity anywhere in the ruined city. Just the beasts and plants of deathworld, now strangely quiet and sluggish with their enemy gone, the motivations of hatred that had enraged them for so long now vanished. They stirred and reared when the ship passed over, quickened to life again as the raw emotions of the surviving Pyrrans impressed upon them.

"They can't all be dead," Teca said in a choked voice. "Keep looking."

"I am quartering the entire area," Meta told him.

Kerk found the destruction almost impossible to look at, and when he spoke, his voice was low, as though he were talking only to himself.

"We knew that it had to end like this—sometime. We faced that and tried to make a new start on a new planet. But, knowing something will happen and seeing it before your eyes, those are two different things. We ate there, in that . . . ruin, slept in that one. Our friends and comrades were here, our entire life. And now it is gone."

"Go down!" Clon said, thinking nothing, feeling hatred. "Attack. We can still fight."

"There is nothing left to fight for," Teca told him, speaking with an immense weariness. "As Kerk said, it is gone."

A hull pickup detected the sound of gunfire, and they rocketed toward it with momentary hope. But it was just an automatic gun still actuating itself in a repeating pattern. Soon it would be out of ammunition and would be still like the rest of the ruined city.

The radio light had been blinking for some time before someone noticed it. The call was on the wavelength of

Rhes's headquarters, not the one the city had used. Kerk reached over slowly and switched the set to receive.

"Naxa here, can you hear me? Come in, *Pugnacious.*"

"Kerk here. We are over the city. We are . . . too late. Can you give me a report?"

"Too late by days," Naxa snorted. "They wouldn't listen to us. We said we could get them out, give them a place to go to, but they wouldn't listen. Just like they wanted to die in the city. Once the perimeter went down, the survivors holed up in one of the buildings and it sounded like everything on this planet hit them at once. We couldn't take it, standing by I mean. Everyone volunteered. We took the best men and all the armored ground cars from the mine. Went in there. Got out the kids, they made the kids go, some of the women. The wounded, just the ones who were unconscious. The rest stayed. We just got out before the end. Don't ask me what it was like. Then it was all over, the fighting, and after a bit everything quieted down like you see it now. Whole planet quieted down. When we could, me and some of the other talkers went to see. Had to climb a mountain of bodies of every creature born. Found the right spot. The ones that stayed behind, they're all dead. Died fighting. Only thing we could bring back then was a bunch of records that Brucco left."

"They would not have had it any other way," Kerk said. "Let us know where the survivors are and we will go there at once."

Naxa gave the coordinates and said, "What're you going to do now?"

"We'll contact you again. Over and out."

"What *are* we going to do now?" Teca asked. "There's nothing left for us here."

"There's nothing for us on Felicity either. As long as Temuchin rules, we cannot open the mines," Kerk answered.

"Go back. Kill Temuchin," Teca said, his power holster humming. He wanted revenge, to kill something.

"We can't do that," Kerk said. Patiently, because he knew the torture the man was feeling. "We will discuss this later. We must first see to the survivors."

"We have lost everywhere," Meta said, voicing the words that everyone was thinking.

Silence followed.

21

THE FOUR GUARDS ran into the room half carrying Jason, then hurled him to the floor. He rolled over and got to his knees.

"Get out," Temuchin ordered his men, and kicked Jason hard on the side of his head, knocking him down again. When Jason sat up, there was a livid bruise covering the side of his face.

"I suppose that there is a reason for this," he said quietly.

Temuchin opened and closed his great hands in fury, but said nothing. He stamped the length of the ornate room, his trailing prickspurs scratching deep gouges in the inlaid marble of the floor. At the far end he stood for a moment, looking out of the high windows and across the city below. Then he reached up suddenly and pulled at the tapestry drapes, tearing them down in a sudden spasm of effort. The iron bar that supported them fell as well, but he caught it before it touched the floor and hurled it through the many-paned window. There was the crashing fall of breaking glass far below.

"I have lost!" he shouted, almost an animal howl of pain.

"You've won," Jason told him. "Why are you doing this?"

"Let us not pretend any more," Temuchin answered, turning to face him, a frozen calm replacing the anger. "You knew what would happen."

"I knew that you would win—and you have. The armies fell before you and the people fled. Your horde has over-run the land and your captains rule in every city. While you rule here in Eolasair, lord of the entire world."

"Do not play with me, demon. I knew this would happen. I just did not think that it would happen so quickly. You could have allowed me more time."

"Why?" Jason asked, climbing to his feet. Now that Temuchin had realized the truth, there was no longer any point in concealment. "You said that by accepting you would lose."

"I did. Of course." Temuchin straightened his back and looked unseeingly out the window. "I just had not realized how much I would lose. I was a fool. I thought that only my own life was at stake. I did not realize that my people, our life, would die as well." He turned on Jason. "Give it back to them. Take me, but let them return."

"I cannot."

"You will not!" Temuchin shouted, rushing on Jason, grabbing him up by the neck and shaking him like an empty goatskin. "Change it—I command you." He loosened his grip slightly so that Jason could gasp in air and speak.

"I cannot—and I would not even if I could. In winning, you lost, and that is just the way I want it. The life you knew has ended and I would not have it any other way."

"You knew this all along," Temuchin said almost gently, releasing his grasp. "This was my fate and you knew it. You let it happen. Why?"

"For a number of reasons."

"Tell me one."

"Mankind can do very well without your way of life. We have had enough killing and bloody murder in our history. Live your life out, Temuchin, and die peacefully. You are the last of your kind and the galaxy will be a better place for your ending."

"Is that the only reason?"

"There are others. I want the off-worlders to dig their mines on your plains. They can do that now."

"In winning I lost. There must be a word for this kind of happening."

"There is. It was a 'Pyrrhic victory.' I wish I could say that I am sorry for you, but I'm not. You're a tiger in a pit, Temuchin. I can admire your muscles and your temper and I know that you used to be lord of the jungle. But now I'm glad that you are trapped." Without looking toward the door, Jason took a short step in its direction.

"There is no escape, demon," Temuchin said.

"Why? I cannot harm you—or help you any more."

"Nor can I kill you. A demon, being dead already,

cannot be killed. But the human flesh you wear can be tortured. That I shall do. Your torture will last as long as I live. This is a small return for all that I have lost—but it is all that I have to offer. We have much to look forward to, demon . . ."

Jason did not hear the rest as he bolted through the door, head down and running as fast as he could. The two guards at the far end of the hall heard his pounding feet and turned, lowering their spears. He did not slow or attempt to avoid them, but fell instead and slid, feet first, under their spears and cannoning into them. They fell in a tangle and, for one instant, Jason was held by the arm. But he chopped with the edge of his hand, breaking the restraining wrist, and was free. Scrambling to his feet, he hurled himself down the stairwell, jumping eight, ten steps at a time, risking a fall with every leap. Then he hit the ground floor and ran through the unguarded front entrance into the courtyard.

"Seize him!" Temuchin shouted from above. "I want him brought to me."

Jason pelted toward the nearest entrance, veering off as it filled suddenly with guards. There were armed men everywhere, at every exit. He ran toward the wall. It was high and topped with gilded spearheads, but he had to get over it. Footsteps sounded loudly behind him as he sprang upward, his fingers closing over the edge of the wall. Good! He heaved himself up, to throw his legs over, climb between the spearheads and drop to the other side to vanish into the city.

The hands locked about his ankle, the weight holding him back. He kicked and felt his boot crush a face, but he could not free himself. Then other hands caught his flailing leg and still more, pulling him back down into the courtyard.

"Bring him to me," Temuchin's voice sounded over the crowd of men. "Bring him to me. He is mine."

22

Rhes was waiting, a tiny figure beside the launch as the *Pugnacious* dropped down from the sky. It was a full-jet, 20G landing. Meta was not wasting any time. Rhes picked his way through the fused and smoking sand as the port opened to receive him.

"Tell us everything quickly," Meta said.

"There's little enough to tell. Temuchin won his war, as we knew he would, taking every city with one blow after another. The people here, even the armies, could not stand against him. I fled after the last battle, with all the others, for I did not wish to see my thumbs hanging from some barbarian banner. That was when I got your message. You must tell me what happened on Pyrrus."

"The end," Kerk said. "The city, everyone there, is gone."

Rhes knew that there were no words that he could say. He was silent a moment; then Meta caught his eye and he continued.

"Jason has—or had—a radio, and soon after I reached the launch, I picked up a message from him. I could not answer him and his message was never completed. I did not have the recorder on, but I can remember it clearly enough. He said that the mines could be opened soon, that we had won. The Pyrrans have won, that is exactly what he said. He started to add something else, but the broadcast was suddenly broken off. That must have been when they came for him. I have heard more about it since that time."

"What do you mean?" Meta asked quickly.

"Temuchin has made his capital in Eolasair, the largest city in Ammh. He has Jason there in . . . in a cage, hung in front of the palace. He was first tortured; now he is being starved to death."

180

"Why? For what reason?"

"It is a nomad belief that a demon in human form cannot be killed. He is immune to normal weapons. But if he is starved long enough, the human disguise will wither and the demon's original form will be revealed. I don't know if Temuchin believes this nonsense or not, but this is just what he is doing. Jason has been hanging in that cage for over fifteen days now."

"We must go to him," Meta said, leaping to her feet. "We must free him."

"We will do that," Kerk told her. "But we must do it the right way. Rhes, can you get us clothes and *moropes?*"

"Of course. How many will you need?"

"We cannot force our way in, not against the ruler of an entire planet. Just two of us will go. You will come to show the way. I will go to see what can be done."

"And I will come, too," Meta said, and Kerk nodded agreement.

"The three of us then. At once. We don't know how long he can live under these conditions."

"They give him a cup of water every day," Rhes said, avoiding Meta's eyes. "Take the ship up. I'll show you which way to go. It does not matter any more if the people in the city here know we are from off-planet."

This was before noon. By drugging the *moropes* and loading them into the cargo bay, a good deal of riding time was saved. The city of Eolasair was built on a river among rolling hills, with a forest nearby. They landed the ship as close as they could without being seen and had the *moropes* on the way as soon as they were revived. By later afternoon they entered the city, and Rhes threw a boy a small coin to show them the way to the palace. He wore his merchant's clothes, and Kerk had put on his full armor and weapons. Meta, veiled as was the local custom, clutched her hands tightly on the saddle as they forced their way through the crowded streets.

Only before the palace was there empty space. The courtyard was floored with gold-veined marble, polished and shining. A squad of troops guarded it, their bearded nomad faces incongruous above the looted armor. But their weapons were in order and they were as deadly as they had been on the high plains. Worse, perhaps, their tempers were not improved by the warm climate.

A chain had been passed between the tops of two of the tall columns that flanked the courtyard and from it, hanging a good two meters above the ground, was suspended a cage of thick bars. It had no door and had been built around the prisoner.

"Jason!" Meta said, looking up at the slumped figure. He did not move and there was no way of telling if he was alive or dead.

"I will take care of this," Kerk said, and jumped from his *morope*.

"Wait!" Rhes called after him. "What are you going to do? Getting yourself killed won't help Jason."

Kerk was not listening. He had lost too much and felt too much pain recently to be in a reasoning mood. Now all of his hatred was turned against one man, and he could not be stopped.

"Temuchin!" he roared. "Come out of your gilt hiding place. Come out, you coward, and face me, Kerk of Pyrrus! Show yourself—*coward!*"

Ahankk, who was the guard officer, came running with his sword drawn, but Kerk backhanded him offhandedly, his attention still fixed on the palace. Ahankk dropped and rolled over and over and remained there, unconscious or dead. Surely dead, with his head at an angle like that.

"Temuchin, coward, come out!" Kerk shouted again. When the stunned soldiers touched their weapons, he turned on them, snarling.

"Dogs—would you attack me? A high chief, Kerk of Pyrrus, victor of The Slash?" They fell back before his burning anger, and he turned to the palace as the front entrance was thrown wide. Temuchin strode out.

"You dare too much," he said, his cold anger matching that of Kerk's."

"You dare," Kerk told him. "You break tribal law. You take a man of my tribe and torture him for no reason. You are a coward, Temuchin, and I name you that before your men."

Temuchin's sword flashed in the sunlight as he drew it, a fine-tempered length of razor-sharp steel.

"You have said enough, Pyrran. I could have you killed on the spot, but I want that pleasure for myself. I wanted

182

to kill you the moment I first saw you—and I should have. Because of you and this creature which calls itself Jason, I have lost everything."

"You have lost nothing—yet," Kerk answered and his sword pointed straight at the warlord's throat. "But now you lose your life, for I shall kill you."

Temuchin brought his sword down in a blow that would have cut a man in two—but it rang off Kerk's blade. They battled then, furiously, with no science and no art—barbarian sword fight, just slash and parry, with eventual victory going to the strongest.

The clang of their steel rang in the silence of the courtyard, the only other sound being the rasping of their breath as they fought. Neither would give way, and they were well matched. Kerk was the older man, but he was the stronger. Temuchin had a lifetime of sword fighting and battles behind him and was absolutely without fear.

It went on like that, a rapid exchange that was broken suddenly by a sharp twang as Temuchin's sword snapped in two. He threw himself backward, out of the way of Kerk's slash, so that instead of gutting him it cut a red gash in his thigh, a minor wound. He sprawled at full length, blood slowly seeping into the golden silk he wore, as Kerk raised his sword in both hands for the last, unavoidable blow.

"Archers!" Temuchin shouted. He would not submit to death this easily.

Kerk laughed and hurled his sword away. "You do not escape that easily, ruling coward. I prefer to kill you with my bare hands."

Temuchin shouted wordless hatred and sprang to his feet. They leaped at each other with the passion of animals and closed in struggling combat.

There were no blows exchanged. Instead, Kerk closed his great hands around the other's neck and tightened. Temuchin clutched his opponent in the same way, but the muscles in Kerk's neck were steel ropes: he could not affect them. Kerk tightened his grip.

For the first time Temuchin showed some emotion other than unthinking anger. His eyes widened and he writhed in the clutch of the closing fingers. He pulled at Kerk's wrists, but to no avail. The Pyrran's grip tightened like that of a machine, and just as implacably.

Temuchin twisted about, got his hand in the back of his belt and pulled out a dagger.

"Kerk! He has a knife!" Rhes shouted, as Temuchin whipped it around and plunged it full into Kerk's side under the lower edge of his breastplate.

His hand came away and the hilt of the dagger remained there.

Kerk bellowed in anger—but he did not release his grip. Instead, he moved his thumbs up under Temuchin's chin and pushed back. For a long moment the warlord writhed, his boot tips almost free of the ground and his eyes starting from their sockets.

Then there was a sharp snap and his body went limp.

Kerk released his grip and the great Temuchin, First Lord of the high plateau and of the lowlands, fell in a dead huddle at his feet.

Meta rushed up to him, the red stain spreading on his side.

"Leave it," Kerk ordered. "It plugs the hole. Mostly in the muscle, and if it has punctured some guts, we can sew it up later. Get Jason down."

The guards made no motion to interfere when Rhes pulled away one of their halberds and, hooking it in the bottom of the cage, pulled it crashing to the ground. Jason rolled limply with the impact. His eyes were set in black hollows and his skin was drawn tautly over the bone of his face. Through his rags of clothing red burns and scars could be seen on his skin.

"Is he . . . ?" Meta said, but could not go on. Rhes clutched two of the bars, tensed his muscles, and slowly bent apart the thick metal to make an opening.

Jason opened one bloodshot eye and looked up at them.

"Took your time about getting here," he said, and let it drop shut again.

23

"No MORE right now," Jason said, waving away the glass and straw that Meta held out to him. He sat up on his bunk aboard the *Pugnacious*, washed, medicated, his wounds dressed, and with a glucose drip plugged into his arm. Kerk sat across from him, a bulge on one side where he had been bandaged. Teca had taken out a bit of punctured intestine and tied up a few blood vessels. Kerk preferred to ignore it completely.

"Tell us," he said. "I've plugged this microphone into the annunciator system, and everyone is waiting to hear. To be frank, we still don't know what happened—other than the fact that both you and Temuchin think that each lost by winning. It is very strange."

Meta leaned over and touched Jason's forehead with a folded cloth. He smiled and put his fingers against her wrist before he spoke.

"It was history. I went to the library to find out the answer, later than I should have—but not too late, after all. The library read a lot of books to me and very quickly convinced me that a culture cannot be changed from the outside. It can be suppressed or destroyed—but it cannot be changed. And that's just what we were trying to do. Have you ever heard of the Goths and the Hunnish tribes of Old Earth?"

They shook their heads no and this time he accepted the drink to dampen his throat.

"These were a bunch of backwoods barbarians who lived in the forest, enjoyed drinking, killing and their own brand of independence, and fought the Roman legions every time they came along. The tribes were always beaten —and do you think they learned a lesson from it? Of course not. They just gathered up the survivors and went deeper in the woods to fight another day, their culture and their hatred intact. Their culture was changed only when they *won*. Eventually they moved in on the Romans, captured Rome and learned all the joys of civilized life. They weren't barbarians any more. The ancient Chinese used to work the same trick for centuries. They weren't very good fighters, but they were great absorbers. They were overrun and licked time and time again—and sucked the victors down into their own culture and life.

"I learned this lesson and just arranged things so that it would happen here as well. Temuchin was an ambitious man and could not resist the temptation of new worlds to conquer. So he invaded the lowlands when I showed him the way."

"And by winning, he lost," Kerk said.

"Exactly. The world is his now. He has captured the cities and he wants their wealth. So he has to occupy them to obtain it. His best officers become administrators of the new realm and wallow in unaccustomed luxury. They like it here. They might even stay. They are still nomads at heart—but what about the next generation? If Temuchin and his chiefs are living in cities and enjoying the sybaritic pleasures thereof, how can he expect to enforce the no-cities law back on the plateau? It begins to look sort of foolish after a while. Any decent barbarian isn't going to stay up there in the cold when he can come down here and share the loot. Wine is stronger than *achadh* and they even have some distilleries here. The nomad way of life is doomed. Temuchin realized that, though he could not put it into words. He just knew that, by winning, he had left behind and destroyed the way of life that had enabled him to win in the first place. That's why he called me a demon and strung me up."

"Poor Temuchin," Meta said, with sudden insight. "His ambition doomed him and he finally realized it. Though he was the conqueror, he was the one who lost the most."

"His way of life and his life itself," Jason said. "He was a great man."

Kerk grunted. "Don't tell me that you're sorry I killed him?"

"Not at all. He attained everything he ever wanted; then he died. Not many men can say that."

186

"Turn off the annunciator," Meta said. "And you may go, Kerk."

The big Pyrran opened his mouth to protest, then smiled instead, and turned and went out.

"What are you going to do now?" Meta asked as soon as the door was closed.

"Sleep for a month, eat steaks and grow strong."

"I do not mean that. I mean where will you go? Will you stay here with us?"

She was working hard to express her emotions, using a vocabulary that was not suited for this form of communication. He did not make it any easier for her.

"Does that matter to you?"

"It matters, in a way that is very new." Her forehead creased and she almost stammered with the effort to put her feelings into words. "When I am with you, I want to tell you different things. Do you know what is the nicest thing that we can say in Pyrran?" He shook his head. "We say, 'You fight very well.' That is not what I want to say to you."

Jason spoke nine languages and he knew exactly what it was he wanted to say, but he would not. Or could not. He turned away instead.

"No, look at me," Meta said, taking his head in both hands and gently turning his face toward hers. Her actions said more than any words could and he was ashamed of his inability to speak. Yet he still remained silent.

"I have looked up the word 'love,' just as you told me to do. At first it was not clear because it was only words. But when I thought about you, the meaning became clear at once."

Their faces were close, her wide clear eyes looking unflinchingly into his.

"I love you," she said. "I think that I will always love you. You must never leave me."

The direct simplicity of her emotions rose like a flooded river against the shored-up dikes of his conditioned defenses, the mechanisms that he had built up through the years. He was a loner. No one was on his side. I'm all right, Jack. Take a woman, leave a woman. The universe helps those who help themselves. I can take care of myself and . . . I . . . don't . . . need . . . anyone. . . .

"Dear stars above, how I do love you, too," he said, pulling her to him, his face pressing into her neck and hair.

"You will never leave me again," she said.

"And you will never leave me again. There, the shortest and best marriage ceremony on record. May you break my arm if I ever look at another girl."

"Please. Do not talk about violence now."

"I apologize. That was the old unreconstructed me talking. I think that we must both bring gentleness into our lives. That is what you, I and our pack of growling Pyrrans need the most. That's what we all need. Not humility, no one needs that. Just a little civilizing. I think that we can survive with it now. The mines should be opening here soon, and the way the tribes are moving to the lowlands, it looks like you Pyrrans will have the plateau to yourselves."

"Yes, that will be good. It can be our new world." She hesitated a moment as she weighed his words. "We Pyrrans will stay here—but what about you? I would not like to leave my people again, but I will go if you go."

"You won't have to. I'm staying right here. I'm a member of the tribe—remember? Pyrrans are rude, opinionated and irascible, we know that. But I am, too. So perhaps I've found a home at last."

"With me, always with me."

"Of course."

After this there was no more that could be said.

Don't Miss These
Bestsellers From Dell

THE SECRET OF SANTA VITTORIA Robert Crichton 95c

GAMES PEOPLE PLAY Eric Berne M.D. $1.25

THE FIXER Bernard Malamud 95c

THE DIRTY DOZEN E. M. Nathanson 95c

THE PAPER DRAGON Evan Hunter 95c

TAI-PAN James Clavell 95c

THERE IS A RIVER: THE STORY OF EDGAR CAYCE
Thomas Sugrue 95c

I, A WOMAN Siv Holm 75c

A DANDY IN ASPIC Derek Marlowe 75c

AN ODOR OF SANCTITY Frank Yerby 95c

THE DOCTORS Martin L. Gross $1.25

PEDLOCK & SONS Stephen Longstreet 95c

THE MENORAH MEN Lionel Davidson 75c

CAPABLE OF HONOR Allen Drury $1.25

BILLION DOLLAR BRAIN Len Deighton 75c

If you cannot obtain copies of these titles at your local bookseller's just send the price (plus 10c per copy for handling and postage) to Dell Books, Box 2291, Grand Central Post Office, New York, N.Y. 10017. No postage or handling charge is required on any order of five or more books.

41 weeks on the Best Seller List!

CAPABLE
OF
HONOR

ALLEN DRURY

Now $1.25

Walter Dobius was the most powerful columnist in the nation and with the right turn of a phrase he could either make or break a senator, a governor, perhaps even . . .

But no, that was impossible. This was America, a democracy; that sort of thing just couldn't happen here. Or could it?

"Allen Drury has written another terrific political novel . . . hurdles you into the middle of Washington's big-time intrigue with the same exciting style of writing that gained literary fame for his Pulitzer Prize-winning ADVISE AND CONSENT. . . . breathless reading." —*Tampa Tribune*

"Outstanding" —*Fort Wayne News-Sentinel*

A DELL BOOK

The #1 bestseller that dazzled the nation

MADAME SARAH

CORNELIA OTIS SKINNER
95c

On stage she was the greatest actress the
world has ever known. Off stage she was
a woman who made her own rules for life
and love. Passionate, willful, breathtaking,
maddening, and wonderful, she reigned
supreme over a glamorous and glorious
age. Her name—
SARAH BERNHARDT

"One of the most beautiful of human stories."
—*New York Times Book Review*

"Dramatic . . . tempestuous . . . scintillating . . .
this book is a 'must'."
—*Los Angeles Times*

"Racy . . . romantic . . . memorable."
—*Life Magazine*

A DELL BOOK

If you cannot obtain copies of this title at your local bookstore, just send
the price (plus 10c per copy for handling and postage) to Dell Books, Box
2291, Grand Central Post Office, New York, N.Y. 10017. No postage or
handling charge is required on any order of five or more books.